NEW
TRICKS

NEW TRICKS

DAVID ROSENFELT

GRAND CENTRAL
PUBLISHING

NEW YORK   BOSTON

Rosenfelt

Grand Central Publishing
Hachette Book Group
237 Park Avenue
New York, NY 10017

Visit our Web site at www.HachetteBookGroup.com.

Printed in the United States of America

First Edition: August 2009
10 9 8 7 6 5 4 3 2 1

Grand Central Publishing is a division of Hachette Book Group, Inc.
The Grand Central Publishing name and logo is a trademark of Hachette Book Group, Inc.

Library of Congress Cataloging-in-Publication Data
Rosenfelt, David.
    New tricks / David Rosenfelt. — 1st ed.
        p. cm.
    Summary: "Edgar-award nominated author David Rosenfelt's hilarious hero, Andy Carpenter, plunges into a high-profile murder case in which a Bernese puppy and his golden retriever play instrumental roles"—Provided by publisher.
    ISBN-13: 978-0-446-50587-1
    1. Carpenter, Andy (Fictitious character)—Fiction. 2. Trials (Murder)—Fiction. 3. Dogs—Fiction. 4. New Jersey—Fiction. I. Title.
    PS3618.O838N48 2009
    813'.6—dc22   2008022269

b12609249

I am raising a literary glass in a toast to a long and wonderful life for Oliver Baron Rosenfelt.

NEW TRICKS

• • • • •

"ANDY CARPENTER, Lawyer to the Dogs."

That was the *USA Today* headline on a piece that ran about me a couple of months ago. It was a favorable story overall, but the headline was obviously designed to make a humorous comparison between me and those celebrity attorneys who are often referred to as "lawyers to the stars."

While you would naturally think it would have exposed me to ridicule from my colleagues in the legal profession and my friends, it really hasn't. This is because I don't hang out with colleagues in the legal profession, and my friends already have plenty of other reasons to ridicule me.

Actually, referring to me this way makes perfect sense. Last year I went to court to defend a golden retriever who had been scheduled to die at the hands of the animal control system here in Paterson, New Jersey. I saved his life, and the media ate it up with a spoon. Then I learned that the dog was a witness to a murder five years prior, and I successfully defended his owner, the man who had been wrongly convicted and imprisoned for that murder.

Three months ago I cemented my reputation as a dog lunatic by representing all the dogs in the Passaic County Animal Shelter in a class action suit. I correctly claimed that my clients were being treated inhumanely, a legally difficult posture since the opposition took the position that a key part of "humane" is "human," and my clients fell a little short in that area.

With the media covering it as if it were the trial of the century, we won, and living conditions in the shelters have been improved dramatically. I'm in a good position to confirm this, because my former client Willie Miller and I run a dog-rescue operation called the Tara Foundation, named after my own golden retriever. We are in the shelters frequently to rescue dogs to place in homes, and if we see any slippage back to the old policies, we're not exactly shy about pointing it out.

Since that stirring court victory, I've been on a three-month vacation from work. I find that my vacations are getting longer and longer, almost to the point that vacationing is my status quo, from which I take infrequent "work breaks." Two things enable me to do this: my mostly inherited wealth, and my laziness.

Unfortunately, my extended siesta is about to come to an unwelcome conclusion. I've been summoned to the courthouse by Judge Henry Henderson, nicknamed "Hatchet" by lawyers who have practiced in his court. It's not exactly a term of endearment.

Hatchet's not inviting me to make a social call, and it's unlikely we'll be sipping tea. He doesn't like me and finds me rather annoying, which doesn't make him particularly unique. The problem is that he's in a position to do something about it.

Hatchet has been assigned to a murder case that has dominated the local media. Walter Timmerman, a man who could accurately be referred to as a semi-titan in the pharmaceutical industry, was murdered three weeks ago. It was not your everyday case of "semi-titan-murdering"; he wasn't killed on the golf course at the country club, or by an intruder breaking into his mansion. Timmerman was killed at night in the most run-down area of downtown Paterson, a neighborhood filled with hookers and drug dealers, not caddies or butlers.

Within twenty-four hours, police arrested a twenty-two-year-old Hispanic man for the crime. He was in possession of Timmerman's wallet the day after the murder. The police are operating on the safe assumption that Timmerman did not give the wallet to this young man for safekeeping, knowing he was soon to be murdered.

This is where I am unfortunately going to enter the picture. The accused cannot afford an attorney, so the court will appoint one for him. I have not handled pro bono work in years, but I'm on the list, and Hatchet is obviously going to stick me with this case.

I arrive at the courthouse at eight thirty, which is when Hatchet has instructed me to be in his chambers. The arraignment is at nine, and since I haven't even met my client-to-be, I'll have to ask for a postponement. I'll try to get it postponed for fifty years, but I'll probably have to settle for a few days.

I'm surprised when I arrive to see Billy "Bulldog" Cameron, the attorney who runs the Public Defender's Office in Passaic County. I've never had a conversation of more than three sentences with Billy in which he hasn't mentioned that he's overworked and under-funded. Since both those things are true, and since I'm personally underworked and overfunded, I usually nod sympathetically.

This time I don't have time to nod, because I'm in danger of being late for my meeting with Hatchet. Lawyers who arrive late to Hatchet's chambers are often never heard of or seen again, except for occasional body parts that wash up on shore. I also don't get to ask Billy what he's doing here. If I'm going to get stuck with this client, then he's off the hook, because I'm on it.

I hate being on hooks.

• • • • •

"YOU'RE LATE," says Hatchet, which is technically true by thirty-five seconds.

"I'm sorry, Your Honor. There was an accident on Market Street, and—"

He interrupts. "You are under the impression that I want to hear a story about your morning drive?"

"Probably not."

"For the purpose of this meeting, I will do the talking, and you will do the listening, with very few exceptions."

I start to say *Yes, sir,* but don't, because I don't know if that is one of the allowable exceptions. Instead I just listen.

"I have an assignment for you, one that you are uniquely qualified to handle."

I nod, because if I cringe it will piss him off.

"Are you at all familiar with the case before me, the Timmerman murder?"

"Only what I've read in the paper and seen on television." I wish I had more of a connection to the case, like if I were a cousin of the victim, or if I were one of the suspects in the case. It would disqualify me from being involved. Unfortunately, I

4

checked my family tree, and there's not a Timmerman to be found.

"It would seem to be a straightforward murder case, if such a thing existed," he says and then chuckles, so I assume that what he said passes in Hatchet-land for a joke. "But the victim was a prominent man of great wealth."

I nod again. It's sort of nice being in a conversation in which I have no responsibilities.

"I'm told that you haven't taken on any pro bono work in over two years."

Another nod from me.

"I assume you're ready and willing to fulfill your civic responsibility now?" he asks. "You may speak."

I have to clear my throat from lack of use before responding. "Actually, Your Honor, my schedule is such that a murder case wouldn't really—"

He interrupts again. "Who said anything about you participating in a murder case?"

"Well, I thought—"

"A lawyer thinking. Now, that's a novel concept. You are not being assigned to represent the accused. The Public Defender's Office is handling that."

Relief and confusion are fighting for a dominant position in my mind, and I'm actually surprised that confusion is winning. "Then why am I here?"

"I've been asked to handle a related matter that is technically before Judge Parker in the probate court. He has taken ill, and I said I would do it because of my unfortunate familiarity with you. Are you aware that the victim was very much involved with show dogs?"

"No," I say. While I rescue dogs, I have little or no knowledge of dog shows or breeders.

"Well, he was, and he had a seven-month-old, apparently a

descendant of a champion, that his widow and son are fighting over. The animal was not included in the will."

This may not be so bad. "So because of my experience with dogs, you want me to help adjudicate it?"

"In a manner of speaking."

"Glad to help, Your Honor. Civic responsibility is my middle name."

"I'll remember to include it on the Christmas card. I assume you have a satisfactory place to keep your client?"

"My client?"

He nods. "The dog. You will retain possession of him until the issue is resolved."

"I'm representing a dog in a custody fight? Is that what you're asking me to do?"

"I wouldn't categorize it as 'asking,'" he says.

"I already have a dog, Your Honor."

"And now you have two."

● ● ● ● ●

TARA KNOWS SOMETHING IS GOING ON.

I don't know how she knows, but I can see it in her face when I get home. She stares at me with that all-knowing golden retriever stare, and even when she's eating her dinner, she occasionally looks up at me to let me know that she's on to me.

I take her for a long walk through Eastside Park, which is about six blocks from where I live on 42nd Street in Paterson. Except for a six-year span while I was married, it is where I've lived all my life, and no place could feel more like home. No one that I grew up with lives here anymore, but I keep expecting to see them reappear as I walk, as if I were in a *Twilight Zone* episode.

It's home to Tara as well, and even though the sights and smells must be completely familiar to her, she relishes them as if experiencing them for the first time. It is one of the many millions of things I love about her.

It's been really hot out lately, but the evenings have been cool, and tonight especially so. All in all it's a perfect couple of hours, but the ringing phone when I get home is a reminder that perfection is fleeting, and not everything is as it should be. I can see by the caller ID that it's Laurie Collins calling from her home in Wisconsin. The Wisconsin that is nowhere near New Jersey.

"Hello, Andy."

Every time I hear Laurie's voice, every single time, I am struck by my reaction to it. It is soothing, and welcoming, and it makes me think of home. But I'm already home, and Laurie isn't here.

We talk for a while, and I tell her about my day, and my new client. I glance over at Tara to see if she's listening, but she seems to be asleep. Laurie tells me about her day as well; she's the police chief of Findlay, Wisconsin, and has been since she moved back there, a year and a half ago.

We broke up when she first moved, and those first four months were maybe the worst of my life. Then I went up to Findlay to handle a case, and we reconnected. Now we have a long-distance, committed relationship, which is feeling more and more like an oxymoron. Telling her about my day isn't really cutting it. I want her to be an actual part of my days.

"So when are you getting the dog?" she asks.

"Tomorrow."

"Have you mentioned it to Tara?"

"No. I think she'll be okay with it, but it'll cost me a truckload of biscuits."

"You seem a little quiet, Andy. Is something wrong?" she asks.

Of course something's wrong. It's wrong that you're in Wisconsin and I'm here. It's wrong that we only talk on the phone, and we sleep in beds a thousand miles away. It's wrong that we only see each other on vacations, and that we can't be making love right now. These are the things I would say if I weren't a sniveling chickenshit, but since I am, all I say is, "No, I'm fine. Really."

Laurie is coming here on a week's vacation starting in a few days, and we talk about how nice it will be to see each other. Talking about it is enough to cheer me up, and it puts me in a more upbeat mood.

I hang up and turn to my sleeping friend. "Tara, my girl, there's something we need to talk about."

Tara takes the news pretty well, though the fact that she keeps falling asleep during my little speech means she may not be fully focused. She's sleeping a lot more than she used to, a sure sign of advancing age. It doesn't worry me, though, because Tara is going to live forever. Or even longer.

I settle down to read about my new client in a three-page report prepared by the probate court. The dog is a seven-month old Bernese mountain dog named Bertrand II, which strikes me as a pretty ridiculous name for a puppy, or a dog of any age, for that matter.

The dog is currently living at the home of Diana Timmerman, the widow of the murder victim. I have been told to arrive promptly at her house in Alpine, half a mile west of the Palisades Interstate Parkway, at ten AM. I'm a punctual person, and pretty much the only times I'm ever late are when someone instructs me to arrive promptly. I get to the Timmerman house at ten forty-five.

Actually, it's less a house than a compound, or maybe a fortress. There are two guards on duty at the gate, one inside the gatehouse and one patrolling outside. The one outside is actually wearing a gun in a holster. He's at least six five, 260 pounds, and would probably only need the gun if the intruder happened to be a rhinoceros.

"Name?" the guard inside the gate asks me.

"Carpenter." I'm a man of as few words as he is.

He picks up a clipboard and looks at it for a few moments, then puts it down and says, "Drive up and park to the left of the house. Someone will be out to get you."

I go along a driveway that slopes upward until I come to the house, an amazingly impressive structure that looks straight out of *Gone with the Wind*. I consider myself independently wealthy, having inherited over twenty million dollars from my father a few years back. If I were willing to part with all of it, I could probably afford the Timmermans' garage.

Because civil disobedience is my thing, I park to the right of the house, not the left. I get out of the car and wait, and after about five minutes the front door opens and a young man, probably in his early twenties, comes out. He starts to walk toward his car, then sees me and heads over.

"You're here for Waggy?" he asks, and when he sees that I look confused, he adds, "The Bernese."

"Yes," I say.

"I'm Steven Timmerman," he says, which means he is Diana Timmerman's stepson, and one of the two people fighting for custody of the aforementioned "Waggy." He offers his hand, and I shake it.

"Andy Carpenter."

He nods. "Please take good care of him, Mr. Carpenter." He starts to walk back toward his car, but stops and turns. "He loves to chew on things, especially the rawhide bones. And he goes crazy over tennis balls." He grins slightly at the recollection, then turns and goes to the car.

As soon as he pulls away, the door opens again and a woman comes out of the house. She is dressed fashionably; my arrival definitely didn't interrupt her in the process of cleaning out the attic or scrubbing the toilet.

"Mr. Carpenter?" she asks.

"Andy. You must be Ms. Timmerman?"

She smiles, apparently with some embarrassment. "No, I'm Martha. Martha Wyndham. I'm Mrs. Timmerman's executive assistant."

"Nice to meet you. What do you executively assist her at?"

Another smile. "Being Mrs. Timmerman. You're here for Waggy?"

"Waggy? Is that what everybody calls him?"

She shakes her head. "Just Steven and me. But it would be best if you didn't mention that to Ms. Timmerman. Bernese mountain dogs were originally bred to pull wagons. That seemed so funny in this case that Steven and I call him Waggy. You love dogs, I understand?"

"Guilty as charged. I'm a certified dog lunatic."

"As am I. But you might want to let him stay here while you make your determination. It could be upsetting for him to be thrust into a strange environment."

"He'll be fine; my house is dog-friendly. Where is he?" I ask.

"In his room. But Mrs. Timmerman would like to talk to you first."

That's not completely appropriate; she is the other one of the litigants pressing for ownership of Waggy, and I really shouldn't be speaking to her without the opposing party present. On the other hand, appropriateness was never my forte, and I did say hello to Steven, so what the hell.

I let Martha lead me into what they probably refer to as the library, since the walls are covered with packed bookshelves. Most of them are classics, and few look like they have been read in a very long time. This may be a library, but it's not a reading room.

Five minutes go by, during which Martha and I engage in small talk, mostly about baseball. She's relatively likable, but I'm starting to get annoyed. "Where is she?" I finally ask.

"I'm sure she'll be down in a moment."

"Give her my regards, because I'm not waiting any longer. I'll take Waggy and be on my way."

"Mr. Carpenter."

I look up and see Diana Timmerman, tall and elegant and completely unconcerned that she kept me waiting.

"Good guess." I turn and ask Martha to bring me Waggy, and Diana nods that it is okay to do so.

"I'm sorry to keep you waiting," Diana lies. "I'm Diana Timmerman."

At that moment the phone rings, and Diana says to Martha, "I am available for no one today." Martha goes off to tell the caller just that, and then to get Waggy.

"It's nice to meet you," I say. "I'm sorry for your loss."

"Thank you; it's been a difficult time. Walter was a wonderful man. And with the authorities searching the house three times, going through his things as if he were the criminal, it's been hard to get back to anything approaching a normal life."

I nod understandingly, but all I really want to do is get out of here. "Murder investigations can be intrusive things."

"Yes. Now, I did want to talk to you about Bertrand."

"I'm sorry, but that would be improper. All conversations about the subject can only take place with both litigants present."

She smiles without humor. "Well, then it's unfortunate you didn't get here fifteen minutes earlier. The other 'litigant' was just here. I'm surprised you didn't hear him yelling at me from your car."

She's obviously talking about her stepson Steven, and I sense she wants to engage me in a conversation about him. But I'm getting more than a little tired of this; I feel like I'm trapped in an episode of *Dallas*. "It's been great chatting with you, but it's time for me and my client to leave."

Diana looks toward the door, where Martha has silently reappeared with one of the cutest dogs I've ever seen. It's a Bernese mountain dog puppy, a smile on his face and his tail wagging so hard that it shakes his entire body along with it. There was clearly more than one reason to name him Waggy.

I walk over and kneel on the floor next to him and start to pet him. He seems about to burst with excitement; his energy level is overwhelming. Finally I get up and take his leash. "Let's go, buddy. But you might want to calm down a little before you meet Tara."

"Will you be needing his crate?" Martha asks.

"Why would I need a crate?"

"He lives in his crate," she says.

"Not anymore," I say. "Not anymore."

Martha walks me to the door and outside to my car. "Does Steven live here?" I ask.

She shakes her head. "No, he doesn't."

Martha says good-bye, petting Waggy before she gets into her car. She starts the engine and is beginning to pull out when I see Waggy's ears perk up slightly. Somehow he senses what is coming before I do, but I don't have long to wait.

The explosion is deafening, shocking, and somehow disorienting, and at first I can't tell where it is coming from. But then the windows explode from inside the house, and the flames follow. Martha stops her car, and I can see her mouth open in a scream. Waggy barks, but both of their sounds are overwhelmed by the noise of the house coming apart.

There seems to be a second explosion, not nearly as loud, and then I see security guards come running, but it doesn't matter how big they are or how many guns they're carrying. If their job is to protect Diana Timmerman, they are now officially unemployed.

CRIME SCENES are really boring places to be once the crime is over.

The police on the scene want to question everyone who has the misfortune to have been there, but first they want to spend hours walking around looking thoughtful and consulting in hushed tones with one another. The rescue efforts ended a while ago, and Diana Timmerman's body has been found and carted off by the coroner, but the place is still crawling with police, firefighters, and investigators.

I'm told to wait by my car for a detective to talk to me. It's better than waiting in the house, since at this point there pretty much isn't a house. Martha is waiting her turn in the back of a police car, though after maybe twenty minutes she gets out and stands next to it. If she thinks her visibility will speed things up, she hasn't been at many crime scenes.

Waggy is hanging out with me, and not that happy about it. He still has that irrepressible smile, but he wants to get out and explore the area and hopefully get petted by the cops. I'm impatient as well, but I have considerably less desire to be petted.

The state police are in control of the operation, probably be-

14

cause of the nature of the incident. If it can be determined that the bomb is the work of a terrorist, then I'm sure the FBI will be called in. I'm not sure what distinguishes a terrorist from a regular person who blows up houses, but it's probably a matter of intent and the message they are sending.

It hasn't quite hit me yet that if I had been willing to chat with the late Ms. Timmerman a few more minutes, then Waggy, Martha, and myself would be leaving this area in jars. I can see and hear Martha periodically breaking into sobs, but I'm feeling pretty stoic. I'm sure later I'll start twitching and moaning, but right now it just feels surreal.

Based on his tail movements, Waggy has already moved on.

It's hot out, and I'm getting very cranky by the time Detective D. Musgrave of the state police finally comes over to question me. I know his first initial because D. MUSGRAVE is written on his shirt; I assume there are other Musgraves in the state police from whom he's trying to distinguish himself.

"This your dog?" D asks, backing up in a defensive posture as Waggy tries to jump on his leg.

"Actually, he's a ward of the court," I say.

"What does that mean?"

I proceed to explain to D how Waggy came to be my client, but he doesn't seem that interested, jotting only a small note on his notepad.

"So you were in the house before the explosion?" he asks.

"Yes."

This causes a prolonged note-writing flurry; there seems to be no discernible relationship between the length of what I say and the time it takes him to transcribe his version of it.

D questions me about my visit to the house. In real life, the event took about ten minutes; under his excruciatingly slow questioning, it takes about an hour and a half. My mind wanders during his note taking, but most of the time I'm hoping that Waggy will piss on his shoe.

He doesn't.

It's starting to hit me just how close I came to dying, and I'm feeling a need to get home. I make it clear to Musgrave that he's gotten everything from me that he's going to get, and he gives me permission to leave. I want to say something to Martha before taking off, but she's still being questioned, so I take Waggy and head for home.

En route, I call Kevin Randall, my associate in my two-lawyer firm. Kevin supplements his income by running the Law-dromat, an establishment at which he dispenses free legal advice to customers who come in to wash their clothes. It is there that I reach him.

"Hello, and thank you for calling the Law-dromat," he says when he answers the phone.

"Hey, Kev, it's Andy. How ya doin'?"

"You mean other than the obvious?" he asks. Most people regard *how are you?* or *how ya doin'?* as just meaningless chitchat. Not Kevin; those are questions that he takes quite seriously.

"Which obvious might that be?" I ask.

"Can't you hear how nasal I sound?"

He sounds the same as always. "I thought it was my phone," I say. "I have a very nasal-sounding phone."

"I have unresponsive congestion," he says.

"Does that mean you talk to your congestion, but it doesn't answer?" Kevin is a total hypochondriac, which gives me something to torture him about.

His annoyance is obvious. "No, it's one that doesn't respond to traditional medicinal regimens."

"I hate when that happens," I say. "You want to come meet our new client?"

"We have a client?' he asks, his surprise evident and totally rea-

16

sonable, since we haven't taken one on in a while. "It's not another golden retriever, is it?"

"Of course not," I say. "It's a Bernese mountain dog."

"Andy . . ."

"This one's not my fault. I swear . . . Hatchet assigned me to the case. We're actually getting paid for it."

"Paid for what?"

"It's sort of a custody case, although the number of people claiming him has recently been reduced by one. And there may be some complicating circumstances."

"Like what?"

"Did you hear about the explosion at the Timmerman house?" I ask.

"Of course. It's all over the news."

"Well, our client lived there, and he and I were in the house before it blew up. Had we stayed there another two minutes, we wouldn't be responding to traditional medicinal regimens."

• • • • •

KEVIN IS WAITING FOR ME on my front porch when I get home.

I asked him to come over so I could pick his brains about the situation regarding the now one-sided custody fight, and because I didn't want to leave Waggy and Tara alone without first knowing that they get along. He's beaten me home because I hit traffic on Route 4 in Paramus.

"Sorry I'm late," I say, as I take Waggy out of the car. "I ran into some unresponsive automotive congestion."

"You never let things go, do you?" he asks.

I smile. "It's one of my most appealing traits."

He points to Waggy. "This, I assume, is our client?"

"In the hairy flesh," I say.

I ask Kevin to take Waggy around to the backyard, and I enter the house through the front door. Tara is there to meet me as always, and I take out one of the biscuits I keep hanging in a bag by the door. We play a little game whereby she won't take the biscuit from my hand, but instead feigns disinterest until I put it on the floor. Then she slowly eats it while I watch.

Once she finishes, I say, "Tara, I've got someone I want you to meet. And I want you to keep an open mind about it."

18

I take Tara out back to the yard, and Waggy goes berserk when he sees her. He starts jumping on Tara's back and head, and poor Tara just stands there and takes it, as if she has no idea what to make of this lunatic. I do detect a slight wag of Tara's tail, which I take as a positive sign.

The meeting having gone reasonably well, we all go back into the house, and I'm about to bring Kevin up to date on all that has gone on when Laurie calls. I put her on the speakerphone, and am therefore able to update them both simultaneously.

As I tell the story, I can feel the delayed-reaction anger building inside me at the person who planted the bomb that killed Diana Timmerman and almost killed Martha, Waggy, and myself.

"Are there any suspects?" Laurie asks.

"I have no idea. I'll call Pete Stanton and ask him to see what he can find out." Pete is a lieutenant with Paterson PD, and pretty much my only friend in law enforcement. Fortunately, he knows everyone there is to know, and often serves as a reluctant source of information for me.

"But someone has already been arrested for the original murder?" Laurie asks.

"Right. And from what I understand, it's a kid from the inner city. He had Timmerman's wallet when they picked him up, so they think the motive was robbery. Since he's not someone who's likely to be blowing up mansions in Alpine, especially from prison, I would say his defense just got a bit easier."

In my view, which is shared by Kevin and Laurie, there are no such things as coincidences in murder cases. Walter Timmerman and his wife being murdered separately, less than four weeks apart, certainly wouldn't cause us to change that view. The two murders absolutely must be connected, and since the accused is in jail and unable to have blown up the house, he's most likely on his way to being off the hook.

"This is all fascinating," Kevin says. "But why do we care? The dog goes to the son, since he's the only person alive with a claim to it. And then we're out of it."

"Diana Timmerman was killed today by a bomb that could have killed me and Waggy. I would sort of like to have someone to blame for that."

"I understand that," Kevin says. "But we have no role to play here. The police will find the bad guys, the son will get Waggy, and who knows, maybe someday we'll find a client without a tail."

"I think Kevin's right about this one, Andy," Laurie says. "Starting your own investigation would be a waste of time and money."

I'm not sure what I want to do about this. "I know, but . . ."

She presses it. "You'd be on the outside looking in. For all you know, the police have a suspect already."

As much as I hate to admit it, she's right, and so is Kevin. "Okay. I'll let it go. I'll represent Waggy, and then I'm out of it."

"Are you telling the truth, or just telling us what we want to hear?" Laurie asks.

"I have no idea."

• • • • •

BILLY "BULLDOG" CAMERON arrived at my office at nine o'clock, which means he was alone for an hour. When I show up at ten, he is sitting in a chair in the hallway, just outside my locked door, eating a peach he bought from the fruit stand on the street level. My office is on Van Houten Street in downtown Paterson, which is unlikely to be confused with prime real estate.

"What are you doing here?" I ask, and then follow that with, "Did we have an appointment?"

He chooses not to answer either question, but instead asks one of his own. "It's hot as hell in here. You can't afford better than this dump?"

"It keeps me in touch with my roots," I say as I let him into the office.

He looks around at the receptionist area. "You might want to get yourself some new roots. This place makes my office look like the Museum of Modern Art."

I turn on the wall-unit air conditioners and then ask, "You know how to make coffee?" It's a process I've never quite mastered.

"Of course," he says, and walks toward the coffeemaker. "What time does your assistant come in?"

"Probably October," I say. He's talking about Edna, who's been with me since I started the practice, and who makes me look like a workaholic.

We take the coffee and go back to my office. I remove a pile of papers and soda cans from the sofa, and he sits down, a little warily. "So I hear you were at the Timmerman house yesterday."

I nod. "Just before it went 'boom.'"

"Must have scared the shit out of you."

I shake my head. "I laugh in the face of danger."

"So I've heard. Will you give me a statement describing what happened?"

"What for?"

"So I can use it to help get my client out of jail," he says.

"Why would he need me for an alibi?" I ask. "Wasn't he in jail at the time?"

He nods. "Yes. Your testimony is just icing on the cake for my time line. I've got other things to point to that indicate my client was in the wrong place at the wrong time when Timmerman took the bullet."

"Or when he took the wrong wallet from the wrong body."

Billy won't confirm that, of course, but he does ask an interesting question. "I understand you can place the son, Steven, in the house just before the explosion?"

"I can. Why?"

"Well, you didn't hear it from me, but I believe he's about to become the focus of the investigation."

"They're looking at him for killing his father and his mother?"

"Stepmother, and only for two years at that. And the word is they hated each other. With her dead, he stands to inherit almost four hundred million dollars."

"And with her alive?"

He shakes his head. "Zippo."

"Four hundred million is substantially more than zippo," I point out.

"You got that right. In fact, with that kind of money, you could fix this place up really nice."

Diana Timmerman mentioned to me just before the explosion that her stepson had been yelling at her a few minutes before, and she sarcastically commented that she was surprised I couldn't hear it from my car. I repeated this to the police, but I don't see any reason to mention it to Billy.

Edna still hasn't quite made it in yet, so I type out and sign a one-page statement for Billy. He thanks me and leaves, but not before mentioning how understaffed and underfunded his office is. I nod.

I now have something of a dilemma. I am representing a dog in a custody fight between two people. One of those people is dead, and the other might well be a suspect in her murder, a murder in which the dog would have died, too, had I not shown up at that time.

It doesn't leave me with too many good choices for Waggy.

• • • • •

Pete Stanton and Vince Sanders

are waiting for me when I get to Charlie's.

They are at our regular table along the back wall of the most fabulous sports bar in America. When I say that they are "waiting" for me, I mean that in a limited sense. They are already eating burgers and fries, watching baseball, drinking beer after beer, and leering at the single women who always seem to be in attendance. But they would rather hang themselves than ask for the check before my arrival; that is an honor left to me.

It has been that way since I inherited my fortune. Pete earns a decent but underwhelming salary as a police lieutenant, and though Vince does somewhat better as the editor of the local newspaper, they share a common cheapness and simultaneous disregard for my money.

"Where the hell have you been?" is Vince's warm greeting for me when I walk over to the table. Vince's gruffness is skin-deep; it extends from the skin on the front of his body to the skin on the back.

"Why? You were afraid you would have to pay the check?"

Vince smiles. "I do not fear the impossible."

"I was almost killed in an explosion yesterday," I say.

24

"Are your credit cards okay?"

I proceed to tell them my story, though they're already familiar with what happened at, and to, the Timmerman house. They didn't have any idea that I was there.

"You were there to pick up a dog?" Pete asks.

"Not just any dog. He is my client."

"Don't you think you're taking this dog thing a bit far? Maybe you should try some human companionship?"

I stare for a few moments at Pete, then Vince. "Maybe someday I'll try that."

I ask Pete if he can use his contacts to find out the status of the investigation, and after about ten minutes of grumbling he agrees.

Then I turn to Vince. "You knew Timmerman, didn't you?" Vince has mentioned him to me in the past, but even if he hadn't, the overwhelming likelihood is that he did know him, since he knows virtually everyone. He has a separate closet in his office just for his Rolodexes.

He nods. "One of the worst low-life scumbags who ever lived. May he rest in peace."

"I take it you didn't like him?"

He grunts. "When he came up with that arthritis drug . . . he didn't give me an exclusive on the story."

In Vince's mind, giving someone else a story is original sin. "That was fifteen years ago," I say.

It takes Vince a lot longer than that to give up a grudge. "Feels like yesterday."

"Who did he give the story to?"

"*The New England Journal of Medicine,*" he says, frowning at the recollection. "Those hacks."

Unlike most pharmaceutical semi-titans, who own or run companies in which other people do research and make discoveries, Walter Timmerman was himself a chemist and researcher. Twenty years ago he developed a drug called Actonel, which revolutionized the study of DNA by allowing for a much smaller sample to result in a reliable test. The implications to the justice system were enormous.

As important as that discovery was, it was not what made Timmerman absurdly wealthy. That came later, when he developed a drug that greatly reduced the pain, and therefore increased the mobility, of arthritis sufferers.

"Do you know the son?" I ask. "Steven?"

Vince nods. "Yeah. Good kid. Nothing like his father."

"You like him?" I ask, making no effort to conceal my astonishment.

"Hey, I'm not in love with him. He's a good kid, that's all. He did me a favor once."

"What kind of favor?" Vince generally doesn't like to ask for favors, for fear of having to return them. I've done him a couple of major ones, though he's done more for me.

"He got his father to make a big donation to a charity of mine. And then he showed up and worked a couple of events; just rolled up his sleeves and did whatever was needed."

Vince is a huge fund-raiser for an organization called Eva's Village, a Paterson-based group whose mission is to feed the hungry, shelter the homeless, treat the addicted, and provide medical care for the poor. It is such an amazingly worthwhile charity that I don't know how Vince ever got involved with it. But he hits me up for a donation every year.

"You think he could have committed two murders?" I ask.

Vince sneers, which is pretty much his natural facial expression. "I said he's a good guy. How many good guys murder their parents?"

I can't think of too many, and I've already reached my three-beer quota, so I call for the check.

Vince and Pete are fine with that.

• • • • •

Before I go to sleep, I call Laurie.

At times like these, I like to tell her what I'm thinking, so she can tell me what I'm really thinking.

This time I reveal that I'm getting semi-obsessed with the Timmerman murders, even though I know very little about the circumstances and only barely knew one of the victims. "It must be because I was almost a victim myself," I say.

"Or because you're anxious to get back to work," she says.

"Excuse me?"

"Andy, when you're working on a case, you're engaged intellectually in a way that's unlike any other time. I think you need that more than you like to admit."

"That's crazy. I had a very satisfying intellectual discussion with Vince and Pete tonight at Charlie's."

"I can imagine," she says. "What did you talk about?"

"Faulkner and Hemingway."

"What about them?

"Vince said neither of them can hit the curveball, and Pete said that Vince is an asshole."

Laurie laughs, probably as appealing a sound as exists in the world. Then, "I'm serious, Andy. I'm not telling you to get involved in this case, other than to take care of Waggy, but I do think it might be a good idea for you to get back to work."

By the time I wake up in the morning, I've decided that it's possible Laurie knows what she's talking about. I place a call to Steven Timmerman at the number that was in the records the court provided me. He answers the phone himself, which for some reason surprises me.

I tell him that I'm trying to determine the proper home for Waggy, and that while I know this is a tough time for him personally, he should let me know when he would be ready to meet with me.

"How about today?" he asks.

I'm fine with that, and I tell him so. He asks where I would like to meet, and I suggest his home. Since I might wind up putting Waggy there, I want to get a sense of what it's like.

He tells me where he lives, and I'm not pleased when I learn that it's in New York City. I love the city, but it's my least favorite place in the world to drive.

Waggy a city dog? I don't think so.

I find a parking place at 89th Street and West End Avenue. The Upper West Side is the part of Manhattan I like best; it has the excitement and pace of the city, but with the feel of a real neighborhood. Just by walking on the street you know that real life is being lived there.

Steven lives on the fourth floor of a brownstone between Riverside Drive and West End on 89th. There is nothing pretentious about it at all, though I'm sure that it's expensive, real estate prices being what they are.

I'm not put off by the fact that there is no yard for Waggy to ultimately run around in. Many people have the mistaken notion that dogs shouldn't live in apartments, because they therefore won't get exercise. The truth is that dogs don't go outside by themselves to do calisthenics; they have their needed physical activity when their owners take them out. New York has dog owners as good as anywhere in the country. You only need to take a walk through Central Park to realize that.

I ring the buzzer at the street level, and Steven's voice comes through the intercom. "Come on up," he says.

"Okay. Where's the elevator?"

"There isn't any. The stairs are on your left."

"It's a walk-up?" I say, trying to mask my incredulity.

He laughs; I guess I'm not real good at incredulity-masking. "Yes. I hope that's okay."

"It's fine," I lie.

Waggy a walk-up dog? I don't think so.

The inside of Steven's apartment is as unassuming as the exterior. My guess is that he didn't put a dent into his father's fortune by decorating this place.

He shakes my hand when I enter and notices that I'm still out of breath from the three flights of stairs. "Sorry about the stairs," he says. "I'm used to it, but most people aren't."

"No problem," I gasp. "You mind if I borrow your oxygen tent?"

He laughs and gives me a chance to catch my breath. While I'm doing so, I notice that there are a number of pictures of Steven and his father, but images of his late stepmother are nowhere to be found. One of the pictures, in which Steven appears to be no more than ten years old, includes the now destroyed house in Alpine.

He sees me staring at it and says, "I guess we got out just in time, huh?"

"That's for sure," is my less-than-clever retort. The incident has left me a little shaken, and seeing the house triggers that feeling again.

"I loved that house. I guess you always love the house you grew up in. You feel that way?"

I nod. "I do. That's why I'm still living in it."

"I envy you," he says. Then: "You feel like a slice of pizza? There's a place on Broadway that's the best in the city."

Now he wants me to go back down the stairs? "Why didn't you suggest that before I climbed Mount Brownstone?"

"I figured you wanted to see my place, because hopefully Waggy will be living here soon. Now that you've seen it, we can talk over pizza," he says. "Or we can stay here; whatever you like."

I opt for the best pizza in the city. The stairs on the way down fortunately turn out to be far easier to navigate than the same stairs on the way up.

I think it's a gravity thing.

• • • • •

New York has by far the best pizza
in the world.

This is not a debatable issue among serious-minded pizza eaters, of which I am one. And not only is the pizza the best, but it is everywhere. There are apparently thousands of pizzeria owners who have mastered the art, and they've all chosen to gather on this tiny piece of real estate called New York City. If you live here and throw a dart out your window, you will hit a great piece of pizza.

What is bewildering to me is why it has come to this. I can't imagine there is anything about the ingredients or expertise necessary to make New York pizza that would disintegrate if transported across city or state lines. Why doesn't one of these pizza geniuses set up shop in Teaneck? Or Philadelphia? Or Omaha? They would throw parades for him; he would be presented with ceremonial keys to those city's ovens and hailed as an unchallenged genius.

Instead they fight among themselves for a small "slice" of the pizza market, and the rest of the country is left to munch on pizza that comparatively tastes like cardboard soap.

Steven takes me to Sal and Tony's Pizzeria, on Broadway and 101st Street. Either Sal, or Tony, or both, are truly artists, the pizza is beyond extraordinary. They serve the slices on those cheap, thin, paper plates that cannot even support the weight of the slice, but that's okay. They clearly are investing their money in the proper place, in the pizza.

Steven starts telling me about Waggy, though he admits he doesn't know very much. Waggy is the only son of Bertrand, a Westminster champion who was widely regarded as the finest show dog this country has ever produced. Bertrand died suddenly in his sleep about a year ago, an event that sent the dog show world into mourning.

"What about his mother?" I ask.

"Another dog in my father's stable. I think she did some shows for a while, but Bertrand was the star of the family. Apparently they all hoped that Waggy would follow in his father's footsteps."

"They?" I ask. "Not you?"

He grins. "Personally, I don't give a shit. I think a dog should be a dog, not a performer. Waggy should have fun."

"He would have fun living with you?"

He nods, perhaps a little wistfully. "I think so. I know a lot about fun, or at least I used to."

"Not anymore?" I'm finding myself liking him, much as Vince had predicted.

"No."

"Why not?"

"I don't know . . . it's all tied in to my father . . . I'd rather not go there. Self-psychoanalysis isn't a requirement to take care of Waggy, is it?"

"Have the police talked to you about the murders?"

"Twice, including this morning. I think they're floundering, because the guy in jail couldn't have blown up the house. Maybe they think I did it."

"Does that worry you?"

He shakes his head. "No, I just figure the truth will win out. That's more your field; isn't that the way it works?"

"In theory," I say. "Do you have any idea who could have done it?"

"Blowing up the house? Or killing my father?"

"Let's start with your father."

He shrugs. "I assume the guy they arrested. But I can tell you one thing for sure. My father didn't go to downtown Paterson looking for drugs or a hooker."

"Those things didn't appeal to him?" I ask.

"It wouldn't matter if they did, he could have made any drug he wanted in his lab, and he would have had the hookers come to him. It would never have been my father's style to do what they say he did; he would never put himself in a situation he couldn't completely control."

Steven gets up to get us another couple of slices, and I use the time to check my phone messages at home. There are two. The first is from Laurie, giving me her flight information for her trip here. No matter what the next message is, it can't be as good as that one.

It isn't. It's from Pete Stanton, telling me that he's done some checking into the Timmerman murders, and he's learned that Billy Cameron's client has been released, and that Steven is going to be arrested. "The kid lives in the city," Pete says. "They'll probably take him down there. Looks like you've got yourself a second dog."

While waiting for Steven to come back to the table, I find myself with a dilemma. He clearly has no idea what is about to hit him, and will be unprepared for it. Besides the emotional jolt, he will not have time to take care of any matters he might want to before going into custody.

I would not be breaking any confidences by telling him about the impending arrest. Pete attached no such restrictions on it, and in any event I wouldn't mention Pete. My instincts tell me that

Steven was not involved in the murders, but my instincts have been known to be wrong on many occasions. For example, I'm positive the Knicks will win the NBA title every year.

On the other hand, I could conceivably be exposing myself to some legal jeopardy by telling him. Were he to take flight to avoid arrest, I could be subject to an obstruction of justice charge. I'm confident I could beat it, but in the hands of a prosecutor who disliked me, it would be a major annoyance. And the percentage of prosecutors who dislike me hovers right around one hundred.

I still haven't decided what to do when Steven comes back with the pizza.

I take a bite. "This really is good," I say.

End of discussion.

• • • • •

I CAN SEE THEM as we approach Steven's apartment.

There are at least half a dozen men standing and sitting in strategically positioned places within a hundred feet of the entrance to the building. To me they are so obvious that they might as well be singing the Miranda warning a cappella, but Steven has no idea what awaits him.

I only walked back here because my car is parked along the way, but I decide to pass the car by and continue walking. I may not have prepared Steven for what is about to happen to him, but I'm not about to abandon him when it does.

As we approach I see the men pretending to be carefree and moving aimlessly, but actually executing a pincer movement. Suddenly they close in, and their actions are so swift and stunning that they take me by surprise—and I knew exactly what was going to happen.

One of the officers grabs Steven and turns him toward the building, while another moves me away so that I can't physically intervene. Obviously, being New York cops, they don't know me, so they are unaware that I am not a physical intervener. But I'm a hell of a verbal intervener.

35

Steven is stunned and is muttering something unintelligible as the officer tells him that he is under arrest, and then quickly recites his rights to him. The officer concludes with, "Do you understand what I have just told you?"

Steven does not answer; it's possible he isn't even aware that the man is speaking.

"Do you understand what I have just told you?" the officer repeats.

Finally Steven nods and says, "Yes . . . yes."

"Do you wish to speak with me now?" the officer asks.

This time Steven doesn't speak; he just turns to me. The look on his face is a desperate plea for help.

"No, he does not wish to speak to you now," I say.

"Who are you?" the officer asks, looking at me for the first time.

"I'm his attorney."

"Well, isn't that a happy coincidence."

Steven is taken to the Manhattan County jail, where he is booked and fingerprinted. Before they leave, I instruct him not to talk to anyone at all, and I assure him that I will meet him down there.

I do so, and while I am there I formally agree to waive extradition so that he can be transferred to New Jersey. Lieutenant Dennis Simmons of the New Jersey State Police expresses his appreciation for my cooperation, though we both know I had no choice. Refusing permission would have only delayed the process by a day or so, while Steven would have been sitting in a jail either way.

By eight o'clock in the evening, Steven has been rebooked and is probably not very comfortably settled in the Passaic County jail. I know from having other clients recount their experiences what he is going through; the fear is palpable, and unfortunately warranted.

I won't be able to see him until the morning, so I go home and call Kevin. I bring him up to date on the day's events, and assure him that for the moment we have a client who is not another canine.

"Andy, you and I both know that it doesn't matter whether he is guilty or innocent; he's entitled to the best defense he can get. And he'll get it no matter who represents him."

That is such an obvious statement that I have no idea why Kevin felt the need to voice it. "I know that, Kevin."

"Do you also realize that if he's guilty, then he left the house that day thinking you were going to go inside and get blown apart? Along with his stepmother and the dog?"

Amazingly, that hadn't occurred to me. "I hadn't thought about that until you just said it."

"Do you still want him as a client?"

"You know what? I'm not sure."

"Think about it, Andy. Because if they really wanted to, they could charge him with attempted murder of his own attorney."

I call Laurie to discuss it with her, but she's not at home. Since it's nine o'clock in Wisconsin, my mind would ordinarily start imagining her out to dinner with Brett Favre or some other member of the Wisconsin jet set. The truth is that right now my mind is so preoccupied that I don't even have the time or energy for petty, ridiculous jealousies. This situation is screwing up my priorities.

My most reliable mind-clearing technique has always been to take Tara for a long walk. It somehow feels like getting down to basics. She is in complete touch with her world; the way she sees and smells everything . . . the way her ears perk up at any unusual sound . . . it somehow encourages me to trust my own instincts the way she trusts hers.

It's a little more difficult tonight, since I'm walking both Tara and the maniac known as Waggy. He is positively crazed with excitement by this walk, though we've pretty much followed the same route every day since he's been here.

I am taking very seriously Kevin's comments about that day at the house. If Steven planted the explosives, or caused them to be planted, then he is obviously a cold-blooded murderer. And because he saw me outside the house, and knew I was going in, then he was fully content to be a cold-blooded murderer of me.

But I was basically a stranger to him, and it seems silly to feel he is entitled to a vigorous defense if charged with killing his father and stepmother, but not for the attempted murder of an unwitting bystander. On the other hand, I keep coming back to the fact that the unwitting bystander was me.

I cut the walk a little short, not because I am seeing things with total clarity, but because my arms ache from trying to restrain Waggy. We get home, and I pour myself a glass of wine.

Laurie calls me back and is as supportive as she can be, while we both understand that the decision is both personal and mine. I think about it some more, and then decide to discuss it with Waggy, who is sleeping next to Tara on the end of the bed.

I'm nuts to do anything to wake up Waggy; I could be opening myself up for another session of his running around the house like an Olympic hurdler. But I say, "Wag, old buddy, here's the situation. I'm going to try to help your friend Steven. If we win, you live with him. If we lose, you stay here. Either way you'll be fine."

He just looks at me, gives a little wag of his tail, and lays his head on Tara's back.

I take this as a sign that he approves of the plan.

• • • • •

I PICK KEVIN UP AT THE LAW-DROMAT
at eight AM.

His car is being repaired, and we're going down to the jail for an early-morning meeting with Steven. Though from our point of view the meeting could wait until later in the day, we will be there early for his sake. If he's like every other client I've had in this predicament, he is scared out of his mind and needs to see a friendly face. Someone on his side.

When I arrive, there are about five customers sitting around, waiting for an interruption in the whirring sounds of the washers and dryers that means their clothes are done.

Kevin is in intense conversation with a woman, maybe seventy years old, who is sitting but still leans against a small cart that she would use to transport her laundry. He waves to me and says that he'll just be a couple of minutes.

I sit down about ten feet away and see that they have papers spread out on the chair between them. I am close enough to hear them talking, which is of little benefit because they are speaking Spanish. I had no idea Kevin could speak Spanish, and certainly not as fluently as it appears. It's disorienting; I feel like I'm watching a dubbed movie.

They talk for ten more minutes, interrupted only by the woman getting up to put more quarters in her dryer. Finally they finish, and the woman gathers up her papers before retrieving her clothes.

Once Kevin and I are in the car, I say, "I didn't even know you could speak Spanish."

"I had to learn, because for so many of my clients it's a first language."

"Clients? I thought you give legal advice for free down there."

"I do, but I still consider them clients. I'm representing that woman on a probate matter. Her husband died, and his will wasn't correctly prepared or filed."

What I'm hearing is pretty amazing. "So you actually represent these people? In court?"

"When I have to."

"For free?" I ask.

He nods. "For free; most of them couldn't afford to pay anyway. But they wouldn't take their laundry anywhere else."

Kevin has obviously become a pro at pro bono. "How many of these clients do you have?"

He thinks for a moment. "Right now? Probably about seventy."

I don't know how to respond to this, so all I say is, "Oh."

On the way to the jail, Kevin tells me that he has checked and learned that Richard Wallace has been assigned to prosecute the case. It's a mixed blessing for us. I know Richard well; my father trained him many years ago. He is cooperative and professional, but he is also smart and tough.

Once we're in the small, private visiting room reserved for lawyers and their clients, Steven is brought in to see us. The look on his face immediately tells us he has had a long, horrible night, and the truth is that it will only be the first of many.

The police and prosecutor made an embarrassing mistake in initially arresting and charging the wrong person for the Walter Timmerman murder. They would not then have moved so hastily to arrest Steven had they not been very confident that the embarrassment would not be compounded by another early release. They may not have the goods on Steven, but they damn sure think they do.

I introduce Kevin, and Steven immediately starts pressing us for information on his situation. He's hoping I'll tell him something positive, something to give him a reason to hope, when in actuality I've got nothing to tell him at all.

"Here's how it works at this point," I say. "For now I am more of a collector than a provider of information. And one of the most important sources of that information, maybe the most important, is you."

"What does that mean?" he asks. "I don't know what the hell is going on, so how am I going to tell you anything that you can use?"

"You know more about your family than anyone else, and the secret to all this is almost definitely in your family. So I want you to think very carefully about it, and look at it from all different angles. Write down anything that comes to mind; we'll spend a lot of time talking about it."

He seems unconvinced, but promises to do as I say. Then he asks the question that every single person asks the first time they face what he is facing. "How long will I be in here?"

"It depends on their evidence. If they have enough to take you to trial, and they probably do, you'll be in here at least until that trial is over. There will not be bail granted, not in a case like this."

"I didn't do this . . . please believe me . . . I did not do this. Nothing that they can have can be real, or true."

"We have to convince a jury of that. But there's another thing we need to talk about now."

"What's that?"

"Your representation. Do you have a criminal attorney?"

He seems offended by the question. "Of course not."

"You can hire one of your choice, assuming you have financial resources. You should not feel obligated to hire us simply because I happened to be there when this went down."

"I want you. Everybody says you're terrific." He looks at Kevin, who nods, apparently confirming that assessment.

"You checked me out as a criminal attorney?" I ask, since this seems to fly in the face of his previous apparent unconcern at the possibility of being arrested.

He shakes his head. "No, I was doing research about you because you were going to decide what happens to Waggy. I wanted to see what kind of person you are. In the process, I read about cases you've handled and people you've helped."

I continue to make sure he understands that he can talk to or hire a different attorney, but he adamantly refuses to entertain the possibility. We discuss my fee, which is considerable but doesn't seem to give him pause.

"I have a trust fund," he says. "I'm supposed to get money from it each quarter, but I always put it back into the fund. I'm sure I can have access to it now."

"How have you supported yourself?" I ask.

"I make furniture. People hire me and I custom-design it to their specifications."

"Where do you do this?"

"I have space downtown in the West Village. There's a small showroom in the front, and I do the work in the loft."

Soon I'll know everything about Steven Timmerman that there is to know, but right now I see him as an unspoiled, hardworking dog lover.

On the other hand, he may be a cold-blooded killer who murdered his parents, and almost me as well.

My father served many years as the lead prosecutor for Passaic

County. When he would start on a case, before he fully examined the evidence and well before it went to trial, he would simply say, "We will see what we will see."

Yes, we will.

● ● ● ● ●

RICHARD WALLACE agrees to see me right away.

It's not a surprise to me, it's consistent with how I know he will handle this case. It's the duty of the prosecutor to share all the evidence with the other side, and Richard understands that he needs to do that on a timely basis. He's not interested in inhibiting the defense; he's interested in proving his case.

Arriving at Richard's office triggers significant nostalgic feelings about my father. I used to come to his office often and just hang out, particularly on weekends. It was his way of balancing the extraordinary hours he worked with his desire to spend time with his son.

On the way home we would stop at the restaurant of my choice, usually a place called The Bonfire, before heading home. Those were great days, and if anything the passing years have made them greater.

"Takes you back, doesn't it?" Richard asks when he sees that I am lost in thought. Richard is a good fifteen years older than me; he was just starting out back then.

I nod. "Sure does. This very office is where I should have developed a work ethic."

He smiles. "You've done okay for yourself. Your father was proud of you, and he'd be prouder now."

As usual, I'm somewhat uncomfortable with emotional feelings, so as usual I try to deflect them. "So you'll drop the charges against my client?"

He smiles. "Afraid not." Then: "We're preparing a package now." He's talking about copies of police reports and other existing evidence.

"How about a preview?"

"Well, you've got a bit of an uphill climb," he says. "Walter Timmerman had just removed Steven from his will."

That's unfortunate, but not a huge problem, and certainly not conclusive evidence. It goes to motive, but it can be dealt with. I don't bother pointing this out to Richard, because we're not arguing the case now.

Richard continues: "Steven's stepmother was to get all the money, unless Steven outlived her. Which he did. He also hated her, and they argued frequently, including a few minutes before her death. I understand that you know firsthand that he was in the house just before the explosion."

"Perhaps."

He smiles. "Don't worry, I won't call you as a witness. I have other people who can place him there."

"There were a lot of people there that weren't killed," I say. "Any one of us could have planted the bomb."

"Were you also seen in downtown Paterson near where Walter Timmerman's body was found at around the same time? Did you also have traces of his blood in your car?"

There's nothing I can say to this, so I just keep listening. It's getting ugly.

"I told you this is a bad one, Andy. And it gets worse."

"Let's hear it," I say, even though I don't want to.

"Steven spent three years in the marines, very much against his father's wishes. His specialty was explosives, and he had specific expertise in the type used to blow up the house."

Kaboom.

I head back to my office a little shaken by what I've heard. I've been doing this far too long to believe anything when only one side of a story has been presented, but Richard's presentation was quite ominous.

Obviously, I'm going to give Steven the opportunity to explain away whatever he can, but before I do so I want to familiarize myself with everything the prosecution has. I still find it hard to picture Steven at the house, knowing I was going inside, telling me to take good care of Waggy and make sure he had chewies and tennis balls, while aware all along that Waggy and I were going to be dead in a few minutes.

It doesn't compute, but the truth is that murder cases rarely do.

Kevin is waiting for me at the office, and Edna has made her appearance as well. Kevin seems content to sniffle and pretend to sneeze, while Edna is on the phone dealing with a crisis of her own. Her cousin Stella's neighbor's daughter is getting married, and Stella has not received an invitation. Edna has clearly been called upon to advise Stella on how to handle this potential slight, and within five minutes I hear Edna advise her to talk to the neighbor about it, ask other neighbors about it, and forget it and ignore it completely. The fact that her advice is self-contradictory does not seem to give her pause.

I bring Kevin up to date on what Richard told me, and he agrees that we should wait to get the discovery documents, which will be delivered in the morning, before confronting Steven with any of it.

Since there is little to do before the documents arrive, I decide to go home and start preparing for Laurie's arrival tonight. Those preparations will be basic. They start with changing the sheets on the bed, something I haven't done in quite a while. I can't actually remember the last time I did it, but it must have been a long time ago, because I think the sheets were white at the time. Now they're a dull gray.

After that I'll shower a couple of times, brush my teeth until my gums bleed, and try to find underwear and socks without any holes in them. Thus finished with the personal-hygiene portion of the preparation, I'll plug one of those electric air fresheners into a socket in the kitchen. It hasn't been smelling so great in there lately; I think I may have dropped a frozen pizza behind the stove a few weeks ago.

These tasks will have to be delayed for a while, because as I'm ready to leave the office, Martha Wyndham shows up unannounced. I'm not a big fan of unannounced show-ups, but since I had planned to meet with her anyway, I decide to make an exception in this case.

I bring her back to my private office, which in the area of cleanliness makes my house look like a sterile operating room. I can see her eyes scanning the room, trying to find a relatively clean place to sit down. Unable to do so, she picks the least dirty place and sits in the chair opposite my desk.

"What can I do for you?" I ask.

She hesitates a moment. "I feel as if we have something of a bond, seeing as how we both could have been in that house."

I can't believe she's here because of this imagined bond, so I just nod and wait for her to continue.

"I understand you're representing Steven," she says.

"How did you know that? I haven't even officially registered with the court."

"He called me and told me so," she says. "From the prison."

"You and Steven are friends?"

"I guess so, though I never really thought of it that way. We talked a lot; we have the same view about a lot of things." She thinks for a moment. "I consider him a friend . . . yes."

At this pace, Laurie will have landed at the airport, met someone new, and gotten engaged by the time I get home. "So what can I do for you?" I repeat.

"I want to help Steven in any way I can."

"Good," I say. "He can use all the help he can get."

"So tell me what I can do," she says.

"How long did you work for Mrs. Timmerman?"

"One week."

She sees my surprise, so she continues. "I was Mr. Timmerman's personal assistant, and when he . . . died . . . Mrs. Timmerman asked me to work for her."

"So you know a lot about them?" I ask.

She nods. "To a degree. They were difficult people to get to know. But I can certainly be a source of information, if that's what you need."

"That's helpful," I say. "I'll need a road map to help me navigate their lives. Steven may not have killed them, but someone did. Someone with a reason to do so."

"I'm afraid I don't know who that might be," she says.

"Not yet. Tell me about Steven's relationship with his father."

"It was complicated; I don't even think Steven understood it. Steven idolized him, and loved him, and was intimidated by him, and probably hated him. And every one of those emotions made sense. Walter Timmerman was an amazing man, in ways both positive and negative. Not an easy man to have as a father."

"But you don't think Steven could have killed him?"

"No."

"What about his stepmother?"

"That's another story."

• • • • •

LAURIE'S PLANE IS DUE at Newark airport at eight o'clock.

I'm there just before seven, which is about normal for me. For some reason I have a compulsion to arrive at airports well in advance, especially when I'm picking someone up. It makes no sense, because planes almost never arrive early. And on the rare occasions that they do, they compensate for it by arranging for the arrival gate not to be ready, so that the plane has to sit on the tarmac until it is.

And the ugly truth is that planes could be early, if the airlines so desired. Nothing is more annoying than sitting on a plane that is late in taking off, and having the pilot announce that he will "make up time in the air." If they could fly faster when they're late, why not fly faster all the time? Can you imagine a bus driver on a seventy-mile-per-hour highway arbitrarily deciding to go forty?

So once again I spend an hour looking at the arrivals screen, checking to see if other planes are arriving early, as if that might signify a pattern. They're not.

By the time the plane lands and Laurie gets her bags, it's past eight thirty. It's been an almost nine-hour trip for her; she's had to switch planes twice. Some people might look tired or disheveled

49

from that kind of day, but not Laurie. She would look great if she traveled cross-country strapped to the top of a covered wagon.

I'm not much for public hugging, but I make an exception in this case. We hold it for at least fifteen fantastic seconds, at which point she pulls back and looks me right in the eye. "Andy, I have missed you so much."

"Oh?" I ask. "Have you been away?"

We make it home in less than thirty minutes. It's about fifty feet from the garage to the front door, then another forty feet to the twelve steps leading upstairs, then another twenty feet or so to the bedroom. My plan is to navigate this distance and have Laurie in bed in less than twenty-eight seconds, which would represent a new record.

Unfortunately, Tara and Waggy have other ideas. Tara goes nuts as soon as she sees Laurie, and Waggy goes nuts because he is nuts. Within a few seconds Laurie is on the floor rolling around, petting them and laughing. The look on her face is pure delight.

"You look tired," I say. "Ready to turn in?"

"Tired? Let's take them for a walk."

"A walk?" This is not going according to plan, so I shake my head. "No can do. I tried walking them this morning. They hate walks; they refused to go. We argued about it."

She smiles. "That's a shame. A nice walk would have put me in the mood to make love with you. But if they don't want to walk . . ."

"Hey, they're dogs," I say. "We'll just show them who's boss. Let's go."

I take Waggy and Laurie takes Tara, and we walk for about an hour through Eastside Park. By the time we get back we're all a little tired and ready for bed, except for Waggy. Waggy wouldn't get tired if we walked to New Zealand.

Laurie and I are undressed and in bed within a few minutes of entering the house. She stretches out her arms. "You changed the sheets," she says.

"I change them every day," I say. "Force of habit."

"You're lying," she says.

I nod. "I also lie every day. It's another habit."

She pulls me close to her. "Let me show you something you don't do every day."

And she does. It would be nice if it could become a habit.

While Laurie makes breakfast the next morning I tell her all I know about the Timmerman case. The depth of my knowledge is such that I would have time to relate the entire story even if she were making instant oatmeal, but she's making pancakes. Her pancakes occupy a prominent spot on the list of things I miss when she is in Wisconsin.

"So where will you start?" Laurie asks after hearing my spiel.

"The father. He was the one with the money and the power."

She nods. "That's what I would do." Then: "You're going to be a busy boy."

She's verbalized what I already knew, and was feeling terrible about. I'm going to be consumed by a case while Laurie is making one of her rare visits. "I'm sorry; the timing is not great," I say.

She shrugs. "It is what it is. I can use the downtime, and there's a lot of friends I can catch up with. Plus, I'll be here to help if you need it."

"I could hire you on a temporary basis, maybe try it for ten years or so, see if it works out. Fifty bucks a week, but you'll always have a place to sleep." It's a pathetic attempt to suggest she move back, but it's as close as I'll come to broaching the subject.

She doesn't take the bait. "That's an incredibly appealing offer," she says. "I'll talk about it with my agent."

I head down to Timco Pharmaceuticals, the company Walter

Timmerman founded and ran for the last twelve years. Company-naming was obviously not his strong suit.

I usually find that calling ahead in these situations is not the best way to get people to speak to me, especially when I have no idea who those people are. I can be more insistent and obnoxious in person, or at least that's what everybody tells me.

Timco is located on Route 17 in Mahwah, in a building much smaller and less expensive than I would have expected. It looks like one of those mini medical center complexes that have sprung up everywhere. The entire thing looks like it could have fit in one of the bedrooms of Timmerman's now exploded home.

The small lobby is not exactly a beehive of activity, matching the feeling that the exterior gives off of a slow-moving environment. Not what one would expect from the cutting-edge company that Timmerman was said to run.

The directory still lists Walter Timmerman as the chairman and chief executive officer, with Thomas Sykes next in line as chief operating officer, so when I approach the receptionist I give her my name and ask to speak to Sykes.

"Is Mr. Sykes expecting you?"

"Anything's possible," I say, "but only he can really answer that."

"What is it about?"

"I'm representing Steven Timmerman."

She picks up the phone and relays my message to whoever answers. The response is obviously positive, because within moments a young woman comes out to lead me back to Sykes's office.

The main part of the building is surprisingly alive. It is one large laboratory, with what appears to be the most modern equipment, and a large staff of earnest people using them. If anyone is over thirty-five, they're aging well. The average basketball team is older than this group.

Sykes himself seems under forty, though he is clearly the elder statesman here. He smiles and shakes my hand, welcoming me to Timco, as if I am joining the team. I thank him and enter his modern, well-appointed office, which has a large painting of Walter Timmerman looking down from the wall, as if he were Chairman Mao.

"Thanks for seeing me," I say.

"No problem. But I doubt I can help you much; I don't know Steven very well. The truth is, I'm not sure I'd want to help you if I could."

"Why is that?"

"Well, if Steven . . . if Steven did this . . ."

"That, as we say in legal circles, is a big 'if.'"

Sykes nods vigorously. "I understand. Innocent until proven guilty. I get it." He shrugs. "But I really don't know him well at all."

"I'm more interested in learning about Walter Timmerman."

He smiles. "Walter, I knew."

"Good. Please tell me about him."

"What do you want to know?" he asks.

"Everything. I'm looking to fill in the blanks, and right now blanks are all I have."

He nods agreeably. "Okay. Well, there's Walter Timmerman professionally, and privately. Two very different people."

"Start with professionally," I say.

"One of a kind," he says. "An amazing, amazing man."

"I'm going to need a little more specificity than that."

"He was collaborative, inquisitive, brilliant . . . all he cared about was the science and the idea. He treated everyone whose ability he respected as an equal, even though he had no equal."

"What exactly did he do?"

This question sends him headlong into an extended scientific dissertation, of which I understand maybe ten percent. When I hear the word "biology," I interrupt. "So he was a biologist?"

"Are you a basketball fan?" he asks.

"Yes."

"Asking if Walter was a biologist would be like asking if Michael Jordan was a shooter. Of course he was, but he was so much more. Think of it this way. Usually you have chemists and microbiologists working side by side. Walter was the best of both; I like to say he lived at the intersection of Chemistry Boulevard and Microbiology Avenue. It was an incredible advantage for him in what he was doing."

"What was he doing? Particularly recently."

"Well, I can't say exactly, because lately he wasn't very talkative about his work, and whatever he did was in his lab at home. But for years he was studying the physical aspects of life; he understood it better than anyone who ever lived. He understood that the human body, any living organism, is a collection of chemicals."

"So you're talking about his discoveries in DNA?"

"That was just scratching the surface."

We talk some more about Timmerman's work, though Sykes keeps pointing out that in recent months he was utilizing his lab at home and keeping to himself. This doesn't seem to fit in with the "collaborative" person Sykes described, but he doesn't see the contradiction, so I don't point it out.

When it comes to the personal Walter Timmerman, Sykes is much less expansive. He professes to know little about Walter's home life, but his sense is that Walter could be a demanding husband and father.

"Had you met his wife?" I ask.

"Twice, but just to say hello. At industry dinners. Walter hated events like that, but he was receiving awards at both, so he couldn't get out of it."

"What was your impression of her?"

He grins, but doesn't look particularly happy. "She was a handful. Knew what she wanted, and how to get it. But Walter seemed crazy about her."

"With everything you know about Walter Timmerman, can you think of any reason someone would want him dead?"

He thinks about it for a moment. "Walter Timmerman was a person who pushed at the limits of science and knowledge. So who might kill him? I guess someone with an interest in preserving those limits."

Then he shrugs. "Or not. Who knows?"

• • • • •

I CALL KEVIN AT THE OFFICE, where he's
been wading through the discovery documents.

As bad as they are, he doesn't seem too distressed about it. Most of the incriminating facts in there are those that Richard has already alerted us to, so it's not quite as awful as Kevin was fearing.

But it's bad.

I decide not to go back to the office, since it might make me late for the arraignment. Hatchet wouldn't look too fondly on that, and I certainly don't want to get on Hatchet's bad side at the beginning of a murder case. Or at any other time, for that matter.

Kevin is not going to join me at the arraignment. There would be nothing for him to do there anyway, and we're better off with him spending the time getting familiar with the facts of the case. Or at least those items that the prosecution considers facts. Hopefully we'll have a different interpretation.

My plan is to talk to Steven before the arraignment about some of the discovery information, but that plan is thwarted when a screwup results in him being brought over too late for us to meet. We only have about thirty seconds before the hearing starts, leaving me barely enough time to tell him what to expect, and how to behave.

It is rare that an arraignment is eventful, and this one doesn't break any new ground. Richard states the charges clearly and concisely, and tells Hatchet that the prosecution is current on providing discovery information.

Hatchet asks how Steven pleads, and he answers "not guilty" in an understandably shaky voice. If I were facing two charges of murder in the first degree, I would barely be able to squeak.

I request bail, pointing out that Steven has never before been accused of a crime. Richard takes the opposite viewpoint, pointing out the heinous nature of these particular crimes, and adding that a person of Steven's means is a particular flight risk.

Hatchet disdainfully denies bail, as I knew he would. I can see Steven flinch when he hears it, even though I had told him we had no chance to prevail and were basically going through the motions.

Richard requests a trial date in two months, and is clearly surprised when I agree to it. Steven has begged me to, since he doesn't want to spend one day longer than necessary in prison. He isn't quite focusing on the fact that a loss at trial means he'll never leave that prison. Besides, I can always request a delay if it seems we won't be ready.

It's almost four o'clock, so my options are to go to the office or go home. Edna and Kevin are in the office, and Laurie is at home. It's not exactly a decision to agonize over, so I ask Edna to have a messenger bring copies of the documents to my house.

"So I have to copy them?" she asks. I can feel her cringing through the phone. It's standard procedure for her to have copied them when they arrived, but Edna evidently is trying a new approach.

"Not by hand," I say. "You can use the copying machine."

She reluctantly agrees to perform this heroic task, and I head home. When I get there, Laurie is cooking dinner, Tara is lying on the living room couch, and Waggy is jumping on her head. Laurie tells me that this particular head-jumping exercise has been going on for about an hour and a half, and if anything it has gained in intensity.

"It's amazing how much patience Tara has with him," I say.

Laurie smiles. "Saint Tara of Paterson."

"Waggy," I say, "give it a rest."

"He's just excited that they were talking about him on television today."

"What do you mean?" I ask.

"It was on the news. They were talking about the Timmerman case, and they mentioned that you had custody of him. His father was apparently a legend in the dog show world."

I'm surprised and a little annoyed that the word has gotten out; I hope people don't start coming around trying to get a look at him. I glance over at Waggy, who has jumped off Tara and is now smacking a tennis ball with his paw and then chasing it around the room. "I'm not so sure he'd be proud of his son."

We have dinner and then settle down to drink wine and watch a movie. It's nights like these that give me a weird, certainly unwarranted feeling of continuity. As soon as Laurie arrives it's as if she never left, and my remembering that she'll soon be leaving again is both surprising and jarring.

The movie we watch is called *Peggy Sue Got Married,* a Francis Ford Coppola film made in the 1980s about Kathleen Turner magically going back to high school and reliving those difficult years, with the benefit of knowing what life has in store for her.

It's something I occasionally think about. What would I do if I could start over, knowing everything that has happened since? I don't really know, but I'm pretty sure it wouldn't involve law school. And I'd make a fortune betting on sporting events of which I already know the outcome.

When it's over I ask Laurie what she would do differently now that she knows how things have worked out. My hope is that maybe she'll say she wouldn't have moved to Wisconsin.

"Nothing," she says. "Because I don't want to know how things will work out. That's not what the real world is about."

"I understand that. I'm just presenting a fake-world hypothetical. What if you could go back, knowing what was going to happen in your life? How would you change it? What would you do differently?"

"I'd eat less chocolate."

"You're not taking this seriously," I say.

She nods. "Correct. Because if I knew what was going to happen in my life, it wouldn't be living. I take each day as it comes."

I shake my head in frustration, though I'm not sure why I keep pushing this. "Of course you take each day as it comes. Everybody does; there's no choice. What I'm trying to do is get you to imagine knowing about the days before they come."

"Andy, would you like to know what is going to happen before it does?"

"Of course."

"And it would change your behavior?" she asks.

"Absolutely."

"Okay, let's try it. If you keep talking about this, we're not going to make love tonight, and I'm going to sleep in the guest bedroom."

"Can we drop this whole thing?" I ask. "I mean, it's just a stupid movie."

"Maybe it works after all," she says.

• • • • •

I SET AN EARLY MEETING with Sam Willis to bring him on board.

Sam has been my accountant for as long as I can remember, and has an office down the hall. In the last couple of years he has also taken on assignments as a key investigator for me, a task that he accomplishes without even leaving his desk.

Sam has mastered cyberspace and can navigate it to find out pretty much anything. He is simply a genius at hacking into government agencies, corporations, or any other entity naive enough to think it is secure. If I need a phone record, or a bank statement, or a witness's background, all I need to do is put Sam on the case. The fact that it's not always strictly legal is not something that has kept either of us awake nights.

I set the meeting at nine o'clock, because I'm due in Hatchet's chambers at ten thirty to give him an update on what is happening with Waggy. It's a meeting that was arranged before I took Steven on as a client, and I'm hoping the new situation will at least get me off the Waggy hook.

I'm in the office at nine sharp, and Sam arrives ten minutes later. Sam always has a disheveled look about him, and it's exaggerated in the summer, when he's hot and sweaty. Today is a particularly stifling day, and he comes in looking much the worse for wear. Sam has often said he would rather the temperature were ten than eighty.

"Hot out there," I say after he has grabbed a cold soda.

He nods. "You ain't kidding. Summer in the city. Back of my neck gettin' dirty and gritty."

Sam and I are practitioners of a juvenile hobby we call "song-talking," during which we try to work song lyrics into our conversations. Sam is a master at it; if they gave out rankings in song-talking he would be a black belt.

He's opened with a Lovin' Spoonful gambit. Fortunately, I am somewhat familiar with it, so hopefully I can compete. I nod sympathetically. "Isn't it a pity. There doesn't seem to be a shadow in the city."

He doesn't miss a beat, walking over to the window and looking down on the street. He shakes his head sadly. "All around the people looking half dead, walking on the sidewalk, hotter than a match head."

"You're too good for me," I say. "You ready to start the meeting?"

"If we have to," he says, with some resignation.

"I need some help on a case."

He brightens immediately. "You do? Why didn't you say so?"

"I just did. That's how you found out about it."

"I mean when you called me. I figured you wanted me to do some boring accountant stuff."

"Sam, you're an accountant."

"And you're a lawyer, but I don't see you jumping for joy on the judge's table."

"Bench," I say. "The judge sits behind a bench."

"Whatever. What do you need me to do?"

"Find out whatever you can about Walter Timmerman."

"The dead drug guy?" he asks.

I nod. "The dead drug guy."

"What do you want to know about him?"

"Ultimately, I want to know why he's not still a live drug guy, but don't limit yourself. I want to know about his money; how he earned it and where he spent it. I want to know who he spoke to on the phone in the last month before he died. If he sent e-mails I want to see them, if he traveled I want to know where he went and who he went with. Basically, anything you can find out about him interests me."

"What's the time frame?" he asks.

I just stare at him and frown. He knows that everything is a rush.

"Okay," he says. "I'm on it."

"Thanks, Sam. As always, I appreciate it."

He shrugs. "Hey Andy, you just call out my name, and you know wherever I am, I'll come running."

I'm pretty sure he's doing James Taylor. "Winter, spring, summer, or fall?" I ask.

He nods. "All you have to do is call."

This could go on forever, so I attempt to end the conversation, though I can't resist a final jab. "Okay, Sam, we're done here. My body's aching and my time is at hand."

"No problem," he says. "But Andy . . ."

"Yes?"

"Remember, you've got a friend. Ain't it good to know? You've got a friend."

Hatchet is handling an arraignment when I arrive at the courthouse, and I have to wait about half an hour outside his chambers. When he finally arrives, he forgets to apologize for the slight, and keeps me waiting another five minutes before calling me in.

Once I come in, he says, "Have you resolved the issue?"

"About the dog?"

"What other issue is there?" he asks.

"Well, Your Honor, as you are well aware, I'm now representing the defendant in the case. It seems like a clear conflict."

"Then resolve it, and the conflict will go away."

"Well, Your Honor, there has been something of a change in circumstances regarding the two people seeking custody of the dog. One is dead, and the other is in prison."

"Well, then I have a new contender for you to consider." He searches through some notes on his desk. "Judge Parker's office forwarded this. A man named"—he squints to read the name—"Charles Robinson has contacted the court seeking custody of the dog. He represents himself as a close friend of Walter Timmerman, and a partner of his in the showing of dogs."

Charles Robinson is someone I'm vaguely familiar with, and I know him to be a multimillionaire who has made his money in oil and real estate. There have always been vague accusations that his dealings are shady, but as far as I know he has never faced any criminal charges. "Thank you, Your Honor, I'll certainly consider Mr. Robinson. But I do need to make sure the dog is placed in a loving—"

Hatchet interrupts. "Have I given you the impression that I care what happens to this dog?"

"Well—"

"Resolve the matter. Either give him to Robinson or find another solution."

"Yes, Your Honor. Right away."

The phone on Hatchet's desk rings, and he looks at it as if it were from another planet. He picks it up. "Clara, I told you that I was not to be disturbed. Now . . ." He stops, an expression on his face that I haven't seen before. "I see . . . put him on." Another pause, and then: "Just a moment."

He hands the phone to me, the last thing I would have expected. "It's for you," he says.

I am gripped by tension. For Hatchet to allow himself to be interrupted by a phone call for me staggers, and scares the shit out of, the imagination.

"Hello?"

I hear Pete Stanton's strained and nervous voice. "Andy, it's Pete."

"What is it? What's going on?"

"Andy, I'm at the hospital. Laurie's been shot."

I can feel my knees start to buckle, and I half fall toward Hatchet's desk. "Is she all right? Pete, is she all right?"

"Andy, I don't know . . . I just don't know."

"Pete, tell me the truth. TELL ME THE GODDAMN TRUTH!"

"Andy, they don't know if she's going to make it."

• • • • •

I THINK HATCHET SAYS SOMETHING,

some expression of sympathy or concern, but I'm not sure.

Everything seems a blur, and I literally stagger out of his office, heading for the elevator to take me downstairs. I think Pete said there was someone or something waiting for me down there, but I could be wrong.

When I reach the street level, two uniformed policemen seem to be waiting for me. "Mr. Carpenter?"

I nod.

"We'll be taking you to the hospital."

I nod again and follow them to their car. It could be the next-to-last car ride I will ever take, because if Laurie does not pull through, I am going to get in my own car and drive it off a cliff.

I don't ask the officers what they know, because they probably don't know anything, and wouldn't be authorized to tell me if they did. The horrible fear that keeps popping up, easily overwhelming my well-developed sense of denial, is that Laurie might already be gone. If she was, Pete wouldn't have told me over the phone. He would have done just what he did, which was cushion me for the blow by telling me how badly she was hurt.

65

The Barnert Hospital is on Broadway in Paterson, about fifteen minutes from the courthouse. There is little traffic, but it feels as if the trip takes three weeks. They finally pull up to the emergency room entrance, and I rush to jump out, only to find that the car door is locked.

"Open the door!" I yell. "Open the damn door!"

I hear a popping noise and this time when I pull on the handle the door opens. I get out and run into the emergency room. Kevin is there waiting, and the stricken, anguished look on his face tells me that Laurie is gone.

But she's not.

"She's in surgery, Andy. She went in half an hour ago."

I am having trouble processing words. "She's alive? Is that what you're saying? She's still alive?"

"Yes. That's what they told me."

My feet suddenly feel unable to support my weight, and I move over to some metal chairs. Kevin sits down next to me. "Please tell me everything you know," I say. "Everything."

It turns out that Kevin doesn't know much. Laurie was in the front yard of my house throwing a tennis ball with Tara and Waggy when she was shot. She took the bullet in the upper thigh, which became horribly serious because it happened to sever the carotid artery, causing massive blood loss. Only the quick actions of my neighbor, who called 911 and then rushed over to put pressure on the wound, kept her alive.

For now.

I'm about to hit Kevin with a barrage of questions, when I look up and see Pete Stanton standing over me.

"Pete, tell me . . ."

"All I know is that she's in surgery, and she's getting massive transfusions. It's touch and go, Andy."

It flashes through my mind that this sounds like the same injury that killed Sean Taylor of the Washington Redskins. Pete must know that, but he has the good sense not to mention it. Kevin would likely never even have heard of the Washington Redskins.

"Who did this?" I ask.

Pete shakes his head. "Don't know. According to the neighbor, it was a drive-by. But he got a model, color, and partial plate, so we've got a shot at it."

"Where can I wait for the doctor?" I ask.

"There's an empty room on the floor; he's going to come there when he's finished. By the way, I told them you were the husband."

"Why?"

He shrugs. "Gives you access; if you're not family you have no rights."

I nod. "Thanks."

Pete, Kevin, and I go up to the seventh floor, which is the surgery ward. We go to an empty room, with a bed, small bathroom, and two chairs. I suppose this is going to be Laurie's room if she needs one. Please let her need one.

We wait for almost three hours, during which it feels like my head is going to explode from the pressure. The waiting is simply horrible, yet I am clearheaded enough to know that it must mean Laurie is still alive. Otherwise the surgery would be over.

During all the time we're there, I don't think five words are spoken, except for Pete getting an occasional cell phone call updating him on progress in the investigation. There doesn't seem to be much, but it's early, and I'm not focused on that right now.

I finally realize that Tara and Waggy are alone and unattended, and I mention this to Kevin.

He shakes his head. "I had Willie pick them up. I hope that's okay."

As my partner in the Tara Foundation, Willie is as big a dog lunatic as I am, so it's more than okay. "Thanks, Kevin. That's perfect."

Finally, the door opens and a doctor comes in. He's surprisingly, almost annoyingly, young, certainly under forty. If he isn't bringing good news, he's never going to get any older, because I'm going to strangle him with his stethoscope.

I stand as he walks over. I can't read his expression, which bothers me. I wish he were smiling, or laughing, or doing cartwheels. But he's not, and I'm scared shitless. The combined pressure of waiting for every verdict I've ever waited for pales next to this.

"Mr. Carpenter, I'm Dr. Norville."

I don't say a word; I can't say a word.

"Your wife has come through the surgery. She has an anoxic brain injury, due to blood loss, and she remains in very critical condition. She is currently in a coma."

"Will she survive?" I manage.

"We'll have a better idea of that in forty-eight hours. She lost a great deal of blood. And you need to understand that survival is not the only issue."

"What does that mean?" I ask.

"It is likely that her brain was deprived of sufficient blood for an undetermined period of time. There is the potential for injury." He pauses, then adds, "Irreparable injury."

I find my voice and ask as many questions as I can think of, but I can't get any more out of him, other than the fact that the shorter the coma, the better. It's going to take time until we know more.

He can see my frustration, and before he leaves, he says, "Mr. Carpenter, she's alive. At this point, with what she's been through, that's saying a great deal, believe me."

I nod my understanding.

"One step at a time," he says. "One step at a time."

• • • • •

I GO HOME to get some clothing and toiletries to bring back to the hospital. The front yard is cordoned off with police tape as a crime scene, and a squad car with two officers is in place guarding it. I identify myself to them and go in through the back; I wouldn't be able to stand seeing Laurie's blood on the lawn.

My feeling right now is that if Laurie never makes it back to this house, then I will never live here again. Certainly I can't tolerate the idea of staying here now.

Back at the hospital they still won't let me in to see Laurie; she is in intensive care and very susceptible to infection. An intensive care nurse tells me that Laurie is a fighter, and I know that's true. I also know that the cemeteries are full of fighters.

I've got to get a grip.

I lie down on the hospital bed, fully clothed, at about eleven o'clock, and start to cry. It's the first time I can remember crying since my father died, and if memory serves, this feels even more painful.

A nurse opens the door to see if she can help, but when I ignore her, she leaves me alone. Soon I lie down on the bed, and before I know it, it's four o'clock in the morning. For a brief moment on awakening I forget where I am or why I'm here, and the quick realization is like taking a punch in the gut.

I stagger down to the nurses' station and ask if there's any word on Laurie's condition. The nurse smiles and says, "She's resting comfortably."

"She told you that?" I ask.

"Well, no . . . she . . ."

"She's in a coma. How would you know if she's comfortable?"

"Maybe I should call the head nurse."

"Never mind," I say, and head back to the room. I've accomplished nothing except attacking a young woman who was only trying to help and make me feel better.

Feeling better seems a ways off.

My cell phone starts ringing at seven o'clock and simply does not stop. Every friend that Laurie has, and that includes pretty much everyone she has ever met, is calling to find out how she is, and to offer whatever help they can provide.

Edna calls at seven thirty. I don't think I've ever heard Edna say a word before nine o'clock, ever, but she has many to say now. It's a mixture of outrage at the animal who could hurt Laurie, and pleading with me to let her help. She tells me that she is going to come to the hospital and sit in the lobby, so as to be there in case I need her. I tell her not to, but I'm actually touched by her reaction, and Laurie will be as well, I hope.

Kevin comes at eight o'clock, and Dr. Norville arrives half an hour later, as part of his rounds. He has nothing new to report, except to say that Laurie spent a comfortable night. I resist the urge to torture him as I did the nurse.

They let me see Laurie through a glass window into the intensive care unit. She looks better than I would have thought, very pale but peaceful and extraordinarily beautiful. I want to go to her, to touch her and hold her hand, but they won't let me.

I go back to the room, where Kevin is waiting. I know he wants to talk to me about the Steven Timmerman case, but he doesn't know how to bring it up.

I save him the trouble. "Kevin, I want to take a day or two to think about things. I may withdraw from the case, if I can't give it the attention it deserves."

He nods. "That's very reasonable. Shall I tell Steven what's going on?"

I nod. "He has a right to know."

We hear noises out in the hallway, and Kevin goes to the door to see what has people so excited. He comes back a moment later.

"What's going on?" I ask.

"You're about to find out."

After a few seconds, Marcus Clark walks in the door. Marcus is one of the quietest people I know, silent and invisible when he wants to be, but he creates instant commotion wherever he goes. Actually, "commotion" might not be the right word. It's closer to panic, bordering on terror.

I've used Marcus as a private investigator on a number of occasions, more frequently since Laurie gave up that job and moved to Wisconsin. Marcus has also served as my personal bodyguard when cases have placed me in some physical jeopardy. He is uniquely qualified for both jobs, because he is the most frightening human being on the planet.

With Marcus walking down the corridor, the nurses must have reacted like the cinematic Japanese citizenry when they saw Godzilla wandering the streets of Tokyo. Actually, Marcus and 'Zilla are similar in a number of ways. They are both basically nonverbal, fearless, and perfectly willing to kill anything in their path. I think Marcus has fresher breath.

Laurie first introduced me to Marcus, and I've always been struck by the change in his demeanor when he's around her. He becomes borderline human, and I've even detected a hint of emotion. He likes her, which is why I try to remind him at every opportunity how disappointed she would be if he killed me.

Marcus doesn't say hello; I don't think I've ever heard him say hello or good-bye. He just looks around the room and is probably disappointed when he sees only Kevin and me. "Laurie," he says, and I think it's a question.

"She's in intensive care," I say. "She's unconscious."

He takes a moment to digest that information. "She'll be good," he says. "The shooter . . . nuh."

That probably represents as long a speech as I've ever heard from Marcus, and with that he turns around and walks out, sucking all the air out of the room with him. When talking about celebrities and politicians, it's often said that when people with real presence, real star power, walk into any room, they take it over. They become the center of everything. That's the way it is with Marcus, and when he leaves there's a void left behind.

Kevin stares at the door, openmouthed. "Did he just say what I think he said? That he's going after the guy who shot Laurie, and that he'll do something bad to him when he finds him? Maybe kill him?"

"Not in so many words, but yes."

"That's vigilante justice," says Kevin.

"I prefer to call it good old-fashioned vigilante justice."

Kevin thinks for a moment. "Me too," he says.

I don't know who or where the shooter is, but if he's smart, he's getting his affairs in order and choosing a casket.

Kevin goes down to the jail to update Steven Timmerman, and I go back to returning cell phone messages. This one is from Cindy Spodek, a good friend of Laurie's and mine who is an FBI agent in Boston. She is one of the people I turn to for information if my cases involve the bureau in some fashion, and she has been as helpful as she can be while maintaining professional confidences.

Her call was to inquire about Laurie, and I tell her what I know, which is unfortunately not much.

"She'll make it, Andy. She's a fighter."

I know everybody is being well intentioned, but that line is starting to drive me crazy. "Right."

"Any leads on the shooter?" she asks.

"I think so. They got the make of the car, and a partial license. Pete Stanton is the lead detective on it."

"Good," she says. She knows Pete, and the kind of cop that he is.

"And Marcus has vowed revenge," I say.

"Game, set, and match," she says. "You going to ask for a delay on Timmerman?"

I'm surprised she's even aware that I am representing Steven. "I'm going to take a couple of days to figure that out. How did you know I was on it?"

"Are you kidding?" she says. "You cost me an assignment."

"What does that mean?" I ask.

"There's a task force on it. I was going to get assigned, but then you came on board, and they reworked it because they knew we were friends."

This is bewildering to me. "Why was the bureau investigating Walter Timmerman?"

"That I don't know; I hadn't gotten briefed yet. And you know I couldn't tell you if I did know."

"Understood," I say. If she doesn't know anything, there's no sense trying to cajole her into revealing more.

It's only when we get off the phone that I realize exactly what she said. If I cost her the assignment, then the bureau's task force is still in existence, even after Timmerman's death, because I obviously got involved well after the murder.

It's not that the bureau "was" investigating Walter Timmerman. It's that the bureau "is" investigating Walter Timmerman.

The question is why.

• • • • • .

AT FIVE O'CLOCK the nurse comes in to speak to me.

It's really just an update; she doesn't have any new information to share. She reaffirms the doctor's comments that the shorter the coma lasts, the better the prognosis is for future recovery, though she won't come close to committing to specific time frames.

What's encouraging to me is her focus on Laurie's chances for recovery, rather than survival. As the doctor said, one step at a time.

Richard Wallace calls me to express his concern for Laurie, whom he knows fairly well. He apologizes for not having called earlier, but he was in court all day.

"Andy, if you need to ask for a continuance on Timmerman, I certainly won't contest it. Take all the time you need."

"Thanks, Richard. I appreciate that. Right now Kevin's working on it while I figure things out."

"Kevin's a great lawyer. Much better than you," he says, trying to lighten the mood.

"Right," is my clever retort. While Laurie is down the hall in a coma, I am resistant to any mood lightening. "By the way, Richard, why is the FBI on Timmerman?"

"What does that mean?"

"They have a goddamn task force investigating Timmerman."

He is silent for a few moments. "I didn't know that."

This doesn't seem possible. "No idea?"

"No idea, Andy. Are you sure about this?"

"I'm sure, though please do not reveal where you heard it. Do you have a guess as to why they might care about him?"

"You've got all the information I've got, Andy. Nothing has come up that should interest the feds."

Coming from certain other prosecutors, I would suspect that they were dissembling, or outright lying. Coming from Richard, I'm sure that he really is in the dark. I'm also sure that he must be pissed off about it.

I call Willie Miller to make sure that Tara and Waggy are okay, and he assures me that they are. He also wants to help in the search for Laurie's assailant, but when I tell him that Marcus is on the case, he backs off some. Willie knows that Marcus is usually sufficient, in the same way that a marine battalion is usually sufficient.

I go down to the hospital cafeteria to have dinner, after telling virtually every employee of the hospital where I'll be should there be any change in Laurie's condition.

The food is set up in self-serve-buffet style, and I choose what appears to be either very dark-colored chicken or very light-colored meat loaf. The first few bites don't shed much light on the question, so I decide just to shovel it in quickly and get back upstairs.

I'm almost finished when I look up and see Pete Stanton, who was just upstairs looking for me and inquiring about Laurie's condition. "You up for talking about the case?" he asks.

"Sure," I say, somewhat reluctantly. I desperately want the shooter to be caught and punished, but I also have this need for my mind to be focused on Laurie's recovery. It's stupid, I know, but it feels like if I relax my concentration on her and her condition, she could suffer for it. I know better, but I feel on some level as if my power of thought is helpful to her.

"Our feeling is that the shooter was a pro," Pete says. "He used a Luger thirty-eight, not exactly your gangbanger's weapon of choice. And he only took one shot, which means he was confident it was all he'd need."

"But he pretty much missed," I say. "He couldn't have wanted to shoot her in the leg. If it hadn't hit an artery, she'd be out jogging by now."

"Right. But your neighbor said that just before the shot, she was kneeling down in front of one of the dogs, petting it. The neighbor called to her and she stood up, just as the shot was fired. It could be that the shooter was aiming low, and missed because she stood up."

It's certainly possible, though at this point unknowable. "So if it was a pro, then it wasn't random, and it wasn't cheap. Whoever was gunning for Laurie had the money to hire help."

"Right," he says. "You got any idea who that might be?"

"She's a chief of police, Pete. She could have made a lot of enemies."

"I called her second in command in Findlay, a Captain Blair. He says that the whole town is praying for Laurie; they've organized a candlelight vigil."

"Did he say she's a fighter?" I ask.

"Yeah . . . how'd you know that?"

"Never mind."

"He's going through all the files and talking to everybody in the department, but he doubts the shooter had anything to do with Findlay. I tend to think he's right."

"Why?"

"It doesn't make sense. Why come here to do it, when they could have done it there, probably easier? It wasn't like she was leaving there forever; she had a job, so they would know she'd be back."

"She was also a cop here, Pete. And an investigator after that. That should give you a long list of possibilities."

He nods. "And we're checking them out. I was just wondering if it could be a result of any case she worked on for you."

"Off the top of my head, no. But I'll give it some thought."

"Good," he says, standing up. "You feel like coming down to Charlie's for a beer? Might do you good, and they'll call you if there's any news."

I shake my head. "I'd rather stay here."

He nods. "Vince said you'd say that. You speak to him?"

"This morning," I say.

"I've never seen him this upset. He got his paper to offer a reward."

"He's a better guy than he lets on," I say.

Pete grins. "I won't tell him you said that."

• • • • •

A NURSE WAKES ME at three o'clock in the morning.

I experience an instant wave of panic, which is just as quickly relieved by the fact that the nurse looks excited and pleased. "Mr. Carpenter, come with me. Your wife is responding to stimuli."

I throw off the covers and rush out into the hall before the laughing nurse makes me realize that I'm in my underwear. I go back to the room and put on my pants, since the last thing I need is a floorful of sexually aroused nurses, ogling me. I'm still zipping up as I go back into the hall.

They let me in Laurie's room for the first time, and I am disappointed to see that she is still unconscious. The head nurse is there, and she tells me that they put patients like Laurie through a regimen of stimuli four times a day, things like pressing a sharp item onto her feet, legs, and arms. For the first time since she's been there, she has had a slight reaction.

"Talk to her," the nurse says. "Take her hand and talk to her. If she's going to respond to verbal stimuli, it will most likely be a voice she knows."

I take Laurie's left hand. It feels warm but lifeless, and I have to fight off a need to cry. That's been happening to me a lot lately,

78

if I'm not careful I could forfeit my membership in Macho Men International.

"Laurie, it's me, Andy. Laurie can you hear me? Squeeze my hand if you can hear me."

She doesn't squeeze my hand, doesn't react at all. I try it again, and again there's nothing. I squeeze her hand, gently, as if I'm showing her how to do it.

Nothing.

I talk to her until about four thirty. I talk about Findlay, and Paterson, and movies, and baseball, and politics, and anything else I can think of. I keep asking her to squeeze my hand, and she keeps refusing.

I doze off until about a quarter to six, then wake up and start the process again. I've given a lot of closing arguments, and tried to convince a lot of juries, but I've never wanted to get through to anyone as much as I want to get through to Laurie right now.

"Laurie, squeeze my hand. Please. It's me, Andy. I love you, and I want you to squeeze my hand."

And she does. At least I think she does; it's slight and almost imperceptible, so slight that I almost can't tell if it's me squeezing or her. So I try it again, and this time I know for sure.

Laurie can hear me.

I run out in the hall yelling to the nurses, and three of them come running. I get Laurie to repeat her performance for them, and they confirm for me that it's real. And that it's a damn good sign.

They send me out so that they can run some tests, and I head back to the room, my feet barely touching the floor. For the first time since this began, I'm feeling some optimism.

I take a shower, dress, and check back with the nurses. Laurie is still upstairs, so I go back to my room. Kevin has arrived and is of course thrilled to hear about Laurie's progress.

"That is fantastic," he says. "Beyond fantastic."

"She's a fighter," I say.

Kevin brings me up to date on his meeting with Steven Timmerman. Steven is understanding and sympathetic to a point; he expressed his concern for Laurie and me, and will accept whatever decision I reach. He just wants it to be fast. He wants his trial to take place as quickly as possible. It's a reasonable position for him to take.

Dr. Norville comes in for the daily update on Laurie's condition. I basically understand about every fifth word he says, but the gist of it is that the brain scans they performed do not show damage, but that I shouldn't take too much encouragement from that, because they are notoriously unreliable at this early stage.

He is pleased by her responses to the stimuli, but again cautions me in doctor-talk not to read too much into it. Laurie is not out of the woods, and won't be until she wakes up. Ever willing to grasp on to straws with both hands, I like the fact that he doesn't say "if" she wakes up.

Kevin, whose favorite place in the entire world is a hospital, seizes upon the occasion to ask Dr. Norville about his own "unresponsive congestion."

"How long have you been experiencing it?" Norville asks.

"About three weeks," says Kevin.

"Do you have an internist?"

"Of course," says Kevin, slightly miffed. You name the type of doctor, and Kevin has one.

"You might want to see him," Dr. Norville says, and extricates himself from the conversation and the room.

Kevin is obviously not pleased with the interaction. "Does he really think it's possible I haven't consulted with my internist about this?"

I shake my head in feigned sympathy. "What planet is that guy living on?"

Sam Willis drops by to ask if I want an update on his progress in digging into the now concluded life of Walter Timmerman. The truth is that I don't, but he's worked hard and quickly on it, so I agree.

It is truly amazing how much of a person's life is available on computers if you know where to look, have the expertise to do so, and are willing to skirt all applicable federal and local laws. Sam fits the bill on all those counts, and he brings me a treasure trove of information on Timmerman, he says—far too much to go through now. And he'll have much more later on, when he really has time to get into it.

"Can you give me an overview?" I ask.

"Well, the guy was as rich as the media reports made him out to be; I would estimate his net worth at between four hundred and four hundred fifty million. And he didn't spend much of it; he had the nice house, spent a lot on jewelry for the current wife . . ."

"Was Steven's mother his first wife?"

Sam nods. "Yes. Died about six years ago. Cancer."

"No recent unusual transactions?" I ask.

"Could be; I'm not sure. At this point I was more into gathering the information than analyzing it," he says. "I've also got copies of the e-mails he sent and received for the last three months from his private and business addresses, but I didn't read most of them."

"How did you get that?" I ask.

"You don't want to know," he says, and he's right about that. "By the way, I did happen to see one strange e-mail."

"What was that?"

Rather than tell me about it, he searches through the reams of paper and finds a copy of it. It is from Robert Jacoby, whose e-mail sign-off identifies him as the director of laboratory operations at the Crescent Hills Forensics Laboratory.

The e-mail conveys what seems to be an annoyance on Jacoby's part with Timmerman, though it is expressed rather gently:

Walter

I've chosen to report back to you in this informal way because of the unusual results we have gotten on the sample you submitted. As you no doubt are aware, the DNA from the sample is your own, as it is a perfect match from a previous sample of yours we have on file.

Did this represent something of a test you felt we needed to pass? That would surprise me, and the fact that you requested the results on a priority basis only adds to my puzzlement. Can you enlighten me?

All my best to you and Diana. Looking forward to getting you back on the golf course.

Robert

I won't be able to place this in any kind of context until I go through everything Sam has brought, though he says he didn't see a reply to Jacoby's questions. Certainly the fact that a man who was soon to be a murder victim was experimenting in any way with his own DNA is at least curious, and something for me to look into carefully if I stay on the case.

But a nurse comes in and asks me to quickly come to Laurie's room, so right now everything else is going to have to wait.

• • • • •

"ANDY."

Laurie says it as I walk in the door. She sort of mumbles it, and it's hard to make it out, but it is without a doubt the most beautiful rendition of my name that I have ever heard.

There is a searing pain in my throat as I fight back the need to cry. I don't want her to see me cry, not now, because I don't want her to misinterpret it. She might think I am upset about her condition, when I have actually never been happier than I am at this moment.

I walk to her side. "I'm here, Laurie. God, you look beautiful."

I take her hand, and she seems to be struggling to speak. It looks as if one side of her face is unmoving and a little distorted. "Andy . . . don't know what happened . . . to me."

The doctor mentioned that she might have short-term memory loss, so I'm not surprised by this. I decided that I would tell her the truth, and I see no reason to change that decision now. "Someone shot you in the leg when you were in front of my house. You lost a lot of blood, but you're going to be fine now."

"Who?" she manages.

"We don't know that yet, but we will. Believe me, we will."

Tears start to stream down her face, but I see that they are only coming out of her right eye. It scares me, but I try not to show it. I assume she is crying at the fact that another human being would do this to her, but that's just a guess. I don't know what perfectly healthy women are thinking, and I doubt my abilities in this area are any better when the woman has a brain injury and is just coming out of a coma.

She doesn't answer, just closes her eyes. I call the nurse over, and she takes Laurie's hand and holds it, probably feeling her pulse. "She's asleep," the nurse says. "She needs to regain her strength."

"Is Dr. Norville here?"

She nods. "He's finishing up a procedure, and then he'll be down."

The "procedure" must require a lot of finishing, because it's almost two hours before Dr. Norville comes down. He spends about ten minutes examining the sleeping Laurie, though she opens her eyes a few times during the process. She doesn't say anything; just closes them again.

After he finishes, he looks at her chart for a few minutes, and makes some notations. I'm beyond anxious, and the process feels like it's taking a week. If he doesn't stop and tell me what the hell is going on, he's going to wind up in a bed in the next room, with tubes stuck in his nose.

He finally puts the chart down and turns to me. "Making excellent progress," he says.

"Any chance you could be more specific?"

He goes on to tell me that Laurie is recovering extraordinarily well, but is suffering the effects of lack of blood, and therefore lack of oxygen, to the brain. It is as if she suffered a minor stroke. Speech will be slightly difficult for a while, and she'll have some loss of movement on her left side.

"But she'll be okay?" I ask.

"With some therapy and hard work, she should return to normal, or near normal. If all goes well."

"Where can that therapy take place? At home?"

He doesn't see why not, though it will be expensive to bring in therapists, and insurance will not cover a good portion of it. That is not exactly a daunting problem for me, and he tells me that the hospital therapist will provide names. If Laurie continues her current progress, and if the proper arrangements are made, he expects she can go home within the week.

I can't wait.

They tell me I have to leave the room so Laurie "can rest," though I'm not quite sure why my being there prevents her from resting. We haven't exactly been doing any dancing, or playing one-on-one basketball. When I resist, they bring over the head ICU nurse to enforce the ruling that I must depart.

The woman is intimidating and physically imposing to the point that she might be able to take Marcus two out of three in arm wrestling. Suffice it to say that I am out of there and in my own room in short order.

A sniffling Kevin is waiting for me when I get back, and he informs me that we have received notice from the court that Charles Robinson has filed suit regarding the custody of Waggy. He has taken an interesting approach: Rather than pursuing custody himself, he is seeking to replace me as custodian. It would have the same practical effect as his winning custody, but it might ultimately be more palatable to the court.

In the short term, though, this new development will likely be an annoyance and major time waster for Hachet—not to mention me—pissing him off at a time when I can't afford to do that. He directed me to resolve the matter and contact Robinson, but I've been preoccupied with more important matters.

Robinson's suit is not something I can afford to focus on, so instead Kevin and I talk about the strange e-mail from the lab director about Timmerman's submitting his own DNA for testing. The lab director was puzzled by it, and Kevin and I both have reacted more strongly than that. Timmerman as a murder victim elevates the mystery of it, and requires us looking into it immediately.

Kevin, after hearing what Sam had to say, has once again been one step ahead of me and gone back to the office for the photos from the murder scene and autopsy report. Timmerman took a bullet in the forehead, but his face should have been recognizable to someone close to him.

I call Richard Wallace and ask him who identified Timmerman's body, since it is not in the discovery materials. He puts me on hold for a few minutes to find out, and returns with the answer.

"The wife. Diana Timmerman," he says.

"She was the only one?" I ask.

"As far as I can tell. There would have been no reason to question her identification, if that's what you're suggesting."

"Nope," I say.

"You have reason to doubt her? His face was mostly intact."

I don't want to share with Richard the knowledge I have about the lab director's e-mail. I don't know if it helps our defense in any way, and if it does, I certainly wouldn't want to tip our hand now. Now that I'm feeling better about Laurie's prospects, I am able to focus more on the case, and feeling like I want to continue representing Steven.

I call Marcus in the hope of learning if he's made any progress in finding the piece of garbage who shot Laurie. I do this with some reservation, since it will by definition require having a conversation with Marcus, a process that is always bewildering and frustrating.

He answers his cell phone on the first ring. "Yuh."

"Marcus?"

"Yuh."

"It's Andy. Everything okay?"

He doesn't answer, which doesn't surprise me. Words are precious to Marcus, and he doesn't want to waste a "yuh" on idle chitchat.

"Any luck on IDing the shooter?" I ask.

"Yuh."

"Who is it?"

"Childs," he says. Or maybe he says "Chiles," or "Giles," or any one of a thousand other names. Marcus on a cell phone is even worse than Marcus in person.

"Childs?" I ask. "Like children?"

"Yuh."

"Do you know his first name?"

"Yuh."

"What is it?"

"Jimmy."

"Have you found him yet?"

"Unh."

"Are you going to?"

"Yuh."

Fascinating as the call is, I extricate myself from it and marvel for a few moments at the terror Marcus must have caused in the informant community to extract this information so quickly.

I then call Pete Stanton and ask him if the police have made any progress on identifying the shooter. Ordinarily he would give me a hard time before telling me anything, but he knows the depth of our shared desire to nail the bastard.

"Nothing yet, but we'll get there," he says.

"The name Jimmy Childs mean anything to you?" I ask.

Pete is silent for a few moments. "You get that from Marcus?"

"Let's just say I got a tip through my crack investigating team."

"Childs is bad news, Andy. He's hired help and doesn't come cheap. He'd get up from breakfast to slit your throat, without his coffee getting cold. Even Marcus might have his hands full."

"Who does he usually work for?" I ask.

"Anybody with enough cash. But the last we had heard he was out of the country."

"Out of the country where?" I ask.

"The Middle East was the rumor, but it wasn't confirmed," he says.

"A high-priced hit man comes six thousand miles to shoot Laurie?" It's bewildering, frustrating, and very frightening.

"What the hell could that be about?" Pete wonders, out loud.

"Marcus will find out," I say.

"Andy, listen to me on this. Tell Marcus to be very, very careful with this guy."

"Maybe you'll find him first. Don't you police do stuff like that for a living?"

He thinks for a moment, weighing the possibilities. "My money's on Marcus," he says.

• • • • •

LAURIE IS NOT IN INTENSIVE CARE when I get there in the morning.

My first reaction is to panic, but then the nurse tells me that she was moved to a private room during the night. In fact, it's the one next to mine, and I didn't even know it.

I take the steps, three at a time, to her new room. When I enter she has her eyes wide open, and she gives me a half smile with the side of the face that she has full movement in.

"It's about time you woke up," I say, and I go to her and give her a hug. I do it gently, so as not to hurt her, but she hugs me back almost as hard as ever. It feels great.

"Andy, you look tired," she says. "You haven't been sleeping." Her speech is still slightly distorted, but much better than I was expecting.

"I've been out partying every night."

"Andy, please tell me what happened. I don't remember anything."

She doesn't even recall what I've already told her, so I relate the details of the incident that I know, and I can see her racking her brain to recall that morning. She draws a blank. "I don't even remember getting up that day," she says.

I nod. "The doctor said that was likely, but that your short-term memory might return over time. What about longer-term memory?"

"I think I'm okay," she says. "Test me."

"Do you remember when you said you would worship and adore me forever?"

She smiles and manages a very slight shake of her head. "Nope. Drawing a blank."

"Laurie, does the name Jimmy Childs mean anything to you?"

She thinks for a few moments. "Should it? Because if I should know it, I'm failing the test."

"He's the guy Marcus said was the shooter."

"Marcus is after him?"

I nod. "Yes. He didn't take too kindly to somebody shooting you."

"Marcus will kill him, Andy."

"I've heard worse ideas," I say. "But Pete thinks Marcus might have his hands full." I go on to tell her what Pete related about Child's résumé. Laurie is as baffled as to who could be behind this as I am.

We're interrupted by a team of therapists coming in to work with Laurie. Feeling incredibly relieved by her condition, I take the opportunity to go down to the Tara Foundation, to check out how things are going, and to find out from Willie Miller how Tara and Waggy are doing.

I am delighted to find out that he has brought the two of them with him to the foundation, rather than leaving them alone at home. They like hanging out with the rescued dogs, especially Waggy, since it gives him an unlimited number of wrestling partners.

Tara seems a little out of sorts. This is probably the longest she's gone without seeing me in a few years. I hardly ever take vacations, and if I do I bring her with me. I'm going to have to provide a ton of biscuits and some serious two-handed petting to get back in her good graces for this one.

Things at the foundation are going well. Willie and his wife, Sondra, have placed eleven dogs in homes this week. I feel guilty that I haven't been helping out, and Willie feels guilty that he hasn't visited Laurie, so we call ourselves even.

Willie of course wants to be brought up to date about everything, and I do so. He is not worried about Marcus's ability to handle Jimmy Childs or anyone else on this planet. Willie holds a black belt in karate and is afraid of no one, but he once told me he couldn't last ten seconds with Marcus.

"Maybe me and Sondra should be careful," he says. "Waggy the psycho dog is bad luck."

"What do you mean?"

"Well, that woman had him, and she got killed in the explosion. Then Laurie had him, and she got shot."

Willie is not smiling when he says this, and he shouldn't be. He's pointing out the coincidence that two people who seemed to be in control of Waggy got killed. I am angry at myself that I didn't even think of it.

I don't believe in coincidences, especially where murders are involved. They might exist, but it doesn't make sense to act as if they do.

I tell Willie to be careful, and not to tell anyone that he has Waggy.

Just in case.

• • • • •

It's time for me to talk to my client.

There is no sense in our trying to construct a strategy to counter the prosecution before we know Steven's version of the events. And time is a-wasting . . .

Kevin makes the arrangements, though I go to see Steven by myself. I find the first significant meeting like this, the one in which the client is called on to state the facts as he sees them, to go better when it's just one-on-one. Clients seem to open up more.

Steven is clearly relieved to see me and hear that I am staying on the case. He expresses the proper concern for Laurie, but he is certainly more focused on his own predicament. I have to admit, if I were facing life in a seven-by-ten-foot cell, I'd be a tad self-centered as well.

What Steven has been living is not a life. He spends twenty-three hours a day in his cell, eats food just south of miserable, and is treated with a complete lack of respect and dignity. Any ability to control any part of his own existence has been taken away from him, and the desperation in his eyes is the same I have seen countless times with countless clients. I imagine it's sort of like being a Cubs fan.

What Steven doesn't fully realize is that, compared with most of the inmates, he is living life in the fast lane. Because he has not been convicted of anything, he is isolated from the other inmates in a cleaner area with relatively kindly guards. Should he be convicted, he'll look back on these days with a wistful nostalgia.

I decide to hit him right between the eyes with my first question. "Steven, where were you the night of your father's murder?"

He doesn't blink. "I was home until about seven o'clock, then I drove to Paterson."

"Why did you do that?"

"My father called and asked me to. He said he had something to show me that I needed to see right away."

"Did he say what it was?" I ask.

"No, but he sounded upset, and I was worried because my father never sounded upset. He was always in complete control of everything."

"And you had no idea why?"

Steven shakes his head. "I assumed it had something to do with his work."

"Why would you assume that?"

"He had just been very intense and secretive about it lately. But his calling me might have had nothing to do with that. He certainly wasn't doing any of the work in downtown Paterson."

"Did you meet your father that night?"

Steven shakes his head. "No, I went to the restaurant he speci-fied, I think it's called Mario's, but he never showed up. He told me to wait outside, but after about an hour I went in and had a beer. I waited another hour after that, then tried to reach him on his cell. When I couldn't get him, I went home."

This part of the story checks out. Steven got a parking ticket outside Mario's, probably when he was in having his drink, which is how the police and prosecution knew he was there. Walter Timmerman's body was found about two blocks away.

"Why didn't you tell any of this to the police?"

"They never asked; they never talked to me at all. Then they arrested that other guy, and I figured he had done it, so I didn't think to go to them with it. Is that somehow bad for me?"

"We'll deal with it," I say, even though we may not be able to. "Were you and your father close?"

"Yes and no. It was kind of day-to-day."

"He took you out of his will."

Steven surprises me by laughing. "About a hundred times, but he always put me back in so he'd have something he could threaten me with."

"But you didn't care?" I ask.

"No, and it drove him crazy. I mean the money would have been nice, but having an actual, real-life father would have been nicer. Once I enlisted in the marines, things were never the same between us."

"He was opposed to that?"

"As opposed as a human being could be. Which I'm sure a shrink would say is why I joined."

"And you became an expert in explosives."

He nods. "Is that why they think I blew up the house?"

"It doesn't help," I say. "What did you and your mother argue about that day?"

"Stepmother."

I nod and stand corrected. "Stepmother."

"Waggy. She didn't care about dogs at all, but he was a possession she wanted, because of who he was. A future champion."

"Did you resolve anything?"

"No, I was hoping you would do that. I still am."

"Do you have any idea who might have wanted your father and stepmother dead?"

"None whatsoever."

"Steven, I need to show you a picture of your father's body taken at the murder scene. It's not going to be a pleasant thing to look at, but it's important."

"Why?"

"Some information has come up about him experimenting with his own DNA. We have to make sure that he was really the victim."

"No one identified the body?"

"Your stepmother."

He nods. "Okay, let me see it."

I can see him tense up as I take the photograph out of the envelope. I put it on the table and he looks at it for a few seconds, then closes his eyes and pushes it away before reopening them.

"It's him," he says. "That's my father."

"You're one hundred percent sure?" I ask. I'm disappointed, even though I thought it was very unlikely that Walter Timmerman faked his death. But it would have been far easier to defend Steven from a charge of murdering someone if the victim was not actually dead.

"I am completely and totally positive."

We talk some more, and he asks me how Waggy is doing. It reminds me that Hatchet had been pressing me to find a solution to the issue of at least temporary custody.

"Are you familiar with Charles Robinson?" I ask.

"Sure, he was a close friend of my father's. We called him Uncle Charlie."

"He's trying to get Waggy," I say. "How would you feel about that?"

"Charles shows dogs as a hobby, like my father did. I think they even co-owned a few dogs. He wouldn't mistreat Waggy or anything, but he'd put him into training."

"Anything wrong with that?"

"Depends on your point of view," he says, leaving no doubt what his point of view is.

When I leave the prison my gut feeling is that I'm somewhat relieved. He answered my questions head-on and did not give the appearance of having something to hide.

Which is to say, my gut tells me that either Steven is telling the truth, or he isn't.

In case you haven't noticed, my gut isn't that gutsy.

• • • • •

DR. ROBERT JACOBY readily agrees to talk to me, but he warns he can't talk to me.

I called ahead and told him that I wanted to discuss Walter Timmerman, though I did not mention the strange e-mail that Sam found. Jacoby agreed, but alerted me that he regarded his interactions with Timmerman as confidential.

Crescent Hills Forensics Laboratory is located in Teaneck, not far from the campus of Fairleigh Dickinson University. The outside looks like a white spaceship, with a flat, oval, sweeping roof sitting atop a mostly glass building like a white sombrero. It seems to have been the work of a blindfolded architect who was given the mandate to make the building as modern as possible, so that clients would assume the work done inside was state of the art. He was obviously instructed not to be concerned if the building turned out to be embarrassingly ugly.

Jacoby's office is a study in chrome and glass, with not a test tube or Bunsen burner to be found. He is dressed in a perfectly tailored suit that certainly never knew the indignity of spending a moment on a clothing store rack. This guy has his clothes custom-made as surely as I don't. And if he's going to roll up his sleeves and get to work, he's going to have to take off his gold cuff links first.

I accept his offer of a glass of Swedish mineral water, and then ask him about his business relationship with Walter Timmerman. He smiles condescendingly and then shakes his head. "I'm sorry, Mr. Carpenter, but our communications are confidential."

"I wasn't asking about specifics," I say, though I'm certainly planning to.

"The line is hard to draw," he says, "so I prefer not to say anything. Even though Mr. Timmerman is deceased, our reputation is such that—"

This is getting me nowhere, so I interrupt. "Were you Mr. Timmerman's personal physician?"

"No."

"His lawyer?"

"Certainly not. But—"

"Are you a priest? A rabbi?"

"Mr. Carpenter, Walter Timmerman was a close, personal friend of mine, and I will honor his memory. You need to understand that you cannot come in here and bully me."

"Noted," I say, as I prepare to bully him. "Now, here's what you need to understand. I have a few questions that I need answers for. It will be relatively painless for you. The alternative is that I serve you with a subpoena and force you to sit through a full-blown deposition, which will feel like a verbal rectal exam, conducted with a rusty spatula."

He doesn't say anything for a few moments, no doubt considering his options and visualizing the spatula. I decide to continue.

"Dr. Jacoby, why did Walter Timmerman send you his own DNA to be tested?"

He reacts to this with apparent shock. "How did you know about that?"

"It came up as part of the investigation."

He sags slightly, which I take as a sign that he is going to drop his resistance to answering my questions. "I'm not sure why he sent me that. I asked him, but he never responded. I found it to be something of an affront, both professional and personally."

"An affront in what way?"

"Well, it seemed to be a test of sorts, yet he couldn't think we would do anything but pass it. Frankly, it was slightly bizarre."

"Could he have just been wanting to get his own DNA on file?"

Jacoby shakes his head. "No, he had done that long ago, and he wouldn't have forgotten that. This was a simple match of DNA in pristine condition. There is not a laboratory in the country that would have missed it."

I have no more idea what to make of this than Jacoby. I could certainly be wasting my time on it as well; it likely has nothing whatsoever to do with Timmerman's murder. "And the DNA was absolutely identical?" I ask.

"A perfect match."

"You're positive?"

He looks at me with clear disdain. "Mr. Carpenter, do you know anything about DNA?"

"I wouldn't know it if it came in here and bit me on the ass."

He frowns. "Well, my associates and I know plenty about it. But we were novices compared with Walter Timmerman. Think of us as watchmakers, with DNA as the watch. We understand watches, we can fix them, we know what makes them tick. But Walter Timmerman knew *why* they tick, he understood them at their core. He knew that the DNA he sent us was his, he knew it was uncontaminated, and he knew that we would find it as such. Why he sent it is a mystery we will probably never understand."

"But he must have had a reason."

"On that we can agree," he says. "Walter Timmerman had a reason for everything he did."

On the way back to the hospital, I try to make sense of what Jacoby told me. He was certainly telling the truth; the e-mail confirms that. But he was not able to shed any light on the mystery, and therefore I did not accomplish much of anything.

One of the most frustrating things about working on a case like this is that we are obligated to follow every investigative road, not knowing where it will lead. Very often we don't find out that it has no relevance to our case until we get to the end of that road. Worse yet, sometimes the road has no end, and we just keep moving forward blindly and unproductively, wasting valuable time and resources.

There is no evidence, not a shred, that the DNA dustup between Walter Timmerman and Robert Jacoby had anything to do with his murder, or that of his wife. All it provides me with is a hunch, and a road to go down.

Which is better than nothing, but not by much.

• • • • •

LAURIE IS COMING HOME.

With special equipment, and her team of therapists, and me, and two squad cars that Pete Stanton is sending along for protection. It will be a glorious procession down Park Avenue in Paterson.

Laurie said that Dr. Norville is delighted with her progress, though it is hard for me to picture him delighted. She swears that he even smiled once. A little.

He told her that she has at least two months of therapy ahead of her, but that over time she should regain full movement and normal speech. She starts to cry as she tells me this; it has obviously been an incredibly emotional and trying experience for her.

I turn away and pretend to help her pack so she won't see me tearing up as well. Crying is for girls; besides, I've been there, done that while Laurie was in a coma.

Laurie understands that she will not be able to work for at least the two months, and she has so notified the city manager in Findlay. Her second in command will fill in, no doubt adequately, since Findlay is not exactly Dodge City. Except for the aberrational murders that I went up there to investigate a couple of years ago, the

101

closest Findlay has come to violence in the streets was when word got out that Brett Favre was going to the Jets.

"Andy, are you okay with my staying at your house through all this?" she asks.

I think for a moment, trying to search my memory to see if I've ever heard a stupider question. None comes to mind.

"Let's try it for an hour or two and see if it works out," I say.

"I'm serious," she says. "It will cause some turmoil." There are some sounds that she is still having trouble saying, and the *oy* sound is one of them. It sounds like *turmill*. I can see the frustration in her face as she hears herself.

"There is nothing that would give me more pleasure than you spending two months at our house."

I'm sure she noticed that I said "our house," but she doesn't correct me. In my pathetic little world, that qualifies as a damn good sign.

Laurie is very shaky on her feet, so she doesn't resist the hospital's policy that patients must use a wheelchair on departure. They will let me do the pushing, and once we make final arrangements for the therapist's equipment to arrive, we're off.

I feel a hell of a lot better leaving than I did the night I arrived.

When we get home, Laurie wants to walk into the house under her own power, though she holds on to my arm as she does. I help her up the steps and into bed, and I can see that the effort has exhausted her.

"Andy, it's so good to be here. I feel better already."

"That's good, because you're going to have to pull your own weight. Light housework, cooking, some gardening, sexual favors, that kind of thing."

Laurie doesn't answer, mainly because she is already sound asleep. I'll have to write that line down to use it later.

I call Willie and ask him to bring Tara and Waggy over. He's busy at the foundation, and promises to do so when they close for the evening. I'm slightly nervous about this, since we have determined that possession of Waggy has proven somewhat unhealthy in the past. But for the time being I won't take the dogs for public walks; I'll just play with them in the backyard, which is surrounded by a fence and can't be seen from off the property.

Laurie wakes up ravenously hungry and anxious to eat the farthest thing possible from hospital food. Since my understanding of cooking ranks with my understanding of DNA, I offer her a bunch of take-out options. She chooses Taco Bell, and I can't say I'm disappointed with the choice.

I go to the Taco Bell on Route 4 in nearby Elmwood Park and pretty much order everything on the menu. When I get back, Tara and the maniacal Waggy greet me at the door. Willie is sitting on the edge of Laurie's bed, and they are laughing and enjoying each other's company.

Things are getting back to normal, and normal is damn good.

Willie takes one look at the bags of food, smacks his hands together, and announces that he is starved. That, coupled with Laurie's previously announced hunger, is going to leave me sucking on the sauce packets for nourishment.

I bring out a large tray and some plates, and we eat right there in the bedroom. I wind up with a steak quesadilla and half of a chalupa, and consider myself lucky. Laurie and Willie eat enough for twelve normal people.

As I'm cleaning up, the phone rings, and Laurie answers it. Her "hello" is soon followed with, "Great! I'm doing great! It's so nice to hear from you."

What follows is a three- or four-minute conversation, mostly about Laurie's condition, job status, and immediate plans. There are long pauses in which she listens to apparently lengthy replies. It all ultimately ends with, "He's right here, Marcus. I'll put him on."

As she hands me the phone, I say, "You've been having that conversation with Marcus? My Marcus?" The longest conversation he and I have ever had consisted of six grunts and a nod. The way this one sounded, Laurie could have been talking to Henry Kissinger.

I take the phone and Marcus says, "Got him."

"Who? Childs?"

"Yuh. Bergen Street."

"Where on Bergen Street?"

"Elevator."

I was once present when Marcus questioned someone in a dilapidated old warehouse at the end of Bergen Street near the Passaic River, hanging him out over a sixth-floor elevator shaft to encourage his truthful responses. It was vintage Marcus, and I think that he's now telling me he has Childs at the same place.

"You got questions?" he asks.

"For him? Absolutely. Should I come down there?"

"Now," he says, and hangs up.

I get up and tell Laurie and Willie about the conversation. Willie insists on going with me, an idea that Laurie encourages. That area can be dangerous at night, and in Childs we are talking about a hired killer, albeit one whom Marcus apparently has under control.

I'd certainly like to bring Willie along, since I'm generally afraid of being alone in my bedroom if it gets too dark. He also shares Laurie's ability to understand Marcus's unique way of speaking. I'm reluctant to leave Laurie alone for an extended time, but she points out that her assailant is obviously not available at the moment to come after her.

Willie and I drive down to the designated meeting place, which if anything is more run-down than it was last time. Marcus signals to us from a window on the sixth floor, and we start trudging up the steps. When we're on the third-floor landing, a rat runs across the floor in front of us, causing me to jump so high I almost fall back down the steps.

"I've got to make some changes in my life," I say, once I've recovered.

By the time we get to the sixth floor, I am gasping for air, or dust, or anything else I can take in. Willie, on the other hand, looks like he could go another fifty or sixty stories.

We enter a large room, lit only by moonlight through the window and a large flashlight that Marcus has rested on a table. He is sitting calmly in a chair, while a man I have never seen before sits on the floor, tied to a radiator. Even in the sitting position, it is obvious he is very large, maybe four inches taller and thirty pounds heavier than Marcus. He looks none the worse for wear; Marcus apparently got him into this position without resorting to violence.

"What you want to know?" he asks.

"Well, to start, whether he shot Laurie."

Before Marcus answers, an obviously unrepentant Childs laughs. "Of course I shot her, I'm just sorry I didn't kill the bitch."

Maybe I've felt more anger and disgust in my life, but I can't remember when. I try to control myself and talk calmly to Marcus. "I want to know who paid him, and why."

Marcus looks at me, expressionless. "S'all?"

"Saul?" I ask. "Who is Saul?" As always, talking to Marcus is leaving me frustrated, so I turn to Willie. "Who the hell is Saul?"

"Marcus is asking if that's all you want to know," he says.

"Oh, sorry." I turn back to Marcus. "Anything you can find out is fine, but that's basically it."

Marcus nods. "Take his gun." He points to a gun on top of the table, which I didn't see before.

I try to talk softly, so Childs can't hear me. "Marcus, I'm not going to shoot anyone, not even him."

"Take the gun," Marcus repeats, and then takes his own gun out of his pocket. "And this."

"Marcus, can you tell me what's going on?"

Willie decides to intervene at this point, and walks over to Marcus. They talk for about a minute or so, with Willie nodding the whole time.

Willie turns to me and talks loud enough for Childs to hear. "Marcus got the drop on this asshole and brought him here. The guy thinks he can take Marcus, so Marcus is going to give him a chance. It will also give Marcus a chance to ask some questions."

Childs laughs when he hears this; his lack of fear of Marcus is giving me the creeps.

I whisper to Willie: "Can't we stay here, with you holding the guns, just in case?"

"I suggested that, but Marcus said no."

"What's he going to do to him?" I whisper.

"The guy shot Laurie," Willie says. "Laurie is just about Marcus's favorite person in the world. I don't think you'd want to sell him life insurance, you know?"

"Willie, are we talking about murder?"

"No, you're talking about murder. Me and Marcus . . . we're talking about self-defense. You're a lawyer; you don't know the difference?"

I've got a bit of a dilemma here. If I just leave and don't try to exercise any influence over the situation, one of these guys might wind up dead. Also, Childs looks every bit as tough as Pete described him, so I cannot be sure if Marcus's confidence, in addition to Willie's, is misplaced.

Even if Marcus prevails, it represents vigilante justice of a kind that I ordinarily do not condone. There is no question but that the proper thing is to turn Childs over to the police. Still, if anyone deserves swift and deadly justice it's Childs, a piece of garbage who admitted to shooting Laurie and vowed to do it again.

The other factor to consider is that there is a far greater chance that Marcus can get Childs to talk than the police could.

I walk over to Marcus. "Marcus, are you sure about this?"

"Yuh."

"This guy is very dangerous. Will you be really careful?"

"Yuh."

"And you'll try your best to avoid killing him?"

"Yuh."

I wish I could let that be the final word.

• • • • •

As soon as Willie and I leave the room, I grab his arm.

"What's the matter?" he asks.

"Sshhh," I say softly, putting my fingers to my mouth to emphasize that I want him to be quiet. I look around, trying to find a vantage point from which I can watch what happens in the room.

Fortunately, there are literally holes in the wall, and I find one that lets me see Marcus and Childs clearly, yet it is small enough that they're unlikely to know I'm there. "I can't just leave him like this," I whisper to Willie. "If something went wrong, I'd never forgive myself."

"Marcus will be really pissed," he says.

"Only if you tell him."

"What are you going to do if Marcus is losing? Shoot Childs?"

I shake my head. "I could never do that. It's still a human life we're talking about. You can shoot him."

Willie just shakes his head in disapproval, but he quickly finds another place from which he can see as well. I also notice that he has one of the guns out and ready.

We watch as Marcus goes over to Childs and starts to untie him.

As he does so, Childs laughs and says, "You're a bigger asshole than I thought."

Marcus doesn't answer; he just continues freeing Childs from the bonds. At the moment he is free, Childs lashes out and punches Marcus in the face. The sound of fist hitting face is a sickening thud, and Marcus staggers back a few feet.

Childs is up and at him like a cat, showing frightening quickness for a man his size. He lands two more punches, one to the side of Marcus's head and another that glances off his shoulder. Marcus backs up a few more steps.

I can see Willie's grip tighten on the gun to the point that I'm afraid he's going to shoot himself. But we keep our positions; it seems too soon to intervene.

Suddenly we see a slight movement, and Childs screams in pain. The punch from Marcus was so quick and short that it was hard to detect, but it leaves Childs holding his stomach and gasping in pain on the floor.

Marcus moves toward him and Childs somehow summons the strength to punch at him again. This time it's done with far less force, probably because it's difficult to punch and wretch at the same time.

Marcus leans down and grabs Childs, lifting him off the floor and over his head as if he were a rag doll. He throws him halfway across the room, and Childs lands in a heap. It is the most astonishing thing I have ever seen in my life.

Marcus walks across to Childs, who is unsuccessfully trying to get up. Marcus pulls his fist back and lifts him halfway up by his collar, preparing to hit the defenseless man in the face. There is no doubt in my mind that it will kill him, and even though I have a great desire to look away, I can't.

I'm cringing, waiting for the blow to be delivered, when Marcus thinks better of it. He relaxes his hand and lets Childs go, and watches as he crumples to the floor.

Willie looks at me, and I just nod. We turn and go down the stairs. I think Marcus can handle the rest of this on his own, and I sure as hell don't want him knowing we stayed to see what happened.

Laurie is sleeping when I get home. I'm certainly not going to wake her, so I don't get to tell her about the events of the lovely evening spent with Marcus and Childs. It's probably just as well: She needs a lot of rest, and dealing with this lunacy can't help.

She's still sleeping when I get up in the morning, and only wakes up after I shower and have coffee. She wants to be updated on the evening's events, and I take her through it. She's anxious to hear from Marcus to learn if he got Childs to talk, as am I, but thinks I did the right thing by leaving when I did.

Two off-duty policemen show up, whom I am hiring to guard the house while Laurie is in it. They will alternate with two other cops, so that the house will always be covered, at least until we decide it's no longer necessary. Even though Marcus has been able to deal with Childs, the fact is that he was hired to shoot her, and whoever did the hiring can find someone else to attempt the job.

Laurie's daytime nurse and two physical therapists show up a few minutes later. I make a note to stock the refrigerator; these people are going to have to eat and drink. I have seemingly overnight gone from hermit to host, and it's not a role I'm used to.

Satisfied that Laurie is well taken care of, I head for the office, where Kevin and Edna are waiting for me. Edna has taken to coming in relatively on time since Laurie was shot; she seems to want to be around to help if she can. It's a side of her I haven't seen before, mainly because it hasn't existed before.

Laurie sleeps late and Edna is coming in to work early. I have undoubtedly entered the bizarro world.

Kevin has characteristically analyzed our case and laid out the things we need to do to really get started. First on the list is a trip down to the Walter Timmerman murder scene. He knows that I always like to start at the beginning and get a feel for myself what happened. I know I'm not going to magically find some evidence that the police missed, but it helps me feel grounded.

We still haven't heard from Marcus, and I'm starting to get a little worried. I also haven't heard from Pete Stanton, though Marcus was supposed to bring Childs to the police when he was done with him.

Kevin and I arrive at the murder scene, and my guess is that if you had given friends of Walter Timmerman's ten thousand guesses as to the location where he might someday die, this actual place in downtown Paterson would have placed behind Mozambique and Mars.

I'm sure the feeling Kevin and I have is different from what we would experience if we came here at night, which is when Timmerman took the bullet. At this hour of the day the feeling is dreary and hopeless; it seems as if all available energy has been sucked out of the neighborhood. The unemployed, many of them probably homeless, get through the day talking on the corners and reclining on the curbs. For some reason I think of the line in the Simon and Garfunkel song, "A good day's when I ain't got no pain. A bad day's when I lie in bed and think of things that might have been." By that standard, these people seem to be experiencing a good day, but their lives have surely long ago started "slip-sliding away."

Were we here at night, we would likely be afraid. It would be a threatening, dangerous environment. Of course, the only way Kevin and I would come here at night would be in an army tank, encased in a bulletproof bubble, guarded by a marine battalion and Marcus.

I can't stop thinking about Marcus. What if Childs somehow prevailed after we left? Maybe he hit Marcus over the head with a pipe when he wasn't looking. Marcus is not invulnerable; even Luca Brazi sleeps with the fishes.

Timmerman was shot in an alley behind a convenience store.

Kevin and I enter the store, which seems to only sell items identified by their Spanish name, and we talk to the clerk behind the counter. He's about eighteen years old, and watches us approach with obvious indifference.

"Hi. We're investigating the murder that took place in that alley awhile back. We'd like to look around, if that's okay with you."

He doesn't say a word; I can't tell if he doesn't understand English or is just not interested in the way we are using it.

"So we'll just look around, all right?"

Again not a word.

"Kev, you want to jump in here?" I ask.

"No, you're doing great."

"Thanks."

I reach for a package of Mentas, which looks and sounds like it must be mints, and hand the clerk a twenty-dollar bill. "Keep the change," I say, and for the first time I see a flicker of understanding.

"We'll be out back," I say, and Kevin and I leave the store.

"Out back" is little more than a few Dumpsters and some garbage that didn't make its way into one of them. It is no longer a protected crime scene, but there remains the faint outline of a chalk mark that identified where Timmerman's body was found. It is covered by an overhang from the building, which is why it hasn't been completely washed away by summer rains. There are also what appear to be faded bloodstains on a cement wall nearby.

There is not going to be anything for us to find here, and I can't imagine Walter Timmerman felt any differently that night. From what I know about him, there does not seem to be a possible reason for him to have come here willingly. In the unlikely event he was out for drugs, or sex, he could have found a much better venue.

It seems far more likely that he was brought here for the purpose of being killed.

"He had to have been forced to come here," I say.

Kevin nods. "That's how I see it as well. Especially at night."

"Why don't you come back here tonight and check it out?" I ask.

Kevin smiles. "You don't pay me enough, boss."

On the way back to the office, I'm feeling somewhat rejuvenated. Going to the murder scene is primarily responsible for this; it has focused me on the case, and at the same time made me more optimistic about its outcome. Nothing like the bloodstained scene of a brutal killing to cheer up Andy Carpenter.

I can see a son like Steven, who perhaps felt wronged his whole life by a domineering father, flipping out and murdering that father in a momentary rage. But I can't see him bringing Walter down to the area we just visited and committing the murder in cold-blooded fashion. It's possible, I know, but I just can't see it.

Laurie's ongoing recovery has also enabled me to concentrate on the case in a way I couldn't while I was in fear for her. It was beyond distracting to be worried about her twenty-four hours a day, and I know now that I could not have continued on the case were she not doing so well.

She is in capable hands, and well protected, and while I will think about her a lot, I won't obsess about it.

My only distraction now is Marcus, and the fact that more than sixteen hours have passed since Willie and I left him with Childs, and I have not heard a word. It's ludicrous to consider myself responsible for Marcus's protection and physical well-being, but if last night somehow ended badly, I don't know that I'll ever forgive myself for leaving him there.

I decide to call Laurie and see how she's doing, only to realize that I neglected to bring my cell phone with me. It was a stupid thing to do: With all that is going on I need to be reachable at all times.

I borrow Kevin's cell and call home, and Willie Miller answers. "Where the hell you been?" he asks.

I'm worried, so I decide I prefer asking questions to answering them. "Is Laurie all right?"

"Yeah, she's fine, but we've been trying to find you."

"Why?"

"Marcus is here."

• • • • •

LAURIE IS DOING PHYSICAL THERAPY

when Kevin and I get home.

Willie is in the den with Tara and Waggy, feet up on the coffee table, drinking a beer and watching ESPN. Tara is working methodically on a rawhide chewie, while Waggy's front legs are going a mile a minute as he furiously tries to burrow a hole in the carpet.

Willie tells me that Marcus is in the kitchen getting something to eat. I have seen Marcus eat once before, and it is seared into my memory. While I have stocked the refrigerator because of all the people in the house, Marcus will clean it out by himself. Then, if memory serves, he will belch once and start hunting for more food.

"What happened after we left last night?" I ask Willie.

"Laurie said to wait for her to finish her therapy. She wants to be there when we tell you. She's almost done."

"I don't want to wait," I say.

Willie shrugs. "You can always ask Marcus."

"I'll wait."

Laurie is finished in ten minutes. During that time I hear noises coming from the kitchen, but I am not about to go in there to see what is going on.

She calls us to the bedroom; she is back in bed and obviously exhausted from her efforts. I have seen her run five miles without breathing heavily, and now a few minutes of exercise wipes her out.

"We talked to Marcus and learned what happened after you left. It's not good news."

"What do you mean?"

She nods. "Marcus asked Childs the questions you and he had discussed. He is confident that Childs had an incentive to tell the truth."

"Who hired him?"

"Childs didn't know; nor did he know why. It was all done in secrecy, and he had no personal contact with the man. He was paid two hundred fifty thousand dollars, with the promise of another two fifty when the jobs were completed."

"Five hundred thousand dollars?" I repeat. It's an amazing figure. Then I realize that Laurie said "jobs." "There was more than one job?"

"Yes. Andy, Childs killed Diana Timmerman. He planted the explosives in the house."

"What?" I look at Kevin, and he is as bewildered as I am. None of this makes any sense; it's connecting two different things that I thought had no connection at all.

"Why the hell would someone want to kill you and Diana Timmerman?"

"Andy, Childs wasn't after me. He was told to shoot the dog. He was told to kill Waggy."

"Waggy?" I point to him. "This Waggy?"

"Yes."

"That doesn't make any sense. Somebody paid a hit man five hundred grand to shoot a dog?"

"Marcus was positive about it," Willie says.

I have no idea what to make of this. It simply does not compute. "Where is Childs now?"

"That's the bad news," Laurie says, and she turns to Willie.

"He went for a swim," Willie says. "But I don't think he got very far, because he has a broken neck."

"Marcus killed him?"

Laurie nods. "He was going to turn him in to the police, but Childs took another run at him, and Marcus got a little carried away. He said he dropped him in the river."

"Damn." Hearing that Childs is dead doesn't exactly bring me to tears, and I'm not likely to reflect that his untimely demise "really puts things into perspective." The problem is that now I have a million more questions to ask him, with no ability to do so.

The truth is that I am defending someone against a charge of double homicide, and I had the real murderer in my hands and let him get away. And thanks to Marcus, he's not coming back.

Had I realized that the shooting of Laurie and the Timmerman murders were connected, I would have gotten all the information out of him that I could, and then turned him in as the real murderer. And I should have realized that the shootings might be connected; as Willie had pointed out, both Diana Timmerman and Laurie were connected to Waggy when they were victimized.

I'm so frustrated by this turn of events that I go into the kitchen to question Marcus personally, to see if he knows more than has been drawn out of him. I have to wait what seems like twenty minutes while he finishes chewing the four or five pounds of food in his mouth.

I ultimately get nowhere; Marcus doesn't even know for sure if Childs is responsible for killing Walter Timmerman. It's not Marcus's fault; he asked the questions I wanted him to ask. It's my fault for not understanding that the events could all be connected, though I still don't know how they possibly could be.

And now it's too late.

Of course, there is always the chance that Childs was playing a game with Marcus, and that he was not telling the truth when he said Waggy was the target. I mean, Waggy can be annoying, but not quite that annoying. The problem with this theory is that Marcus is not the type one would have a tendency to joke with, especially when the potential joker is about to have his neck broken.

But if there is some wealthy lunatic out there who has decided Waggy is to be killed, then I have to be the wealthy lunatic who is going to protect him, especially since he is going to be hanging out with Laurie and Tara.

It makes the custody fight with Robinson all the more important. Hatchet has set a date for the hearing, which will actually be during Steven's trial. It is on the calendar for two hours, and Hatchet made it clear that he is not happy about interrupting the trial. I have not handled Hatchet well in all of this, although Hatchet-handling is a rather delicate task in any event.

The off-duty cops I've hired will stay on, but now that Marcus is free I'm going to bring him on as well. He can be Waggy's bodyguard and double as my investigator. It will make me feel better to have him on the team; Marcus can be a really comforting teammate.

● ● ● ● ●

I CAN TELL that Martha Wyndham considers my request to be a little strange.

I've called to ask her to arrange a meeting for me with someone who knows all there is to know about dog shows. She hesitates for a moment, no doubt wondering how this can possibly help Steven.

"Well . . . sure . . . I guess I can do that," she says. "Is this about Waggy?"

"It impacts on the case in general. It's quite important."

"What is it you want to know specifically? That way I can figure out the best person for you to talk to."

"A person with as much general knowledge about the process as possible. Also with a knowledge of the business end of things."

"The business end?" she asks.

"Right. The value of the dogs, the prize money they can win, that kind of thing." There is always the chance that some rival of Timmerman's on the dog show circuit decided to remove the human and canine competition that Timmerman and Waggy represented. It's far-fetched and ridiculous, but I'm operating in a world where an international hit man targeted a Bernese mountain dog.

She says that she'll get back to me after making some calls, and after I hang up, Kevin and I discuss with whom we might want to share the information Marcus provided about Childs. We decide that there is no upside to telling Richard Wallace what we know; we can always do that later if it is to our advantage.

But I would like Childs's body to be found, if only to prove later on that he was in the area, should we want to do so.

I call Pete Stanton at his office, and he characteristically answers the phone with, "What the hell do you want now?"

"I just had an incredibly weird conversation," I say.

"You're still calling those phone sex lines?"

"No, this was from an anonymous tipster. He called himself A. T."

"A. T.?" Pete asks.

"Yes," I say. "I assume it stands for 'Anonymous Tipster.'"

"You getting to the point anytime soon?"

"Yes. So A. T. calls to tell me that a criminal named Jimmy Childs has died."

"Is that right? Did he mention if this criminal died of natural causes?"

"He said it was a boating accident in the Passaic River, near Bergen Street in downtown Paterson." Of course, there hasn't been a boat there since Revolutionary War days.

"Probably a yacht race gone bad," Pete says. "What did A. T. sound like?"

"I think he was English, probably in his sixties. Very stuffy way of speaking . . . said 'cheerio' a lot."

"Sounds like either Winston Churchill or Marcus," Pete says in his best deadpan voice.

"Couldn't be Marcus. He doesn't say 'cheerio.' He doesn't even eat them; he's a cornflakes guy."

"You got anything else you want to tell me?" Pete asks.

"Not right now."

NEW TRICKS

When I get off the phone, Edna tells me that Sam Willis has been waiting to see me. My mind is a song-talking blank, but I tell her to have him come in anyway. Hopefully he'll let me off the hook.

Sam comes in with a briefcase so large it looks more like a suitcase. He starts to unload it onto the only place in my office that can accommodate all the paperwork, which is the couch.

"What the hell is all that?" I ask.

"Everything you've ever wanted to know about the lives of Walter and Diana Timmerman."

I start to skim through a bit of it while he continues to put the papers on the couch. He's got phone bills, checking accounts, e-mails, brokerage accounts, utility bills . . . it's an amazing display.

"This is unbelievable," I say. "How did you find the time to do all this?"

"Hey, come on, you give me a job, I do it."

"Have you gotten any sleep?"

"Of course," he says. "In fact, last night I was trying to finish, but my head grew heavy and my sight grew dim, so I had to stop for the night."

He's doing the Eagles' "Hotel California," and it's a sign of my level of maturity that I feel a hint of excitement about it. I'm an Eagles fan, and when it comes to their lyrics, I can song-talk anybody under the table.

"I would think it must have been hard to pick it up again in the morning," I say. "You had to find the passage back to the place you were before."

He smiles slightly. The battle has been joined. But while we're battling, I'd also like to hear about the Timmermans. I ask Sam if he noticed anything that seemed unusual.

"If we were talking about my world, everything would be unusual. For them, who knows?"

"What do you mean?"

"Well, Timmerman probably made a hundred international calls in the week before he died. Europe, Middle East . . . he spread it around. And every call was to a different number; he never repeated the same number. Not once."

"How do you read that?" I ask.

"Either he or the people he was calling didn't want anybody to find out who it was. My guess is that the calls were routed to one, or maybe a few, numbers, but in a way that couldn't be traced."

I nod; it's possible he's right, or it could be that Timmerman was just calling a lot of different people. "What else?"

"He had twenty million dollars wired to him from the Bank of Switzerland a week before he died. Now, he didn't need it to eat, believe me, but it's still a nice piece of change."

"Anything about what he was working on in those final weeks?"

"No, and there's a bunch of e-mails where people were asking him about it. There was no way he was sharing it with anybody; it was like he put up a wall. But he kept telling people that he had no time to see them, or go out, because he was so busy. It's all here."

"What about the wife?" I ask.

"She spent money like the world was coming to an end. You name the store, she spent a fortune there. Jewelry, cars . . . unbelievable."

"I know the type," I say. "Her mind was Tiffany-twisted, she got the Mercedes bends."

He smiles. "And my guess is she got a lot of pretty, pretty boys that she called friends."

"Why do you say that?"

"She made twelve phone calls to a hotel in New York in the six weeks before her husband died, one of those places that's so hip they can charge seven hundred bucks a night. And she was there at least twice; she bought drinks on her credit card in their bar."

"Do we know who she called or went to see?" I ask.

"Nope. No way to tell from this. That's going to be up to you. But if you get me a name, I'll take his life apart."

"Maybe somebody at the hotel will remember her," I say.

He smiles. "That's my boy; you can do it. Go get 'em."

"Your confidence is touching. I can feel my eyes filling up with tears."

He laughs. "I mean it. I got a peaceful easy feeling, and I know you won't let me down. 'Cause I'm already standing . . ."

"You're already standing?"

He nods. "Yes, I'm already standing on the ground."

I laugh. "All right, Sam, I want to go though this stuff, so get the hell out of here."

He nods. "Right, boss." He gets up, goes to the door and opens it, but then walks back to me.

"Now what?" I ask.

"Sorry, but every time I try to walk away, something makes me turn around and stay."

This could go on forever; the Eagles have had a long career. "Sam, I've got work to do, beat it."

He nods. "Okay. But all of this is gonna help you with the case, right?"

"Maybe, maybe not."

"What does that mean?" he asks.

I point to the papers. "It means, depending on what I find out, this could be heaven or this could be hell."

• • • • •

I WALK IN THE DOOR and see Laurie coming down the steps to greet me.

She is holding on to the railing and trying to keep her shaky legs steady. She smiles when she sees me, and this causes her to momentarily lose her concentration. She starts to fall, and I can see the panic as she grabs for the railing.

As I so often do in situations like this, I just stand paralyzed, watching. She is unable to regain her balance and falls down the last three steps, landing with a thud on the floor.

Now that it is too late, I rush to her. "Laurie, are you okay?"

"Damnit! Damnit! Damnit!" she screams, pounding the floor. "Andy, I can't stand being like this!"

"Really?" I ask. "I thought you were very graceful. Are you hurt?"

She pauses for a while before answering, as she assesses her own condition. "I don't think so. Just frustrated and embarrassed."

"Where's the nurse?"

"I sent her home. I wanted things to be back to normal tonight."

I help her over to the couch, and though she staggers slightly, she seems to be okay. Tara and Waggy immediately take advantage of the situation to jump on the couch and snuggle next to her, their heads coming to rest on each of her thighs.

Laurie starts to laugh at how quickly they've assumed the comfortable positions, and she pets both of them on their heads. It is amazing how comforting dogs can be.

I didn't see Marcus outside when I arrived, but that doesn't surprise me. Marcus has a way of not appearing to be somewhere until he needs to be there, and I've learned to have confidence in that. I've given him a key, so he can come in and out when he pleases, but I know when he's been inside, because the refrigerator is empty.

"You sure you should be out of bed?" I ask.

"Yes, Andy. Despite my embarrassing performance on the stairs, I'm doing okay. I'm not an invalid."

"Okay. Good."

"I can do things. Really," she says.

"Great. Make me dinner, woman."

"Except that."

"Okay. Let's get naked."

"And except that."

I nod. "So, to rephrase, you can do anything except good stuff."

She smiles. "Right. And I'm especially good at thinking."

"What have you been thinking about?"

"Going home. Getting back to work."

That was not exactly what I was hoping she'd say. "You're not ready for that, Laurie. You must know that."

She nods. "I do. But I have this need to get back to real life."

"Living here is fake life?"

She shakes her head. "I'm sorry, Andy, this is coming out wrong. I love it here, and I love being with you. I just can't stand being helpless like this. I've never experienced anything like it before."

"Laurie, it feels like yesterday that you were in a coma, and you were . . . fighting for your life." My voice catches on these last few words; just the thought of that first night in the hospital is enough to reduce me to a sniveling, unmanly wreck. "You're doing great."

"I know. I'm just impatient."

"So how can I make you less impatient?"

"Maybe you can let me help you with the case. I can read through the files, maybe come up with some ideas. It will give me something to think about, and there's a chance I can contribute something."

This is an easy one for me; Laurie is as good an investigator as I've ever been around, and it can't do anything but help to have a mind like hers on our side. "Absolutely. That's a great idea."

"I know I can't come down to the office yet, but—"

"You don't have to. We'll bring the office here."

"What do you mean?"

"Kevin and Edna would be fine working here instead of the office. It's no hardship at all. And that way you can sit in on meetings and be a part of things."

"Andy, please tell me if I'm being childish."

"Not at all," I say. "It's a great idea." And in fact it is. "Now, what else can I do?"

"You can hold me."

Since Waggy and Tara are still on each side of her, that is going to be difficult. "You seem to be surrounded," I say.

"Not now. Tonight. In bed. I want you to hold me all night."

"You're asking a lot, you know."

She smiles. "I realize that. And I wouldn't blame you if you refused."

"This is not going to turn into an every-night thing, is it?"

"No, I promise," she says. "Tomorrow night I'll find someone else to hold me."

"I'll tell you what. We'll try it with me for a year, and see how it goes."

She smiles again. "I think it will go fine."

Me too.

• • • • •

THE HAMILTON HOTEL is on Hudson Street in
New York City.

At the moment it is considered the hippest part of the entire city,
and I am aware of that because I know people, who know people,
who know people, who are hip.

This is actually known as the Meatpacking District, because
for years it has been the city's center of wholesale meats. Mind-
bogglingly, the meatpacking business is still thriving, even though
hipness is springing up all around it. The area is now filled with
expensive hotels and boutiques in addition to less expensive lamb
chops and veal shanks.

Only in New York.

In front of the Hamilton are velvet rope lines, and even though
it is only three in the afternoon, they are preparing for the influx of
people who will try to get into their rooftop bar tonight. I am told
that people will regularly stand out here for hours in the hope, often
vain, that they will get past the bouncers and gain admission.

Like everything else about the hip world that I've never inhabited, it makes no sense to me. There are half a billion bars in New
York City that you can just walk into and order a drink. They're

more ubiquitous than pizzerias. What could prompt a person to wait hours, and risk rejection, in order to get into this one? And the drinks are probably priced like used cars. So why do people come here? How good could their vodka be?

I enter through the revolving door and walk the fifty feet or so to the concierge desk. On the way there, three employees wish me a good afternoon. They obviously care about me a lot.

I have found that expensive hotels in New York either are very modern or look like they were furnished during the Revolutionary War. This one is modern, and the entire lobby is done in black, white, and chrome. The floor is white with diagonal chrome stripes, and the only carpeting is a few small area rugs in the seating areas. I guess if they raise their room rates to nine hundred a night, they'll be able to afford wall-to-wall.

I know my bias is showing, but I hate hotels like this. The rooms are usually smaller than the average Holiday Inn, and you have to take out a mortgage to eat peanuts from the mini bar. Yet those rooms are always filled, at least until another, even hotter, hotel opens up down the street.

The female concierge is helping a male guest, so I stand behind him and eavesdrop. He has a number of requests: dinner reservations, theater tickets, limousine rental . . . all of which she handles with ease with a phone call.

Each call she makes she starts with, "This is the concierge at the Hamilton Hotel," spoken in the same imperious tone she would use if she were announcing that the queen of England was calling. But it certainly works; this is a woman who gets what she wants, or at least what the guest wants. If I were staying here I would be throwing requests at her all the time; it would be like having my own genie.

When it's my turn, we exchange greetings and I say, "I'd like to speak with the manager, please."

She smiles and says. "Perhaps I can help you?"

"Are you perhaps the manager?"

"No, sir."

"Are you likely to be promoted to manager in the next few minutes?"

"No, sir, I—"

"Then I'm afraid you won't be able to help me. So please tell the manager that I would like to see him."

"Who may I say is calling?"

"My name is Carpenter . . . I'm investigating a double murder."

Apparently among the things concierges don't like to deal with are double murders, since once I say that, she seems rather relieved that I am not asking her to help. She picks up the phone and dials the manager, or at least his office, and within moments I am on the elevator on the way to the top floor. There are video screens on the elevator running old cartoons, which must be another sign of hipness. I should be taking notes on this stuff, so I can impress Laurie with it.

The manager's name is Lionel Paulson, and he seems not to be more than thirty-five or so. He's dressed in a suit that, while I'm no expert, appears to be silk. In fact, it looks so silky smooth that he must have to hold on to the arms of his chair so as not to slide to the floor.

We say our hellos, and I take the chair across from his desk. He asks me to show him some identification.

"You mean like a driver's license?" I ask.

"No, I mean like a badge, or a shield, or whatever it's called that shows me what agency you are employed by."

"I'm an attorney," I say. "We don't get badges, but I can show you our secret handshake."

He is surprised, and tells me that since I had told the concierge that I was investigating a murder, he assumed I was a law enforcement officer.

I assure him that I am not, and I tell him that I want to interview his staff to see if anyone remembers Diana Timmerman. I take out a picture of her that I have and show it to him.

"I certainly have no idea who she is," he says, holding the picture up as he looks at it.

"Was."

"I beg your pardon?"

"Who she was," I say. "She was one of the murder victims."

He drops the picture as if it were on fire. "Oh, my. And she was a guest in this hotel?"

I shake my head. "I don't think so. But she visited someone who was on at least two occasions. I want to know who that was."

"Our guests have an expectation of privacy."

"Then one of them is not going to have his expectations met."

"Your hope is to ask hotel employees if they have seen this woman?"

"I won't be doing the asking. I'll send a few private investigators in; they'll be discreet."

"I can't have disruptions, I . . ."

I shake my head. "A disruption would be if I send a team of big burly guys to serve subpoenas on everyone when you've got a line of people waiting to get into your bar." I'm not being honest about this; I don't have subpoena power, and couldn't get it if I tried.

"When do you propose to have your people here?"

"Tomorrow at five thirty. That's the time of day that she was here both times. And I'll need to know if someone was on duty those days, especially in the bar, who won't be here tomorrow."

He agrees to my request, after getting me to promise to have my people go about their business quietly and professionally. He will convey to the hotel employees that they should answer the questions openly and honestly.

There's always a chance that he will check, learn that I don't have subpoena power, and change his mind. It's unlikely; he will probably just go through with it and hope it doesn't cause any problems.

I thank him and leave, and then call Kevin and tell him to hire an investigation agency that we sometimes use. I somehow forget to mention the part about making sure everyone is quiet and discreet; I want to learn who Diana Timmerman was there to see, and I don't care if they have to set fire to the place to find out.

• • • • •

ANOTHER ONE OF MY STEREOTYPES IS about to unceremoniously bite the dust.

I hate when that happens; I like it much better when my ignorant, knee-jerk opinions about people and events are shown to be one hundred percent accurate.

This particular ill-fated stereotype concerns the people who enter their dogs in prestigious shows. I expect them all to be named Muffy or Buffy (I'm talking about the humans) and to eat watercress sandwiches and sniff about how hard it is to hire decent help these days.

When Martha Wyndham called to tell me she arranged a meeting for me with Barb Stanley in Greenwich, Connecticut, it made perfect sense. Connecticut's snootiness quotient is way up there; as far as I know all people there do is play croquet, drink martinis, and eat bonbons.

Actually, even though I live in what is called the tristate area, which comprises New York, New Jersey, and Connecticut, the latter is sort of a mystery state to me. I don't even know what the people are called. Connecticutites? Connecticuttians?

In any event, my predispositions about the people being snobbish and superior don't seem to be holding true at all. The woman I assume is Barb Stanley is in her early thirties, tall and thin and seemingly possessed of boundless energy. Her place of business, where we are meeting today, is an old warehouse, modernized and designed as a doggy day care facility. People drop their dogs off on the way to work, secure in the knowledge that the animals will have a blast running and playing with friends on some incredible equipment.

When I arrive she is running with the dogs, pausing every so often to roll around on the floor with them. I watch her for about ten minutes, and I don't know how she does it. I wouldn't last thirty seconds. The most amazing part of all is that the NY METS baseball cap she is wearing does not fall off. It must be cemented to her head.

She finally sees me, waves, and then jumps to her feet. She signals to another young woman, whom I hadn't even noticed, and that woman comes over to play with the dogs. Their tongues are hanging, and I think one of them looks over to their imaginary coach to see if they have any time-outs left.

"Can I help you?"

"Yes," I say. "Please tell me you're tired."

She laughs. "Not yet. But you should see me around four o'clock."

"My name is Andy Carpenter . . ."

"Oh, right. Martha said you'd be by. I'm Barb Stanley."

I nod. "She said you were an expert in showing dogs . . . the whole process." I take another look at the dogs, back in play with their new leader. Very few of them look like purebreds. "Are any of these show dogs?"

She shakes her head. "No, although the springer in the back could be."

She invites me back to her office, and when we get there she offers me a drink from a small refrigerator. I choose a bottle of water, and she takes one of the four or five million power drinks that are now on the market. Everybody seems to be drinking them, but I don't think they work. These drinks are selling like crazy, yet the people I see on the street don't seem any more powerful than they were ten years ago. Barb is the exception.

"So where do you want to start?" she asks.

"Do you show dogs yourself?"

She nods. "Sure."

"Have you had any champions?" I ask.

"No, but I just missed a couple of times."

"At Westminster?" I ask.

She laughs. "No, not even close."

"Why do you do it?"

"I love it. I love the dogs, I love being around people who love dogs. It's a lot of work, but I wouldn't trade it for anything. I'm doing a show this weekend; you can come if you'd like."

I say that I'd like that very much. "Is there a lot of money to be won?"

She laughs again. "Not by me." Then, "Sure, the prizes for the big shows are very nice."

"What's the biggest prize you are personally aware of?" I ask.

"I think Westminster Best in Show is a hundred thousand dollars."

So much for the money motive. In the world that Walter Timmerman inhabited, a hundred thousand dollars is tip money. And it is quite unlikely that it would have motivated a rival to go on a murder spree.

"Are you familiar with the Bernese who won Best in Show for Walter Timmerman?" I ask.

"Bertrand. Of course. The most perfect dog I've ever seen. I cried for two days when he died."

"Did you know he had a son?"

"I hadn't," she said. "But I've since read about it. Is he in training?"

"Not yet," I say. "Do you think he should be?"

She shrugs. "Only if he takes to it. Otherwise whoever has him should just let him be a dog."

"Have you ever shown dogs at the same show as Walter Timmerman?"

She nods. "A few times . . . maybe five."

"Do you know if he had any rivalries . . . was there any antagonism between him and another dog owner?"

"I really don't know," she says. "That's a little above my world."

"But have you known emotions to run high, because of the competition?"

She looks at me strangely. "Are you asking if someone could have murdered Walter Timmerman in order to win a dog show?"

I nod. "Yes."

"Mr. Carpenter," she says, "that's crazy."

I'm not prepared to tell her the really nutty part: that Waggy has been the target of a hit man. "Barb," I say, "you don't know the half of it."

• • • • •

A CCORDING TO THE MORNING PAPER, a body was found in the Passaic River last night.

No identification has yet been made, but Pete Stanton, Willie Miller, Marcus, Laurie, and I all know that it will prove to be Jimmy Childs. Soon the world will know it as well. What the world will not know is that Childs killed Diana Timmerman, and almost certainly Walter as well. That particular secret will remain with Steven Timmerman's idiot lawyer, Andy Carpenter.

Ordinarily, for a defense attorney to learn who the real killer is, and have that killer not be his client, is a major positive. It's an out-and-out case winner. Yet I've managed to turn it into a negative by allowing that killer to himself be killed, so as never to be able to reveal all that he knows.

I've scheduled a meeting this morning to go over our current situation with Kevin and Laurie. The trial date is rapidly approaching, and while we have succeeded in accumulating some interesting information about Walter Timmerman, we are not yet able to connect it to a coherent defense for our client. Which is unfortunate, since that is our job.

Kevin brings with him the initial report from the investigators who questioned the employees of the Hamilton Hotel yesterday.

"We finally caught a break," he says. "Five different people remembered Diana Timmerman being there."

"Really?" I say. "I'm surprised."

"Apparently, she was obnoxious. She even accused the bartender of using the wrong kind of vodka in her drink. People remember things like that."

"Did they find out who she was there to see?"

Kevin nods. "Thomas Sykes. In each case he checked in for one night, and Diana Timmerman came to see him."

"Now, that's interesting," I say.

"Who is Thomas Sykes?" Laurie asks.

"The CEO of Timco Laboratories, Timmerman's company. He owned twenty percent of the company."

"So Diana Timmerman was having an affair with her husband's business partner?"

I nod. "And he told me he barely knew her to say hello."

"Lying about a love triangle is not exactly an earth-shattering event," Laurie says.

"But it potentially takes on an added significance when two-thirds of the triangle are murdered by a hit man. It sort of gives new meaning to the word 'isosceles.'"

"According to Marcus, Childs didn't say that he killed Walter Timmerman," Kevin points out.

I nod. "That's true, but probably only because it was another question I didn't tell Marcus to ask."

"So in a normal world," Laurie says, "this would all be starting to make sense. Sykes, who no doubt has a lot of money, hires Childs to kill Timmerman, so as to clear a path for Sykes and Diana. Then Diana starts to pressure him, cause him problems, and he decides to get rid of her as well."

"And then, because he hired the hit man as part of a 'kill two, get one free' promotion, he sends Childs out to kill Waggy."

"I said 'in a normal world,'" Laurie points out.

"Still, it does make Sykes a person of interest," Kevin says.

"Certainly interesting to me," I say. "Let's give him a call."

I place a call to Sykes's office and am told he is in a meeting. I leave word that it is urgent, and he calls me back in half an hour.

"Mr. Sykes, I've been doing some investigating, and I've got a few more questions for you. If we could meet sometime tomorrow, then—"

He interrupts. "I'm afraid I'm very busy, Mr. Carpenter. I can't keep taking the time to—"

I return the interruption. "I understand, but I'll make it as convenient for you as possible. I can come to your office, or if you'd rather we can meet at the Hamilton Hotel."

There is silence on the other end for at least twenty seconds while the message is digested. "Mr. Sykes?"

"I see you're not above dragging people through the mud."

"Actually, I'm not dragging anyone through the mud. I'm trying to clear the mud away so I can see through to the bottom."

He agrees to see me, as I knew he would, but I've got a feeling we're never really going to be buddies again.

Once I get off the phone, I ask Kevin to go down to the jail and ask Steven if he is aware of any particular rival that Walter Timmerman had on the dog show circuit. It still seems like a ridiculous long shot, but I believe in covering every base.

Then I call Cindy Spodek at her FBI office in Boston. Once again I'm told that she's in a meeting, but when I say it's important, the meeting mysteriously ends and she gets on the phone.

"What's up, Andy?"

"You weren't in a meeting, were you?"

"What are you talking about?"

"They said you were in a meeting, but then you got on the phone. I think it was a fake meeting."

"It's a fake meeting that's about to start again, if you don't get to the point," she says.

"I want to talk to the agent heading up the task force on Walter Timmerman."

"You mean the task force you don't even know about because I never told you?"

"That's the very one."

"Forget it, Andy."

"I know who killed the Timmermans, and I thought I should share it with the government, my government, as a way to demonstrate my patriotism."

"I'm getting all misty."

"I would think that a task force investigating Walter Timmerman might want to find out who killed him. That might even be one of their primary tasks." I'm overstating things a bit here, but I'm comfortable with the assumption that if Childs admitted killing Diana Timmerman, then he must have killed Walter as well.

"Was it your client?"

"No."

"Is your client still in jail?" she asks.

"That's another story," I say. "Can you set up a meeting?"

"I'll see what I can do," she says.

"Your country will be forever grateful to you."

• • • • •

I ASSIGN SAM WILLIS THE JOB of giving
Thomas Sykes a cyber strip search.

Maybe it will turn out that all Sykes was doing was getting into
his partner's wife's pants, but I want to know what else he was getting into before the Timmermans died.

Laurie has cooked dinner tonight, the first time she's done so
since she was shot. She's doing remarkably well; though her walk
is unsteady, her facial features and speech are both almost back to
normal. She still tires easily, which drives her crazy. I know that,
because she tells me so.

I have my own, admittedly unscientific, way of measuring how
Laurie is progressing. Basically, my theory is that the more I think
about sex, the healthier she must be.

For a few weeks after the shooting, sex was the farthest thing
from my mind. All I cared about, all I obsessed over, was Laurie
surviving and then someday regaining her health and strength.

Then, as it became clear she was out of the woods and on the
way to a full recovery, the idea of sex as an eventual possibility appeared on the horizon. But it was certainly nothing imminent, and I
just as certainly didn't consider doing anything about it.

But now I detect some faint rumblings out there. It's still not anything I would act on; my fears of rejection and humiliation would simultaneously rule that out. But I am definitely at the point where if Laurie suggested it, it would not provoke a raging argument. It might even be good for her psychologically, and I'm certainly a guy who would do anything to help.

After dinner Laurie makes coffee in two devices she uses, which involve pushing down on the tops and sort of squeezing the coffee out. I think they're called French presses and she considers this the only way to drink coffee. Unfortunately, my taste buds aren't quite sensitive enough to know the difference. I can happily drink any kind of coffee, even instant, while Laurie would rather drink instant cyanide.

"Andy, was there ever a time when you thought I was going to die?"

My knee-jerk instinct is to say no, but for some reason I decide to try the truth, just to see how it goes. "I thought you had died," I say.

"What do you mean?"

I tell her about receiving the phone call in Hatchet's office from Pete, and my desperate fear that he wasn't telling me the full truth, that he was just getting me down to the hospital so he could convey the devastating news in person.

"That must have been awful for you," she says.

"I can't ever remember a worse time in my life. But once I got there, and you came out of surgery, then I knew you were going to make it."

"What made you so sure?"

"It was like, once I could put my mind to it, then I could control it. I thought you had died before I had a chance to focus on your recovery, but once I had that chance, I knew we'd make it."

"We'd make it?"

"I only wanted to live if you did."

"Please don't say that," she says.

I nod. "Okay. I won't say it."

Laurie is quiet for a few moments, then says, "We've never talked about dying, about one of us being left behind."

"We don't talk about a lot of things," I say. "It's natural; we're both busy, and we're usually in different time zones."

She smiles. "We talk about our days; I tell you how my day went, and you tell me about yours."

"I have to come up with more interesting stories. Or more interesting days," I say.

"I love my job, Andy. And I love Findlay. And I love you."

"You've got your cake and you're eating it." It comes off as a little petulant, probably because it is.

"I know you're not satisfied, Andy. And I'm not, either. I just don't know how to make it better."

"For now you should just worry about getting better."

"I am," she says. Then, "I'd like to go with you tomorrow night."

"To the dog show?"

"Yes."

"Why?"

"I need to get out of the house; it will help me feel alive again."

"You think you're up to it?"

"Why? What are you going to do there?"

I shrug. "Hang out . . . I guess look at dogs for a while."

She smiles. "I should be able to handle that. That's what I do here."

I could argue with her, but I'd lose. Which would be fine, because I'd want to lose. "It's a date," I say.

• • • • •

THOMAS SYKES seems less happy to see me this time.

I find that's not unusual in my interpersonal relationships; my sunny disposition is usually good for one relatively pleasant meeting. Two max.

"Let's make this brief, Mr. Carpenter. Say what you came here to say. Ask what you came here to ask."

"Here's the way I work, Mr. Sykes. I ask a lot of questions, and people give me answers. Then I ask some more questions, and sometimes I find out that the previous answers that people gave me weren't true. They were lies. That's what happened in this case, with you."

"Lies?"

"Yes. You told me you barely knew Diana Timmerman. Hardly well enough to say hello. Then I find out that she visited you repeatedly at a hotel in New York. Based on my definition, that qualifies as lying."

Sykes smiles. "Believe it or not, there could be some private matters that I might not want to share with you."

"The woman was murdered," I say. "That makes this a rather public matter."

143

"Our relationship had nothing whatsoever to do with her death. That I can say without fear of contradiction."

"Just what was your relationship?"

"We had an affair."

I'm surprised that he comes right out and says this. "Which was still going on when she died?"

"I don't really know how to answer that. The last time I saw her was about a week before Walter's death. Whether I would have seen her in the future or not, I really don't know."

"So their marriage was in trouble?"

He smiles. "I'm not sure what that means. Obviously, she was not completely faithful, and my understanding was that he was not, either. But to say the marriage was in trouble, does that mean it was nearing an end?"

"Possibly, yes."

"I can't imagine Walter would have given her a divorce. It would have been a public humiliation for him, and a financial disaster."

"No prenup?"

"Diana? No way. I wasn't kidding when I told you she was a woman who knew what she wanted."

"You're going to have to testify to all of this at the trial," I say.

"Why?" he asks, but he doesn't seem fearful or concerned, just amused.

"Because generally in a murder case it's good to explore what the victims were doing, and who they were doing it with."

He shrugs. "I'm not married; I can handle the embarrassment."

I nod. "Can I use your phone?"

He points to the phone on his desk. "Help yourself."

I go to the phone and pick up the receiver. "Do I dial nine?"

Sykes shakes his head. "No, it's a private line."

I dial Sam Willis's number, and he answers on the first ring. "I got the number," he says. "The dope didn't block it."

I pretend that I'm talking to a machine. "Kevin, it's Andy, give me a call at the office later."

Sam laughs and hangs up, and I hang up as well.

"Thanks," I say to Sykes.

He smiles. "No problem." He's held up pretty well under my less-than-withering questioning.

"By the way, you said that it was your understanding that Walter Timmerman was fooling around as well. Any idea who he was doing it with?"

"Not a clue," he says.

As soon as I get outside, I call Sam Willis again and tell him that I've left. He promises to call me back with any information as soon as he can.

When I return to the house, Laurie tells me that Cindy Spodek called: The agent in charge of the task force investigating Walter Timmerman has agreed to see me. She will be setting up the meeting at a convenient time for everyone, and will be coming down to New York to join us.

I'm not surprised that the agent has decided to meet with me; Cindy would have represented me as being credible, and the chance to find out who killed Timmerman must be very appealing to him.

I'm very interested in having that meeting, but my interest increases tenfold when Sam Willis calls me. I instructed Sam to find out who, if anyone, Thomas Sykes called when I left his office. My assumption was that Sykes was at least somewhat worried by what I had to say, and that if he had any kind of accomplice in whatever he was doing, he would call that person and alert him.

"He made one call immediately after you left his office," Sam says. "The call lasted eight minutes."

"Who did he call?"

"The FBI."

• • • • •

LAURIE AND I can barely find a place to park at the dog show, and we've arrived almost an hour before it starts. It's taking place at a large civic center in southern Connecticut, but given the packed nature of the parking lot, you would think we were at Giants Stadium for a play-off game.

"I'm surprised no one is tailgating," I say as we get out of the car.

"You are hereby notified that you have just used up your quota of puns for the evening," Laurie says.

"One? That's all? What kind of quota is that?"

"Sorry, that's my ruling."

We go into the ticket-buying area, where a sign tells us that upper-level seats are the only ones available. That's not a problem for the well-connected Andy Carpenter, because Barb Stanley has left tickets for us at the will-call window.

We get the tickets and hand them to the woman letting people in, and she informs us that we are allowed down in the prep area, which is what Barb had told me. So that's where we go.

We walk into a room that is truly hard to believe. It is divided into walled cubicles, maybe fifty of them, each one containing one

146

dog and anywhere from one to three humans. In each case the dogs are the absolute center of attention, as the humans fuss over them and talk to them, frequently in a baby-talk kind of voice.

It reminds me of a boxing match between rounds, where the fighter sits on the stool and he gets worked on by the cut man and given guidance by his trainer. One major difference is that fighters occasionally pay attention to their trainers, while these dogs couldn't be less interested in what is being said to them.

Barb Stanley sees us, waves, and comes over. "Andy, glad you could make it."

I introduce her to Laurie, and she offers to show us around. The tour really involves little more than what we have already seen, just more of it. We won't be going out into the main area where the competition takes place until later.

All the dogs are very large, and I recognize a Saint Bernard, a bullmastiff, a Great Dane, and a Bernese mountain dog like Waggy. It's a little disconcerting to see big, powerful dogs like this being fussed over; it would be like watching someone apply eye shadow and lipstick to a middle linebacker.

"These are called working dogs," says Barb, but the truth is, I don't think any of them have worked a day in their collective lives. I'm feeling a little envious.

Barb brings us to her own cubicle, where her assistant from the doggy day care business is fussing over Barb's dog, an Australian shepherd. Barb introduces us to her assistant, Carrie, and then says, "This is Crosby. Isn't he beautiful?"

"Crosby?"

She nods. "Yes. My grandfather was a huge Bing Crosby fan. He used to play his records when I came over in the hope that I would stop listening to 'hippie music.' I've been naming dogs Crosby in his honor for as long as I can remember."

"Can we pet him?" Laurie asks.

"Sure."

Laurie and I do that for a few minutes, and then back off so that Carrie and Barb can finish prepping Crosby. Barb says that the dogs really enjoy this, but you'd never know it. They pretty much just sit there impassively. If Waggy ever had to remain this calm, he'd commit doggy suicide.

When the time comes we go out with Barb into the main ring for the competition. It is as bewildering as anything I've ever seen. There is constant motion, owners moving their dogs around the ring when competing and into position when not competing. And all spare time is spent making sure their hair hasn't gotten mussed in any way.

Everything is done strictly to time, and people are expected to have their dogs exactly where they should be at exactly the time they should be there. It's all run by someone called a ring steward, which is dog show language for Kommandant. No one messes with the ring steward.

It only takes about three or four minutes for me to get bored with this, and I'm about to suggest to Laurie that we take off when I hear a voice. "Andy Carpenter, right? I heard you were here."

Standing in front of me holding out his hand is a very, very large man, who must be carrying 320 pounds on a six-foot frame. Everything about him is oversize. His nose is fat; his ears are fat. If he turned around I would expect to see taillights.

"I'm sorry," I say as I shake his hand. "Have we met?"

"We have now. I'm Charles Robinson. Actually, I'm about to fight you in court." He says this in a matter-of-fact, fairly cheery manner.

"So you are."

"I love showing dogs; it's almost as much fun as golf. My entry for today is over there." He points in the general direction of about a thousand dogs. "Name's Tevye."

When I don't say anything, he says, "You know, from *Fiddler on the Roof.* I always liked that song, 'If I Were a Rich Man.'" He laughs at his own joke a little too loudly. Robinson seems relentlessly upbeat and garrulous, and sounds a lot like Santa Claus, without the *ho, ho, ho.* "But between you and me, I don't think he's going to win."

"Don't you have to be with him?"

"Nah, I've got people who do that." He leans in to confide that he wouldn't know what to do anyway, and then goes on to ask, "What are you doing for lunch tomorrow?"

"Probably eating Taco Bell at my desk."

He fake-laughs. "Well, I'll do you one better. Meet me at my club. You play golf?"

"No."

"Smart man. If I had all the time I spent on golf back, I could have saved the world. Come on, maybe we can talk this through and avoid going to court."

I have no desire to have lunch with this guy, especially with the trial date almost upon us. But I have even less desire to spend my time in court on the custody issue, and I can't afford to have Waggy unprotected. So I agree to have lunch with Robinson at his club, which is located in Alpine, about twenty minutes from my house, and he goes back to watching Tevye.

Laurie and I say our good-byes to Barb and wish her luck. On the way home, Laurie says, "So if not for you, Waggy would be doing that?"

I laugh. "Waggy in that ring. Now, that would be worth the price of admission."

• • • • •

I DON'T PLAY GOLF, I don't watch golf, and I don't get golf.

I just can't get interested in anything that requires a "tee time." Even if I wanted to play, if I went for a four-hour walk on the grass without taking Tara, she would turn me into a giant steak bone.

Everything about golf is grossly oversize. First of all, it takes forever. People drive to a club, get dressed, play eighteen holes, and then spend more time talking about it than it took to play. It's a full day's operation; I can watch six college basketball games in that time, and drink beer while I'm doing it.

And the space these golf courses occupy is unbelievable. The one I am driving along now, the one at Charles Robinson's club, is endless. If this amount of land were in a normal city, it would have four congressmen.

The idea of taking turns swinging a stick every ten minutes has no appeal for me. One of the reasons, I think, is that I prefer games where defense can be played. Football, basketball, baseball, even pool, all include attempts to prevent the opposition from scoring. Golf doesn't, and that for me is crucial. It's probably why I became a defense attorney. I don't like golf, or swim-

150

ming, or figure skating, or anything else in which defense isn't a major factor.

As I'm handing my car off to the valet guy, I see Robert Jacoby standing in front of the club, waiting for his car. I'm not surprised he's here; Walter Timmerman was also a member, and Jacoby's e-mail had mentioned that they golfed together.

He waves to me and I just wave back. If I go over to him I'll start talking about the DNA e-mail again, and neither of us would be in the mood for that. When the valet guy gives him his keys he calls him Mr. Jacoby, and he responds, "Thanks, Tim," so I assume he's a member here.

If Charles Robinson has been playing a lot of golf, he's been using a cart. When I enter the dining room he is sitting at a corner table, and he certainly looks to be in his natural habitat.

He sees me from across the room and waves me to the table. He doesn't get up to greet me, understandable since to do so a crane would have to be brought over.

He tells me how delighted he is that I could join him, in the same garrulous way he talked at the dog show. He does this with his mouth full and chewing, and I notice that there are already enough bread crumbs on his plate for Tara to bury a bone in.

A waiter instantly appears and takes our orders. I get a chicken Caesar salad, while Robinson orders veal parmigiana with a side of pasta. The food comes quickly, and we mostly make small talk while we eat. I've got a feeling that in Robinson's case, everything takes a backseat to eating.

Once the plates have been cleared, he gets down to the reason he summoned me. "So you've got your hands full, huh?" he asks.

"You mean with the dog?"

"Hell, no, I mean with the case. The way I hear it your client is in deep trouble."

"Then I hope you haven't gotten any jury duty notices lately."

He laughs far too loudly. Nobody at nearby tables looks over, so I suspect this is not an unusual event.

"Truth is, I know Steven. He used to call me Uncle Charlie. Back in the day. Tough situation, especially if he did it."

There doesn't seem to be a question in there, so I don't bother answering.

"You think you're going to get him off?" he asks.

"I think justice will prevail."

Robinson laughs again. "Uh-oh. Sounds like you really got a problem. So let's talk about the dog, what's his name again?"

"Waggy?"

"Where is he now?"

"On a farm in western Pennsylvania."

"What the hell is he doing there?"

"Mostly plowing, some hoeing, a little weeding. He just loves to work the land."

"Everybody says you're a wiseass," he says.

"Really? Nobody's ever mentioned anything like that to me."

Robinson laughs again; I'm thrilled to pieces that he finds me so amusing. "So how do I get my hands on this dog without us fighting it out in court? He's a champion, and if Walter had lived he'd be competing already."

"But Walter didn't live. And another thing he didn't do was mention you in his will."

"Hell, I know that. But the two people he did mention are dead and in jail. Walter and I were best friends; we played golf here every day. And we were partners on some dogs. He'd want me to have the Bernese."

"He told you that?"

"Nah, if he had lived he wouldn't let me near that dog. He'd want to use it to kick my ass."

"What does that mean?"

"That dog could be a champion, and winning was all that mattered to Walter." He laughs again. "Like me."

"So you were rivals? I thought you were friends?"

He nods. "We were both. All of my friends are rivals."

"But you were in the dog show business together?" I ask.

"That ain't business; that's fun. It's like owning racehorses, except they eat less and shit less."

If Robinson had any chance to get me to give him Waggy, which he didn't, he just blew it. I move my napkin from my lap to the table. It's my way of telling him I'm about to get up and leave. "If your intention in inviting me here was to give you custody of Waggy, it's not going to work. I've been asked by the judge to decide where he should go, and it won't be with you."

For the first time the smile leaves his face, and it is replaced by a cold anger. "You have a problem with me?"

"No, not at all," I say. "But I've got a hunch Waggy would."

The smile comes back to his face, albeit a little forced. "So what do they say? See you in court, counselor?"

I shrug. "It's my home away from home."

• • • • •

FBI Special Agent Damien Corvallis

doesn't look the part.

He's maybe five eight, 160 pounds if you tied weights to his feet. Of course, I have no idea why anyone would tie weights to an FBI agent's feet; I know I wouldn't. But if someone were to tell you that Corvallis was in law enforcement, you would guess library cop.

On the other hand, he has mastered the disdainful stare that all agents must be taught their first day in FBI school. It tells the person at whom the agent is staring that he is inferior and not worth the agent's time.

We are at the FBI offices in Newark, and I'm surprised that the only other person in the room is Cindy Spodek, who flew down from Boston this morning. Usually someone in Corvallis's position would want a bunch of his minions in attendance, so as to intimidate me. That he's kept the meeting so small could be a sign that he wants to talk frankly. At least I hope so.

Cindy is no doubt here because she knows me, and might be of value in getting me to cooperate. She and I know better, that I am chronically uncooperative, but Corvallis has yet to be enlightened as to that fact.

"So, Agent Spodek informs me that you may have some insights as to who may have killed Walter Timmerman."

"In addition to the possibility of having some insights, I also know who did it. And the same person killed his wife," I say. Again, I feel comfortable that if Childs killed Diana, he killed Walter as well. The alternative would be too great a coincidence to believe.

"She also informs me that you can be an irritating pain in the ass."

I turn to Cindy in mock exasperation. "You've betrayed me."

"Let's get this over with as soon as possible," Corvallis says. "What is it you know?"

This guy is annoying me. "Well, for one thing, I know the ground rules for this meeting," I say. "We will exchange information. You'll answer my questions, and then I'll tell you who put a bullet in Timmerman's head."

He stares at me for a few moments, looks at Cindy, and then back at me. "Get the hell out of my office," he says.

I nod and get up. "Have a wonderful day."

I leave the office and go out into the hall. As I knew she would, Cindy follows me out a few seconds later.

"Let me guess," I say. "That bozo sent you out here to tell me that you talked him into giving me one more chance, but that if I don't drop my attitude, I'm not going to find out anything at all, and I will be in deep shit with the bureau."

She smiles. "You took the words right out of my mouth."

I return the smile. "You're incredibly persuasive, Agent Spodek. Now, shall we get this over with?"

We go back in and immediately get down to more serious negotiating. I repeat that I know with certainty who killed Timmerman, but that I can't reveal how I know. I also tell him that I'll need him to answer certain questions, and that I will not reveal where I got any information he provides. But I will, of course, use that information in the defense of my client.

"Agreed," he says. "With the caveat that there will be certain questions I cannot answer."

I insist on asking the questions first, because I'm not about to tell him what I know and then have him clam up. He goes along with that, which I take as a good sign. Cindy obviously told him I can be counted on to live up to my terms of the deal.

"Why are you conducting an investigation into Walter Timmerman's death?" I ask.

"We're not. Our interest in him started well before he died."

I nod. "Okay. Why were you interested in him?"

"In the last year of his life he was doing scientific work that was of extraordinary importance."

"Was he doing the work for you?" I ask.

He shakes his head. "No, but it was a matter of national security. We were intent on making sure that it did not get into the wrong hands. Let's just say that Mr. Timmerman was not quite as concerned about national security as we were."

"So he was going to sell it to the highest bidder?"

"That was a distinct possibility."

"What kind of work was he doing?"

"That I cannot tell you. It would cost me my job, as it should."

"Was he murdered because of his work?" I ask.

"I'll be better able to answer that when I learn who did the murdering."

I ask some more questions, trying without success to probe into the kind of work Timmerman was doing. If I can demonstrate to a jury that Timmerman was doing something involving dangerous people, then I have a better chance of demonstrating reasonable doubt.

I'm reasonably sure that Corvallis is telling the truth, but I decide to play my last card as a test. "Where does Thomas Sykes fit in with all this?"

Corvallis looks surprised. "Timmerman's partner? As far as I know, he doesn't fit in at all."

I stand up and start sniffing the air. "Anybody smell any bullshit in here?"

"What does that mean?" he asks.

"It means that I know you are working with Sykes, but you just told me you aren't. And I know that he called you the other day. So why are you telling me otherwise?"

Corvallis nods. "Sykes has been working with us for months; we've been using him to learn as much as we can about Timmerman. He's still under instructions to call us if he learns anything. He told us about your discovery of his affair with Mrs. Timmerman."

I nod; the explanation makes sense.

"Your turn," says Corvallis. "Who murdered Timmerman?"

"Jimmy Childs."

Corvallis doesn't look surprised, nor does he ask who Jimmy Childs is. Obviously, he is familiar with the man. "How unfortunate for your client that he turned up dead."

I nod. "You got that right."

"Who hired him?" he asks.

"I have no idea. But he was paid half a million dollars for three hits."

"Three?"

"Timmerman, his wife, and their dog."

"Their dog?" Corvallis asks, again not showing any surprise.

"Yes, a Bernese mountain dog puppy, the descendant of a recently deceased champion."

"And Childs was definitely targeting the dog?" Corvallis asks.

"Yes. Any idea why that would be?"

"I'm afraid that's something I can't answer."

"Can't or won't?"

"At the end of the day, does that matter?"

Actually, it does. Especially to me and Waggy. But I'm clearly not going to get any more out of Corvallis, at least not until I have something more to trade, so I look to end the meeting.

"Well, this has been a true joy," I say. "Hard to believe it's ending so soon."

I expect a sarcastic retort from Corvallis, but he surprises me. "Why did you have lunch with Charles Robinson?"

"I have lunch with a lot of people."

"I'm only asking you about one of them," he says.

"He's trying to get custody of a dog."

"The dog Childs was sent to kill?"

I nod. "The very one."

"Did he say why?"

"He wants to train him to become a champion show dog."

"What did you say?"

"I said no, and he said, 'See you in court.' Why are you interested in Robinson?"

Corvallis looks at Cindy, then back at me, and smiles. "This has been a true joy," he says. "Hard to believe it's ending so soon."

As soon as I get back to the house, I meet with Sam Willis and Kevin, instructing them to find out as much as they can about Charles Robinson. If the FBI is interested in him for reasons having nothing to do with Waggy, then I am as well.

Waggy and Tara sit in on the meeting, but they seem preoccupied with gnawing on a pair of rawhide chewies. If Waggy is familiar with Robinson, he doesn't let on.

The only time Waggy looks up is when he finishes the chewie. He sees that we're busy talking and Tara is still chomping away on hers. Since nobody is paying any attention to him, he starts rolling around on his back, playing some kind of weird game that only he understands. Every once in a while he rolls over and jumps to his feet, as if something has interrupted him. Then he flips back on to his back to resume the game.

Life for Waggy is never boring.

• • • • •

"IS THE DEFENSE READY?" is Hatchet's question for me. The presiding judge asks that at the opening of every trial, and I have answered "yes" every time. And every single one of those times I have been lying.

No defense team, at least when I've been in charge of it, has ever been ready. I always want more time, more information, and more exculpatory evidence. But I never have it, so I just always answer "yes."

I have coached and prepared Steven as well as I can for what is about to take place, and he claims to be ready. But he isn't. He's going to watch and listen as the state of New Jersey, using all its power, attempts to take his life and liberty away. No sane person can be fully ready for that.

"This is really a very simple case. Murder cases are not always like that. They can often be very complicated, with a lot of cross-currents, and conflicting motivations, and evidence that is not always clear-cut. But that's not what we have here."

This is how Richard Wallace begins his opening statement to the jury. Richard is not a powerful or particularly eloquent speaker, but he brings an authenticity to the process that makes juries want to believe him.

160

"Steven Timmerman had a falling-out with his father, Walter Timmerman. That can happen between fathers and their sons, and usually differences can be worked out, but sometimes not. There was a unique economic component to these differences, though. You see, Walter Timmerman was worth almost half a billion dollars, and he was threatening to take Steven out of his will.

"Now, Steven's job was making furniture, making it by hand, and while that may be a noble enterprise, one would have to make a lot of tables and chairs to earn half a billion dollars.

"So the evidence will show that Steven arranged a meeting with his father in downtown Paterson, an area that was foreign to both of them. We don't know what he said to get his father to go there, but we do know that once they arrived, he killed him with one bullet through the head. Evidence will place Steven there, and will show that Walter's blood was found in Steven's car.

"But that didn't accomplish what Steven wanted, because he was to find out that the will had already been changed. And the way it was structured, the only way Steven would get the money is if he outlived his stepmother, a stepmother whom the evidence will show he hated.

"Well, that was no problem for Steven. He argued with his stepmother at her house, and fifteen minutes after he left the house it blew up in a massive explosion and killed her. And the evidence will further show that Steven was an expert in the type of explosive that was used.

"So that left nothing standing between Steven and his father's fortune. Nothing except you."

When Richard finishes, it becomes my job to convince the jury that there are two sides to the story, that their natural instinct to call a vote and send Steven to prison for life is somewhat premature.

I've never quite been in this position before. My financial situation allows me to take only cases in which I think the client is worth defending, which means I think he or she is innocent. But it is always simply my belief that my cause is just; I could never be positive about it.

This time I am positive. I know Steven didn't kill his father, because I know who did. Yet there is no way for me to tell this jury what I know; it is unlikely they will ever hear the name Jimmy Childs. Even if I revealed the circumstances behind Marcus's encounter with Childs, it would not be admissible at trial, because it would correctly be ruled hearsay.

My allowing Childs to be killed that night altered this trial in a way I never dreamed possible, and in the process seriously imperiled my client. It is tremendously frustrating, and dramatically increases the pressure I feel to successfully defend Steven.

"Steven Timmerman has not killed anyone," is how I start. "He has also never assaulted anyone, or robbed anyone, or defrauded anyone, or cheated on his tax returns, or gotten a speeding ticket. There is absolutely nothing in his background, nothing whatsoever, that makes it remotely conceivable that he could have done the horrible things that he is accused of.

"Money has never been important to Steven. He has never taken a dime of his father's money, though he was given many an opportunity to do so. He declined a lucrative offer to work in his father's company, choosing instead to follow his artistic instincts and make furniture.

"The truth is, Steven's lack of interest in his fortune drove Walter Timmerman a bit crazy, and he kept taking Steven out of his will in a futile effort to control his son. Yes, Steven was taken out of his father's will nine times, but it never worked, and each time he was put back in. It makes absolutely no sense to believe that this particular time he was driven to murder.

"Walter Timmerman was an extraordinary scientist, and his work has had an enormously beneficial effect on the state of our health, and the state of our justice system. It brought him wealth and acclaim, and all of it was well deserved.

"For much of the last year of his life, Walter Timmerman worked in secret, worked on a project so significant that he kept it from everyone around him. It is reasonable to assume that the work was of tremendous importance, and the evidence will show that the FBI was monitoring him closely.

"It is in that work that deadly dangers lurked, not in the supposed resentment of a son who never displayed any resentment whatsoever. Walter Timmerman feared for his life, and sought to protect himself. But the forces aligned against him were ultimately too great, and those forces had nothing to do with his son.

"Steven Timmerman has been made to look like a villain, and stands accused as a murderer. He has lost his father, and his stepmother, and he is in danger of losing his freedom. I hope and believe that after you hear all the facts of this case, and consider them carefully, you will make sure that does not happen. Thank you."

As his first witness, Richard calls Alex Durant, the guard who was on duty the day the house exploded. He is as large as I remember him, and seems about to burst through the buttons of his suit. My guess is that it's the suit he wore to his senior prom, minus the corsage.

Richard painstakingly takes Durant through the events of the morning, making him detail the procedures he and his associates went through to make sure no one dangerous made it to the house. He has logs that he refers to that show when various people arrived, including me.

"Once Steven went into the house, did you hear any conversations that he might have had?" Richard asks.

"Yes. I could hear him arguing with Mrs. Timmerman. He was screaming at her, and she was screaming back at him."

"Do you know what it was about?"

Durant shakes his head. "No."

"Had you ever heard them argue before?"

"Yes," Durant says, "it happened pretty often."

Finally, Richard leads him to the moment of the explosion, and Durant says that he was in the guardhouse at the main gate at the time.

"How long after Steven Timmerman left did the explosion take place?" Richard asks.

"Maybe fifteen, twenty minutes," Durant says.

"Did you have any conversation with him as he was leaving?"

Durant nods. "Yes. I had noticed that his right front tire was low, and I asked him if he wanted to wait a minute. We had a pump and could fill it for him."

"And did he want to wait for that?"

"No, he didn't."

"Did he say why?"

"He said he was in a hurry, and that he'd deal with it later when he had more time."

"Thank you. No further questions."

Durant has done us considerable damage, and he unfortunately has done so by telling the truth. It makes my job of shaking him that much harder. There is no sense going after him on the facts of the day as he's described them, because he did so accurately.

"Mr. Durant," I start, "how long did you work for Walter Timmerman?"

"About seven months."

"Who did you replace?"

"What do you mean?"

"Who was the Timmerman's head of security before you?"

"There wasn't any."

I feign surprise, though of course I knew what the answer was going to be. "So Mr. Timmerman had a sudden concern about security about seven months ago?"

"He said he would feel safer if people were watching the house."

"How many people?"

"What do you mean?"

"How many people were employed, like yourself, to protect the Timmermans and their house?"

"Around ten."

"And among them, these ten people protected the house twenty-four hours a day?"

He nods. "Yes."

"How long did the Timmermans live in that house, if you know?"

"I believe six years."

"But suddenly, seven months ago, he didn't feel safe?"

Richard objects that Durant could not know how Timmerman felt, and Hatchet sustains. That's okay; my point has been made.

"When I showed up that day, why did you let me go up to the house?"

"Your name was on a list," he says. "You had been approved to enter."

"Had I not been approved, you wouldn't have let me in?"

"That's correct."

"So I wasn't considered a threat to the Timmerman's safety?"

"Right."

"And I assume you were being extra vigilant because Walter Timmerman had recently been murdered?"

Durant won't concede the point. "I was always careful; that was my job."

I nod. "Right. Your job was to only let people in who were

approved, and who were not considered a threat by you or by the Timmermans. Correct?"

He knows where I'm going, but he can't stop me from getting there. "Yeah."

"Which is why you let Steven Timmerman in as well? He was on an approved list?"

"Yes."

"So for the seven months that Walter Timmerman was so concerned with his safety that he built guardhouses and hired ten security people like yourself, Steven Timmerman was always approved to enter?"

"As far as I know."

"You know pretty far, don't you, Mr. Durant?"

Richard objects that I'm being argumentative, and Hatchet sustains, so I rephrase. "Mr. Durant, is there a higher authority than you regarding who was allowed access to that house? Someone else we should talk to, who is more knowledgeable about it than you?"

Durant looks over at Richard, hoping he'll object, but he doesn't. "No," he says.

"So you're the guy?"

"Yeah. I'm the guy."

I turn the witness back to Richard for redirect. He gets Durant to remind the jurors that no one other than the people he already mentioned had gotten through the guards into the house. No sinister mad bombers, no serial killers. The implication is clear: It had to be Steven.

• • • • •

Each night during a trial, I do two things.

I rehash with Kevin what went on in court that day, and then we prepare for the next day's witnesses.

In this case, our rehashing consists of telling Laurie what transpired. She is still doing physical therapy during the day, and therefore cannot attend the court sessions. In this fashion we've inadvertently stumbled on a good way to reflect on the day's events, since she probes us with questions that make us consider and pay extra attention to some things we might have glossed over.

I'm slowly dealing with my guilt about "losing" Childs in the manner that we did. I am doing this by thinking of Childs not as the murderer, but as the murder weapon. He was sent to kill the Timmermans by someone else, and therefore that someone else is the person who had the motive. Childs was just doing a job; the key player in all this is the one that hired him. That is who we have to find.

We have made very little progress in coming up with ways to attack the evidence against Steven. This is of course frustrating; since I know with certainty that Steven is innocent, the evidence had to

167

have been fabricated and planted. But it is also puzzling. I don't understand why the actual killers went to such pains to frame him.

My belief, especially after my meeting with the FBI, is that Walter Timmerman was murdered because of something having to do with his work. It was therefore, as Tom Hagen would say, business and not personal. But someone who could afford Jimmy Childs was not someone likely to fear they would be suspected of the murder. They were doing it from a distance, and that doesn't seem to fit with an elaborate frame-up.

"Whoever hired Jimmy Childs had to know a lot about Walter Timmerman's life, not just his work," I say. "For instance, he had to know all about Steven, about his knowledge of explosives, about his being written out of the will."

"If you have the resources to pay Childs half a million dollars, then you have ways of finding out those things," Laurie points out.

I nod. "Maybe. But I've been thinking of some Middle Eastern jillionaire. Don't forget, twenty million dollars was wired to Timmerman a few weeks before he died. Yet this feels more intimate than that."

"Charles Robinson has that kind of money, and he knows so much about Timmerman's life that Steven called him Uncle Charlie," Kevin says. "And the FBI is interested in him."

I nod. "But we're not close to connecting the dots."

Nothing Sam and Kevin have come up with on Robinson has moved our case forward. He originally earned his fortune as an energy trader, sort of a one-man Enron. His reputation has long been as sort of a shady operator, but if the authorities were ever close to catching him at anything, we can find no evidence of it.

He made worldwide contacts that enabled him to be a facilitator of many things, most of them energy-related. The trading of energy across countries obviously involved huge fortunes, and Robinson has usually put himself in position to get a piece of it.

In recent years he has entered other businesses as well, everything from magazines to a retail clothing chain. But these seem to be secondary to his real business, and showing dogs and racing horses are just hobbies for him.

Kevin and I spend the rest of the evening preparing for tomorrow's witnesses. These are the toughest days in a case like this. One witness after another will lay a solid foundation of apparent proof that Steven is guilty. We'll put a few dents in it, but if we're going to win, it's going to be on the strength of our own case in chief.

I only wish we had a case in chief.

Richard's first witness today is Captain John Antonaccio, the chief of ordnance at Camp Lejeune, in North Carolina. Antonaccio is the person under whom Steven trained in explosives when he was in the service.

Richard takes Antonaccio through his qualifications as an explosives expert. I offer to stipulate as to his expertise, but Richard asks Hatchet to let him detail it for the jury, and Hatchet reluctantly agrees.

To hear Antonaccio tell it, pretty much the only bomb in the last twenty years that he was not responsible for was *Waterworld*. His résumé is impressive, and he is clearly well aware of it.

Next Richard introduces a map of the Timmerman property, and a diagram of the house itself. He gets Antonaccio to show where the bomb went off, near the center of the house, and Antonaccio says that this is where an expert would have planted it, so as to cause maximum damage.

The demonstration is jarring to me, because it reminds me of something that I missed. I will not be able to bring it up on my cross-examination, because I haven't learned enough about it to risk asking a question I don't know the answer to. It's a frustrating mistake on my part, and it's not the first.

Eventually, Richard questions him about his time working with Steven. "Was he competent working with explosives?"

169

Antonaccio nods. "Very much so. One of my best students."

"What qualities did he have that make you say that?"

"He was smart, he was careful, and he had a healthy respect for the materials he was dealing with."

"Some people don't respect the explosives?" Richard asks.

"You'd be amazed how many; they become complacent, over-confident. But Lieutenant Timmerman followed the correct procedures every time."

Richard introduces a document stating that the explosive used at the house was Cintron 321. I don't object, because I know that he could bring in an expert witness to say the same thing.

"Did Mr. Timmerman ever work with Cintron 321?" Richard would never call Steven "Lieutenant," as Antonaccio does. To do so could inspire respect from the members of the jury; I'm surprised Richard hadn't told Antonaccio not to do it as well.

"Absolutely . . . all the time. He knew everything there was to know about it."

"And the detonator that was used, which was set off remotely by a cell phone—to your knowledge he would have the requisite expertise for that as well?"

"It would be a piece of cake for him."

Richard turns Antonaccio over to me. It's been an excruciating two hours, but an effective time for the prosecution. The fact that Steven is an expert in the type of explosive that killed his stepmother is pure circumstantial evidence, but the type that juries eat with a spoon.

"Captain Antonaccio, you testified that you have been teaching the use of explosives for twenty-one years? Is that correct?"

"Yes."

"During that time, how many people have you trained?"

"I don't have an exact number."

"That's good, because I don't need one. Ballpark it."

He thinks for a while and then says, "About three hundred a year."

"So for twenty-one years, that would be more than six thousand?"

"I guess so."

"Are you the only person in the marines who does what you do?" I ask.

"No. Of course not."

"How many such instructors are there? And again, you can ballpark it."

"Maybe a hundred."

"So if we assume there have been a hundred for the last twenty-one years, and each person trains three hundred people a year, then in that time a total of . . ." I turn to Kevin, who has been using a calculator, and he hands me the calculator with the total on it. ". . . six hundred and thirty thousand people have been trained in the use of these explosives?"

Antonaccio is not pleased with the way this is going. "I can't verify those numbers."

"I understand," I say. "Now, do the army and navy blow things up as well? Do they train people in explosives?"

"Of course."

I shake my head slightly and smile at where this is going. "I won't go through the numbers for them, because I'm not a math major. But it sounds like you can't walk down the street without banging into someone who is an expert in explosives."

Richard objects and Hatchet sustains, so I switch to another area. "How would someone no longer in the service go about getting Cintron 321?"

"I wouldn't know."

"Really? For instance, you wouldn't know if it's available on the black market?"

"I'm told if you have enough money you can get anything," he says.

"Including Cintron 321?" I ask.

"I would assume so."

"And detonators?"

"Yes."

"If people had enough money, and they could buy explosives and detonators, could they also pay someone to show them how to use it all?"

Richard objects that I am asking something outside the witness's area of expertise, but Hatchet overrules and makes him answer. "I would think they could."

"Captain Antonaccio, I'd like you to consider a hypothetical. Suppose you sold me Cintron 321 and a detonator to set it off. Would you be able to prepare it in such a way that all I would have to do would be to plant the explosive, and then dial a number on my cell phone to set it off? Would that be possible?"

"Yes."

"So were you to do that for me, all I would have to know is how to dial a phone?"

"Well . . ."

"In my hypothetical," I say.

"Then yes."

"So even though, based on your previous testimony, I seem to be one of the few people in America not trained in explosives, I could blow something up with your help, just by placing a call? Would I have to include the area code?"

Richard objects and Hatchet sustains, but I couldn't care less. My point has been made as well as I can make it. In reality, of course, it's a debating point; the jury is still going to find Steven's expertise in the explosive used to blow up the house to be a damning fact.

And the truth is that they should.

• • • • •

THE MOMENT I GET HOME, I dive into the
discovery documents.

The police and forensics reports confirm what I realized during
Antonaccio's testimony this afternoon. They refer to one explosion as
causing all the damage, the one that took place near the center of the
house.

Yet I was there that day, and I am positive that I heard a second,
much smaller blast, which seemed to come from farther back in the
house. I just assumed, if I thought about it at all, that it was a secondary explosion, perhaps a gas tank or water heater, precipitated by the
first one. It certainly seemed much weaker than the initial blast, and
the damage had already been done.

I still think all of that may be true, but the diagram of the house
shown today reminded me that Walter Timmerman's home laboratory was back in that area of the house where the second explosion
seemed to take place.

I discuss all of this with Laurie, and we kick around what to
do with it. "We're going down the tubes at trial," I say. "And the
courtroom is not the place we're going to win it. If we're going to get

Steven off, it's by understanding what his father was doing, and who wanted to stop him from doing it."

Laurie agrees. Even though she has not been in the courtroom, Kevin and I have kept her up to date. We'll put up a fight there, and we'll score some points, but at the end of the day the existing evidence is on the side of the prosecution.

I alluded in my opening statement to Walter Timmerman's work causing him to be murdered. But the truth is, at this point I can't even introduce evidence of that on a good-faith basis. Of course, we have no hard evidence anyway, but even if we did, we have only guesswork to tie it to the murder.

I call Sam on his cell phone, which is the only phone he ever uses. He answers on the first ring, which I think he has done every time I've ever called him. He must keep the phone taped to his ear.

"Talk to me," he says, his standard greeting.

"Sam, I've got an assignment for you. You can do part of it on the computer, but you may have to do real legwork on the rest."

"Can I carry a gun? I just got a license . . . in case."

Sam has some serious mental issues. "No gun, Sam. This isn't official police business. But you can say stuff like 'ten-four' and 'roger' if you like."

"I copy that," he says.

"Good. I want you to find me the best expert you can on the work that Walter Timmerman was doing."

"What kind of work was he doing?" Sam asks, quite logically.

"I don't have the slightest idea," I admit.

"That's going to make it harder."

"Let's start with DNA. Timmerman was an expert in it, and we have that e-mail about him sending his own DNA in to be tested. So we'll start there. Bring me the mayor of DNA-ville."

"Will do."

"And Sam, if you find someone, but they don't want to help, don't shoot them. Move on to someone else."

But Sam has already hung up, so he doesn't hear me. I turn to Laurie, who has overheard my side of the conversation. "Sam has a gun?" she asks.

"Apparently so."

"You might want to confiscate his bullets."

My next call is to Martha Wyndham, who is not at home. I leave a message that I need to talk to her, and I give her the address of the house, should she be able to come over after court tomorrow.

Laurie and I talk some more about the case, and we then go upstairs to the bedroom. I head into the bathroom to wash up and brush my teeth, and when I come back Laurie is already in bed. This is not a surprise. What is a surprise is that she's naked.

"You're naked," I say, trying not to drool.

"Wow, you don't miss a thing."

I put on a fake Western accent. "Where I come from, when a lady gets herself naked, she's got a reason for it. At least that's what my pappy always told me."

"You had a wise pappy," she said.

This is shaping up as a too-good-to-be-true moment, but I'm also slightly concerned about it. "You're sure you're okay?" I ask. "I mean, you've been through a lot. Are you up for this?"

She smiles. "I was going to ask you the same question."

It turns out that we are both more than equal to the challenge. It also turns out to be one of the most intense, loving experiences of my life.

It wasn't long ago that I thought I had lost Laurie forever, and now she's here, with me, fully and completely.

As Al Michaels once said, "Do you believe in miracles? YES!"

● ● ● ● ●

Robinson arrives at the hearing

with eight lawyers. Since I don't attend bar association meetings, I'm not sure I've ever seen this many lawyers in a group before. I'm not even sure it's called a "group" of lawyers; maybe it's a flock or a gaggle.

The lead attorney is Stanford Markinson, one of the founding partners of Markinson, Berger, Lincoln & Simmons. It is one of the largest law firms in New Jersey, with offices around the state. Robinson must be a hell of a big client to get Markinson to show up personally at a dog custody hearing.

Hatchet makes it clear that he is not at all happy to have to be going through this, and he tells both sides to be economical with their time. This is going to be done before lunch, or he's going to have the attorneys for lunch.

I am very concerned about this hearing, and it has nothing to do with the number or quality of lawyers that Robinson has enlisted to represent him. The fact is that I have very few legal bullets to fire; if I were Markinson I would view this as a slam dunk.

More important are the stakes involved. I don't trust Robinson and view him as a possible suspect in the Timmerman killings, which automatically makes him a suspect in the attempted Waggy killing. Even if he were innocent of all that, I certainly don't trust him to protect Waggy in the way that I have been doing.

Complicating matters is my inability to share with the court the danger that Waggy is facing. Clearly I can't reference what Childs confessed to Marcus, and without that I have no evidence at all of any threat to Waggy.

I am also in the uncomfortable position of not really having a positive goal that I can verbalize. Robinson's is clear: He wants to be named custodian of this dog. My preferred outcome is more vague. I want to maintain my role as the court-appointed decider when it comes to Waggy's future, even though I have done nothing but avoid making a decision for months.

What I want is for Steven to take custody, but I certainly can't guarantee with any certainty at all that Steven will ever again be in a position to do so. Hatchet knows that as well as anyone. I have to try to play a continuing delaying game until I can win Steven his freedom.

Markinson calls as his first witness a trainer named Pam Potter. She has been the primary trainer of Robinson's show dogs for four years, and she describes the conditions that Robinson provides as humane and perfectly acceptable.

"You would be aware if that were not the case?" Markinson asks.

"Oh, yes. I'm around the dogs all the time. I wouldn't stay there if they were being mistreated. I love dogs far too much for that."

"And Mr. Robinson provides whatever veterinary care is necessary?"

"Certainly. Money is never an object."

Markinson turns the witness over to me for cross-examination, but before I can start, Hatchet calls both of us to the bench for a whispered conference. He directs his comments to Markinson.

"What was that witness all about?" he asks.

Markinson is taken aback by the question; he's not used to Hatchet's eccentricities. "Well, Your Honor, we were using her to show that the dog will be well cared for by Mr. Robinson."

"Why?"

"So that you would feel comfortable awarding the dog to him."

Hatchet gives him the icy stare. "This dog is not going to the person who will provide the cushiest life. He is going to the person with the strongest legal claim to him. So stick to the ownership issues."

"Yes, Your Honor."

"I would still like to cross-examine this witness, Your Honor," I say.

"To what end?"

"To challenge what she said."

Hatchet is not very adept at concealing his annoyance. "I just told you that what she said does not matter."

"I understand, but it's still in the record, and I would not like the record to show that it went unchallenged."

"For possible appeal?" Hatchet asks.

"If we don't prevail here," I say. I've got to be careful with this, since Hatchet is not only the judge, he is also the jury. It doesn't make much sense to piss him off.

"If you take more than fifteen seconds to cross-examine this woman, then it's a good bet you won't be prevailing," he says.

I nod, and Markinson and I go back to our respective tables. He has been "Hatcheted" for the first time, and seems a little shocked by the experience.

"I have no questions for this witness," I announce, and I see Markinson smile when I say it.

Markinson calls Charles Robinson to the stand, and studiously avoids asking any questions about how well the dog will be treated. He focuses on his friendship with Timmerman, and their partnership in owning three dogs, none of whom is in competition anymore.

"This dog was special to Walter," Robinson says. "He told me many times that he thought he could be a champion. I know he would want me to help realize that dream." The words would be enough to make me gag no matter who said them, but coming out of the mouth of this slimy worm make them even harder to take.

There is no way I can let this guy have Waggy.

My first question on cross-examination is, "How long has it been since you were in partnership with Walter Timmerman on a dog?"

"A little over four years," he says.

"How many dogs have you owned since then?"

"I'm not sure. I would have to check the records."

"I've checked the records," I say. "Does eleven sound about right?"

"Sounds right," he concedes.

"The records also say that Walter Timmerman has had fourteen dogs since then. Does that sound about right?"

"I wouldn't know," he says.

"You and your close friend and partner didn't discuss these things?"

"We did. I just wouldn't know the exact number."

"So between you, you've had twenty-five dogs since your partnership ended?" I ask.

"Our partnership never ended."

I nod. "I see. You no longer owned dogs together, but you were partners on some metaphysical level. How come your partner didn't leave the dog to you in his will?"

"He left it to his wife. I'm quite sure that if he had any idea she would be killed, he would have included me as well."

"So you believe he made a mistake in leaving you out?"

"Yes. Definitely. It surprised me."

"I can imagine your shock, especially after you left him your dogs in your will."

Robinson doesn't respond, so I ask, "You did leave your dogs to your friend and partner, Mr. Timmerman, didn't you?"

He suddenly becomes more subdued, and it doesn't take Freud to sense an intense anger beneath the surface. "No."

"So you made the same mistake that surprised you so much when Mr. Timmerman made it?"

"I'm afraid that I did."

There's little more I can do with Robinson except get some things on the record in case the worst should happen and he gains custody.

"If you had possession of the dog, what would you do with him? Would he be a household pet?"

"The first thing I would do is have my trainer, Ms. Potter, evaluate him and determine what his potential is as a show dog."

"Because that's what you think Mr. Timmerman would have wanted?"

He nods at finally hearing something he can agree with. "Exactly."

"So he would spend the first month or so at Ms. Potter's training facility, so as to see if he is capable of fulfilling Mr. Timmerman's dream. Is that what you are representing to this court?"

"Yes." He's not happy at the direction this is going.

"And if he were judged incapable of mastering the training necessary to be a successful show dog, you would then have no interest in keeping him?"

"I didn't say that."

"So what do you say?'

"I'd deal with that situation if it came up, but I doubt that it will."

"No further questions." I at least got him on record as promising to keep Waggy at the trainer's facility for a month. I'm not sure how that will help, but I'd feel better if he were there than at Robinson's.

I have no witnesses to call, since my position is that Steven remains the rightful heir. The only place I can make that point is in my closing argument, and I'll get to have the final word, as Markinson will be speaking first.

He's a smart guy and has caught on to Hatchet quickly, so he leaves out anything referring to the health and well-being of the dog. Instead he focuses on Robinson being the court's only real option. Mrs. Timmerman is dead, Steven is obviously not in a position to take the dog, and there are no other candidates.

He adds the importance of a timely decision being reached, since show dogs must start their training at an early age. Obviously Walter Timmerman would have trained Waggy as a show dog, and the court has an obligation to try to follow through on his wishes when they are as obvious as this. If Charles Robinson is named custodian, he will see that Timmerman's wishes come true.

It is a professional, persuasive closing, and the truth is that no matter what I say, it is likely to carry the day.

"Your Honor, as you know, Steven Timmerman is currently on trial for murder. You also know that I believe him to be wrongly accused, but that is now for the justice system to decide. And that decision will be reached in a relatively short period of time.

"Mr. Robinson's alleged close friendship with Mr. Timmerman has not been demonstrated by a shred of evidence before this court, only by Mr. Robinson's own testimony. And their partnership in the showing of dogs, such as it was, has not existed for a number of years. If Mr. Timmerman had wanted to place Mr. Robinson in the line of succession for custody of this dog, he could have. But he did not, and no evidence has been presented to show that his failure to do so was an oversight.

"If a verdict of not guilty had already been reached in Steven Timmerman's trial, we would not be having this hearing. He would have been granted rightful custody of the dog, and justice would be done, and that would be that.

"I would submit that for Steven to lose custody before the verdict is reached would be to deny him his rights. And make no mistake: If Charles Robinson is made the custodian, Steven will never get this dog. The only proper reason for granting Mr. Robinson's petition would be a demonstration that irreparable harm would be done by waiting for that verdict.

"The only such harm even claimed by the plaintiff, though also not supported by the evidence, would be that this animal's future as a show dog would be damaged by a delay in training. Therefore, I will guarantee the court that if a decision is delayed, I will employ a leading trainer to work with the dog until a verdict in the Timmerman trial is reached.

"Thank you for your consideration, Your Honor."

Hatchet does not exactly seem swept up in the emotional power of the arguments. He quickly says that he will consider his decision and announce it when he's ready to do so.

I have absolutely no idea whether I've won or lost, and really don't have the time to worry about it either way. If we lose, I'll try to file an appeal, hopefully delaying a decision until Steven Timmerman is a free man. Or not.

Right now winning that freedom is what I have to be focused on.

• • • • •

RICHARD HAS A BASKETFUL of effective witnesses to call on, and to belatedly start the day he chooses Sergeant Michele Hundley, the forensics technician who was originally called to the Walter Timmerman murder scene in downtown Paterson. The police were smart enough to bring Hundley to the Timmerman house when it blew up, since they knew that the two cases would be connected. Therefore Hundley, whom I know to be good at her job and a terrific witness, would be able to testify to the entire case.

Hundley dresses conservatively in a suit with her hair up and wearing glasses. She reminds me of those women you sometimes see in TV commercials who miraculously transform themselves into knockouts simply by letting down their hair and removing their glasses. I can't be sure about this, of course, since every time I've seen Sergeant Hundley she has rigidly clung to the librarian look.

Richard starts with the Walter Timmerman murder in downtown Paterson, getting Hundley to describe the conditions that existed when she arrived on the scene. Walter died from one bullet to the forehead, and Hundley testifies that the gun had been pressed to his flesh as it was fired.

"So would you describe that as execution-style?" Richard asks.

"Usually we consider it execution-style when the bullet enters the back of the head, not the front."

"So this was perhaps more personal?" Richard asks.

I object that the witness could not possibly know this, and Hatchet sustains.

Hundley then talks about the murder weapon, which was a .38-caliber revolver, but has never been found. Childs used a different gun to shoot Timmerman and Laurie; I assume the Luger he used in the latter case was better for distance.

Hundley goes on to describe the splatter of blood, brain matter, and skull fragments against a wall just behind Walter. I glance over and can see Steven cringing at the testimony, even though I had instructed him to be impassive. I know that Steven is upset at hearing how gruesomely his father died, but the jury might think that he is racked with guilt.

Hundley then talks about the specks of blood that were found in Steven's car.

"Did you test that blood?" Richard asks.

"We did."

"Whose blood was it?"

"Walter Timmerman's."

Richard spends some more time on this, and then shifts to the house in the aftermath of the explosion. Hundley testifies that the explosion came from the upstairs guest bedroom toward the center of the house, the bedroom that Steven used before he moved out.

"It was an extraordinarily powerful explosion," she says, and then goes on to describe the extent of the damage. She concludes that "Diana Timmerman, who was in the den at the time, died instantly from massive head trauma."

I could object a lot more than I do, since Hundley is testifying to some things more properly brought forth by others. For instance, she is not a coroner, and her description of the head trauma as the cause of death is inappropriate. But I know all of what she says is true and Richard can bring in witnesses to prove it, so I don't want to be seen by the jury as attempting to impede the truth.

I need to make at least a few points in my cross-examination. "Sergeant Hundley, it's a difficult subject to talk about, but you testified that Walter Timmerman's blood, brain matter, and skull fragments splattered off the wall?"

"Yes."

"It was something of a mess?"

"Yes."

"So whoever did the shooting would have been sprayed by it, either directly or when it bounced off the wall?"

"Absolutely."

"The blood that you found in the car . . . when was it left there?"

"It's impossible to tell."

"How old is the car?"

"I believe three years old."

"So from what you are scientifically able to determine, it could have been left there any time in the last three years?"

"It's possible."

"Thank you. Who left the blood there?"

Hundley seems slightly taken aback by the question. "Well, it was Walter Timmerman's blood."

"Could it have been planted there by someone else?"

"There is no evidence of that," she says, indignantly.

"Is there evidence against it? Is there anything in what you saw that says that's not possible?"

"Of course it's possible, but that proves nothing."

I smile. "I agree that nothing has been proven."

Hatchet intervenes even before Richard can object, and tells me to cut out the little digs and move on.

I do. "What about the brain matter and skull fragments that you found? Can you determine how long they had been in the car?"

"We didn't find any brain matter or skull fragments in the car," she says.

I feign surprise; over the years I have gotten to be a terrific surprise-feigner. "Only blood?"

"Yes."

"If Steven Timmerman was splattered with blood, brain, and skull, how come he only transferred blood to the seat of the car?"

"That's difficult to say."

"I'm sure it is. Doesn't it make it far more likely that Walter Timmerman, Steven's father, had a cut that bled a little in Steven's car sometime in the last three years? Isn't it reasonable to assume that, considering the lack of brain and skull fragments in the car?"

"I don't make assumptions, Mr. Carpenter. I just report the facts."

I nod. "Just the facts . . . gotcha. Lieutenant Hundley, how many times have you cut yourself in the last three years after which you've bled, even a bit, from a little accident? Could be a paper cut, splinter, torn fingernail, shaving your legs, whatever."

"I really wouldn't know."

"Then guess," I say.

"Maybe four or five."

I smile approvingly. "Then you're very careful; in my case it's a lot more. How many times have you had a little accident that caused you to lose brain matter or skull fragments?"

"Never."

I nod. "Same here. So people bleed all the time, but they rarely get their heads blown up. Walter Timmerman could have left traces of blood in his son's car at any time, but if he had left brain or skull in there, that would have been rather significant. Don't you think?"

"That's not for me to determine."

"And it's equally significant that those things were not there, don't you think?"

"That's not for me to determine," she repeats.

I nod. "Because you just report the facts."

"That's correct."

"Is it a fact that you found clothing of Steven Timmerman's that was covered with his father's blood?"

"No."

"Did you factually find any of that blood in Steven Timmerman's house?"

"No."

"Not in the drains, or the washing machine?"

"No."

"And that's a fact?"

"Yes."

I turn to the scene at the house, though there is little fertile ground for me to cover. As part of my questioning, I ask if all the damage had been done by one explosion, and she tells me that if there were any additional explosions, she is unaware of it.

When I let her off the stand, Richard stands for what I assume will be a redirect examination.

Instead he says, "Your Honor, may we have a discussion in chambers?"

• • • • • •

"YOUR HONOR, we believe we have located the murder weapon. I was informed of it moments ago."

"How convenient for you," Hatchet says. "Where did you find it?"

"In the defendant's downtown loft, where he makes and sells his furniture."

This is not making sense to me. "Richard, I've seen the reports of a previous search of the loft. It didn't turn up then, but it suddenly appeared now?"

"My information on this is not complete; I just thought I should inform the court and defense immediately when this was brought to my attention. But there was apparently a secret, or at least a hidden, compartment in the leg of one of the tables the defendant made. The police discovered the gun in there."

Hatchet obviously finds this as strange as I do. "What made them decide to do another search in the first place?"

Richard is himself looking uncomfortable with this. "There was an anonymous tip, I believe in the form of a phone call."

I argue that the gun should not be allowed to be introduced as evidence, though I really have no solid grounds on which to base my objection. Hatchet delays his decision until the gun is confirmed to be the weapon that killed Walter Timmerman, but he will rule against me. I can tell he's not pleased with this turn of events, but just as I can't come up with a good reason to keep the evidence out, neither can he.

I ask Hatchet if we can adjourn for the day, so that I can talk to my client about this while the tests are run. Richard backs up my request, since if the gun is shown to be what we all think it will be, he'll want to introduce testimony to that effect immediately. Hatchet grants the request, and the jury is sent home until tomorrow.

I arrange to meet with Steven in an anteroom. In a normal situation, I might start by telling him that his loft was searched again, and I would be looking to gauge his reaction for any obvious worry. But once again this case is different; I know that Steven didn't kill his father, Childs did. So it therefore isn't possible that Steven hid the murder weapon.

"They think they found the murder weapon," I say. "It was hidden inside a piece of furniture in your loft."

He recoils as if shot. "That isn't possible. Oh, my God. How is this happening?"

"Do you ever build hidden compartments into your furniture?"

He nods. "Sometimes, when people request it. But it's not for hiding things generally, it's often for storage."

"Who would know about that?"

"Almost anyone who's ever bought a piece of furniture from me."

"That doesn't narrow it down much," I say.

"How bad is this?" he asks. "Is there any chance we can recover?"

"We'll have a better idea about that tomorrow."

When I finish meeting with Steven, I go back into the courtroom, where Kevin is waiting for me. Also there is Martha

Wyndham, who tells me she was in court today. I left word for her to come over to the house after court, and I ask if she'd mind meeting me there. She's fine with that.

I stop at the supermarket before going home, since the four hundred people who seem to be staying at my house have, if anything, started to eat even more than before. I'm not sure, but I think I saw Marcus gnawing on the garage the other day.

Martha beats me home, and Laurie has let her in. When I get there Martha is playing with a crazed Waggy. I could wait for Waggy to calm down before talking to her, but by then Steven would be up for parole.

"Waggy looks terrific," Martha says.

I nod. "And he's matured a lot."

She starts to ask me some questions about the trial, and how I think it's going. Since I don't want to be honest about it, I fend off the questions, including the one about why court was adjourned early. I want to keep the information about the murder weapon quiet until tomorrow, though obviously I have only limited control of that.

I finally get the conversation around to where I want it, which is Charles Robinson. "Did you spend any time with him?"

"Some. Not a lot," she says.

"What was his relationship like with Walter Timmerman?"

She thinks about it for a few moments. "They would have said they were friends. I would describe them as competitors, but with people like that, the line is blurry."

"What do you mean?"

"They were both all about winning, so that's what their friendship was about. They wanted to surround themselves with people who would challenge them, people whom they wanted to beat. I'm not sure they thought about it in those terms, but to them it would make perfect sense."

"Did you ever hear them talking about Timmerman's work?"

"No, when it came to work the only thing they had in common was it made both of them rich. Walter was a scientist; Robinson is some kind of international financier, or trader, or something."

Martha has no real knowledge of Robinson or his activities, and the conversation shifts to her own life in light of the death of her employers. She's saved some money over the years, she says, and her mother left her a decent amount when she died, so finding work immediately is not necessary. She renews her offer to help us with Steven's case in any way she can, but there's really nothing for her to do.

"By the way, did you hear a second explosion that day at the house?"

"No, I don't think so. But all I could really hear was myself screaming." She grins with some embarrassment at the recollection, but I understand her reaction. It was a frightening, surreal moment.

Laurie invites Martha to stay for dinner, but I'm glad that she declines, since I need all available time to prepare for tomorrow's witnesses. Martha offers to help out with Waggy if we need a break, but I decline that offer as well.

After dinner I receive a phone call from Richard Wallace. "Sorry to bother you at home, Andy, but the ballistics test came back and I thought you'd want to know the results."

It's typical of Richard that he would be giving me this heads-up. "Let me guess," I say. "It's the gun that shot Kennedy from the grassy knoll."

He laughs. "Close. It's the one that shot Timmerman from behind the Dumpster."

"Six of one, half a dozen of the other. See you in court, counselor."

• • • • •

HATCHET ALLOWS the murder weapon in as evidence, as I knew he would. Once the ruling is made, Richard calls Detective Roger Manning to the stand. Manning is the officer who led yesterday's search at Steven's loft, and he supervised the ballistics tests that were immediately done.

Manning testifies quite simply that the police received a call in the form of a computer-masked voice, alerting them to the location of the weapon, and that when they conducted a subsequent search, there it was.

He further says that the loft was locked when they arrived, and that they had locked it when they searched it the first time. There was no sign of forced entry, according to Manning.

Richard has him describe the manner in which the ballistics tests were performed, and he introduces photographs of the bullets, allowing Manning to show the jury exactly what he is talking about.

"So there is no doubt that this is the gun that killed Walter Timmerman?" Richard asks.

"No doubt whatsoever."

Obviously I have no ability to challenge the scientific tests, so when Richard turns Manning over to me, I focus on other areas.

"Detective, were there any fingerprints on the gun other than Steven Timmerman's?"

"There were no fingerprints on the gun at all."

I do a double take, as if I am surprised. "Not even Steven's?"

"No," he says. "The gun was wiped clean."

"So your view is that he hid the gun in his own loft, in his own furniture, but wiped it clean so that it couldn't be traced back to him?"

"I can't answer that," he says.

"Can you think of any reason why he would do that?"

"I haven't thought about it."

I nod agreeably. "Why don't you spend some time thinking about it now? We'll wait."

Hatchet, it turns out, has no desire to wait, and he tells me to move on. So I do. "Detective, did you run a trace on the gun, in an attempt to find out its history?"

"Yes. It was not in any database."

"So the gun's only connection to Steven Timmerman is that it was hidden in his loft?"

"The only connection that we could find," he says.

"Okay, for Steven to have done this, he would have had to shoot his father in downtown Paterson, drive an hour or so to his loft, and then hide the gun in the one place it could absolutely be traced back to him."

"Your Honor, is there a question in there?" Richard asks.

"Would you like to try that as a question, Mr. Carpenter?" Hatchet asks. "That is the general procedure that we like to follow."

I nod. "Thank you, Your Honor, I will. Detective, if Steven Timmerman was going to wipe the gun clean, and if it couldn't otherwise be traced to him, why not just leave it at the scene, or throw it into any garbage can between Paterson and New York? Or throw it into the Passaic River? Or leave it anywhere except in his own loft?"

"I can't know what was in his mind."

"Then can you read the anonymous caller's mind? Did he say how he knew where the gun was?"

"No."

"Or why he called now?"

"No."

"But he knew which piece of furniture it was hidden in?"

"He said the leg on the large table."

"Does it bother you at all that you found the gun this way?"

To Manning's credit, he doesn't duck the question. "It would not be my first choice."

I nod. "Thank you for that. Would you say that the anonymous caller, whoever he might be, wants Steven Timmerman to be found guilty in this trial?"

"It would seem so," Manning says.

"That's quite a coincidence, don't you think?"

"What do you mean?"

"The person who wants Steven to spend the rest of his life in jail just happens to be the person whom Steven told exactly where he hid the gun."

I check my cell phone messages when court adjourns, and there is one from Sam telling me that he has found the DNA expert to end all DNA experts. He's a college professor, specializing in genetics. He teaches classes all day and does research at night, so he's going to bring him to the house early Monday morning before court, and I should call him if that doesn't work. It works fine, so I don't bother calling.

When I get home, Laurie is on the phone talking and laughing with a friend from back in Findlay. That is happening with increasing frequency, and I can't say I'm thrilled with it. Pretty soon she's going to want to talk and laugh with those creeps face-to-face, which means she will leave here. That is a day I'm not looking forward to.

We decide to have pizza tonight, and because the smell of pizza always brings Marcus out into the light, I order five large pies. More accurately, I let Laurie do the ordering, since on her pie she always wants a long list of toppings, all of which are healthy. On the other side of the scale, Kevin can have no toppings at all, because every one ever invented sets off his allergies.

I overhear Laurie doing the ordering, and to my horror I actually hear her get artichoke on her pizza. I believe in live and let live, but there should absolutely be a law against artichoke pizza.

Kevin arrives at the same time as the pizza delivery man, and Marcus shows up thirty seconds later. We decide to postpone our trial-day rehash until after dinner, and we dig right in on the pizza.

Marcus eating pizza is a sight to behold. He takes three slices at a time and lays one on top of the other, face-to-face, with the third one in the middle. Then he eats it as a pizza sandwich, in maybe three bites.

Laurie, Kevin, and I don't eat the crusts; instead we feed them to Tara and Waggy. But of course we wouldn't dare suggest that to Marcus. At least I wouldn't.

After Marcus has had four such sandwiches, he stands up, a strange look on his face, and walks toward the back of the house. He doesn't say a word, which is not exactly a news event where Marcus is concerned.

"Where's he going?" asks Kevin.

"Maybe he's going hunting for more pizzas," I say. "They're in season."

The three of us continue eating the cheese portion of the pizza and feeding the crusts to Tara and Waggy. Waggy tries to butt in and get every piece, which clearly annoys Tara, but she's too lady-like to do anything about it. She leaves it to us to make sure she gets her fair share.

Marcus comes back holding what appears to be a hamburger in his hand. "Where'd you get that?" Laurie asks.

"I don't think hamburger hunting season starts until September," I say to Marcus. "I hope the game warden didn't see you."

Marcus puts the hamburger at the edge of the table. "Yard," he says, which I assume means he found it in the yard. It takes a moment for the significance of this to hit me, and during that same moment Waggy moves toward the burger.

"NNNNNNOOOOO!" I scream, as loud as I can, and I make a dive toward Waggy and the table. Waggy, forced to decide whether to keep moving toward the hamburger, or to get out of the way of this screaming, middle-aged lunatic, makes the wise choice. He backs away, huddled down toward the floor, fearful.

I grab the hamburger and, without thinking, run into the kitchen and throw it into the sink. By this time, everyone has followed me into the kitchen, no doubt amazed at behavior that is bizarre, even by my standards.

"What is going on?" Laurie asks.

For the first time in my memory, I am more interested in talking to Marcus than Laurie. "That was in the yard?" I ask. "Just lying there?"

He nods. "Yuh."

"Did you hear anything? Is that what made you go outside?"

"Yuh," he repeats. This conversation is moving right along.

"You think somebody threw it there?" Laurie asks, as it starts to dawn on her. "You think it could be poison?"

"You'd be amazed at how few hamburgers are thrown into my yard at night," I say, which is another way for me to say yes.

"We need to get it tested," Kevin says.

I call Pete Stanton, tell him that I am reporting a possible crime, and ask him to come out with a forensics team.

"What happened?" he asks.

"Somebody threw a hamburger into my backyard."

"Those bastards," he says. "I'm sending out a SWAT team, and I'll tell them to bring ketchup."

"I think they were trying to poison Waggy," I say.

"Who the hell is Waggy?"

"Walter Timmerman's dog. Trust me on this one, Pete. There are some things I haven't told you about the Timmerman murder and Jimmy Childs."

"Are you going to tell me when I get there?"

"If I have to."

"If you don't, I'm not going to get there."

I agree to tell him the story, and he's there within twenty minutes with two officers and a forensics expert. Within fifteen minutes, only Pete remains, and the hamburger has been taken away for a rush test.

"Okay," Pete says after they've left. "Let's hear it."

I'm not sure why I haven't told Pete that Childs had killed the Timmermans and been targeting Waggy; I guess it's just a habit for me to err on the side of not sharing information with anyone not on the defense team. But there's nothing about any of it that causes any additional jeopardy for Steven, and I'm not breaking a confidence, so I bring Pete up to date.

"Marcus is sure about this?" Pete says, directing the question at me even though Marcus is in the room. Pete has as much trouble talking to Marcus as I do.

"Marcus is not involved in this in any way," I say. "The anonymous caller who told me Childs was in the river sounded quite sure, though."

"But he didn't say why Childs killed the Timmermans, or why he wanted to kill their dog?"

I shake my head. "No, he didn't mention that."

"Have you used your tremendous investigating skills to uncover the reason?"

"Not quite."

He pauses a few moments to take this all in. "So your client is on trial for two murders, and not only do you know he's innocent, but you know who actually did it."

"Yes," I say.

"And you can't do shit about it."

"Not yet."

He shakes his head in amazement at my predicament. "You know, I never thought I'd say this, but I actually feel sorry for you."

"That's a great comfort."

Laurie, Kevin, Pete, and I kick it around for another half an hour, accomplishing absolutely nothing. Pete's cell phone rings, and he answers it. "Stanton."

He listens for a while, says "thanks," and disconnects the call.

"Two ounces of pure arsenic. If the dog had eaten that, he'd have been dead inside of a minute."

"Hatchet better rule in our favor," I say. "We cannot let this dog leave this house." I look over at the dog in question, Waggy, who is chewing on a toy and doesn't seem distressed by the goings-on.

But I sure as hell am.

• • • • •

It doesn't take long for my worry to prove justified. Even though it is Saturday, Hatchet issues a ruling on the court Web site directing me to turn Waggy over to Robinson immediately. Robinson is hereby named Waggy's custodian, though the ruling is deemed temporary, and can be revisited at the conclusion of the Timmerman trial. Hatchet does not promise to reconsider his decision in the event Steven is acquitted; he merely retains the right to do so.

Hatchet also directs that Waggy be housed at Pam Potter's training facility for the first month, to be evaluated as to his promise as a show dog. It seems to be a concession to me, but the ruling as a whole is a disaster.

Hatchet's ruling also makes it clear that an appeal will be of no avail. He will not stay his ruling, which means that Waggy will be with Robinson while the appeal is considered. This won't exactly be a high-priority case for an appeals court, and a decision could take months. With the danger Waggy is in, hours could be too long.

Kevin agrees to take Waggy to Potter's facility, since I can't bring myself to do so, and I tell him to ask for a tour when he gets there, and to remember everything he can about the place.

"Why?" he asks.

"So that I can make sure Waggy's well taken care of and safe," I lie.

I go upstairs, where Waggy is hanging out with Tara. "Waggy," I say, "you're going somewhere with Kevin, but you won't be there long."

Waggy seems happy enough about the turn of events, smiling all the while. Tara, however, is significantly wiser, and she stares at me. It is not a trusting look.

"I'm telling you, it won't be long." If Tara is mollified, you can't tell it by her stare. "What, you don't believe me?"

She walks over and licks Waggy's head, which I take as her way of telling me that Waggy is her friend, and nobody screws around with Tara's friend.

I have known Tara for eight years and have never lied to her, and right now, right this minute, she thinks I'm full of shit.

"Tara, he will be back here tomorrow night."

• • • • •

"I'M NOT GOING TO KIDNAP WAGGY,"

I say to Laurie, Kevin, and Marcus.

"You called us here on Sunday morning to tell us that?" Kevin asks.

"Yes, but I would like to discuss, purely on a hypothetical basis, how it could be done if someone wanted to do it."

"Hypothetically," Laurie says.

I nod. "Yes. Perhaps we could then take the information and provide it to his new owner as a guide to how he can protect him better."

"It's good that it's hypothetical," Kevin says, "because if you were really to kidnap him, you would be committing a felony and could face prison time, to say nothing of the loss of your license to practice law."

Everybody in the room knows I am serious about this, and everybody also knows that Kevin is right. Taking Waggy will not be fun and games; it is a serious crime that I am considering.

On the other hand, two attempts have been made on Waggy's young life, and he is now very possibly also in the control of the man who has ordered those attempts. My desire not to break the law is strong, but not quite as strong as my desire to prevent this dog from being killed.

"You're certainly right about that," I say. "So let's leave it as a hypothetical, and let's start by you describing the training facility where Waggy is being kept. Take your time, and do it as completely as you can."

Kevin describes the place in extraordinary detail. It is a large indoor facility about twenty yards from Potter's house. It has twenty holding areas, larger than normal dog runs but too small to be called rooms, and each has an entrance accessible from outside. Unfortunately, he has no idea which one Waggy will be kept in.

Once Kevin is finished, I suggest that he leave. Kevin is far too dedicated to the law to participate in a crime, no matter how worthy he considers its purpose. He seems grateful for the opportunity to get out now, but cautions me to be very careful.

Once Kevin is gone, I ask, "If I were to announce a change in this from hypothetical to real, would either of you want to leave?" I've already talked to Laurie about this, and she has great reservations. She's a police officer, but she's a dog lover, and at this moment I don't know what she'll decide.

"I'm staying," she says.

"Marcus?" I ask.

He nods. "We get the dog."

"Good. I thank you, and Waggy thanks you."

We spend the next few hours planning the operation, and though it seems like a solid approach, I'm feeling very uncomfortable about it. I'm going to be crossing a line I've never crossed before, and it is a very disconcerting feeling.

Laurie will have no active part in the kidnapping; it will just be Marcus and me. Getting in and out would ordinarily not present a major problem, but it will be complicated by the dogs barking like crazy when we arrive on the scene. This will no doubt be exacerbated by the fact that we will have to search room by room until we happen upon Waggy.

The plan is to bring Waggy back here, at least until we can figure out something else to do with him. I don't want to involve more people in this, so asking Willie to take him is out. For the time being he can stay inside, with quick walks out to a small secluded yard on one side near the back of the house, and Marcus will stay around to ward off any intruders.

But first we have to get him, and we wait until cover of darkness to do so. It is Marcus's idea to bring Tara with us; it's possible that her sense of smell will lead us to Waggy's room, so that the operation can be done much more quickly.

The three of us get to the house at almost midnight. It is in an isolated area of Mahwah, and there is little doubt that Potter chose this secluded setting so that there would not be neighbors for her barking dogs to annoy. Obviously, the lack of neighbors works very much in our favor.

We all had different ideas for how to pull this off, but Laurie came up with the best one. We park about two hundred yards away, and both put on gloves. Marcus gets out by himself and throws a few rocks close enough so that the dogs can hear them. They start to bark in unison, and within two minutes lights go on in Pam Potter's house.

From my vantage point at the car, I can see her go out to the dog compound and look around, trying to see what set them off. When she can't find any obvious disturbance, she goes back into her house. Within another minute, the lights go back off in the house.

Tara and I start walking toward the compound, with Tara on a leash. I assume Marcus is executing the next part of the plan, which is to place devices on the front and back doors of the house that will prevent those doors from being opened from the inside. If Potter gets up again to check on what is happening with the dogs, she'll find she can't get out of her house. By the time she realizes it and calls 911, we hope to be long gone with Waggy.

Marcus meets us about fifty yards from the house. "Did you lock her in?" I whisper.

"Yuh."

"Let's go." We move toward the compound with the dogs in it. In the moonlight, it appears to be exactly as Kevin described it.

"Tara, we need you to find Waggy. Find Waggy." As I say it, I cringe with some embarrassment; I feel like Timmy talking to Lassie. But Tara wags her tail, and we head for the dogs.

We're about fifteen yards from the compound when the dogs sense our presence and start to bark. Tara leads us down a long row of rooms, and I'm afraid she's just checking out the place, not Waggy-hunting. But suddenly she stops, and there's Waggy, tail pounding and reveling in the excitement of it all.

Marcus takes out a device and breaks the lock, then steps in and slaps a leash on Waggy. As he does so, I can see the lights go on in the house again. Within moments Potter is going to find out that she's a prisoner, and will call 911. It suddenly strikes me as a mistake that we didn't cut the phone line; I assume that Marcus could have easily accomplished that.

Within seconds we're running to the car, and we get in and drive away, with Marcus and me in the front seat, and Tara and Waggy in the back. I'm exhilarated by what we have accomplished; there's a Bonnie-and-Clyde feeling to it. The only problem is that I want to be Clyde, but Marcus would be rather miscast for the role of Bonnie.

I listen intently for sirens all the way home, but there are none. When we get there, Laurie is waiting anxiously for us. We update her on how flawlessly her plan went, and then Marcus and Waggy head down to their hiding place in the basement, while Laurie, Tara, and I go upstairs to bed.

I lie in bed for an hour, unable to sleep. What we did tonight almost seems surreal. But it wasn't. In fact, the justice system has some very real terms for it, like "breaking and entering," and "grand larceny."

Laurie wakes up and sees me with my eyes open. "Can't sleep?"

"No," I say. "Not so far."

"Does the fact that you're now a felon have anything to do with it?"

"No. I'm just planning my next job. I'm thinking maybe a bank."

"Good night, Andy."

"Good night, Bonnie."

· · · · ·

THEY'RE GROWING A STRANGE CROP

of college professors these days, and Dr. Stanley McCarty is as strange as they come. First of all, he looks like he's about seventeen years old, with hair halfway down to his shoulders. He is wearing jeans and sneakers, with a white buttondown shirt that is buttoned all the way to the neck.

When Sam introduces him to me, he doesn't make any gesture to shake hands, but instead says "hey" and walks past me into the house. He goes to the large-screen TV on the wall in the den and spends about three minutes examining it, even seeming to caress it. Then he says, "Very cool," and comes back to Sam and me.

I've got a feeling that if I bring him in as an expert witness, Hatchet will hold him in contempt before he even opens his mouth.

"So my man here says you need to talk to me," McCarty says, and I have to assume that Sam has earned the designation "my man" in record time.

"I do," I say. "Thanks for coming over."

"No prob."

"You work with DNA?" I ask.

206

He smiles. "The whole world works with DNA."

"But it's your specialty?"

"Hey, I never thought of myself as having a specialty, but let's go with genetics."

"Did you know Walter Timmerman?" I ask.

"Met him once. Didn't really know him, which is okay, because he didn't know me, either."

By this point in the conversation, Sam and I have made eye contact at least a dozen times. If malicious eye contact could kill, Sam's song-talking days would be over for good.

"I need to find out what Timmerman was working on when he died," I say.

"You got his notes?"

I shake my head. "No."

"What do you have?"

"Pretty much nothing."

"Nothing?" he asks.

"Basically. At least no real facts."

McCarty looks at Sam, as if I'm the lunatic in the room. He may be right. Then he turns back to me. "You see the problem here, right?"

I nod as I hand him a copy of the e-mail that Robert Jacoby sent to Timmerman, expressing surprise that he had sent him his own DNA to test. "Take a look at this."

McCarty takes the e-mail and reads it. He's either the slowest reader in America, or he's reading it a number of times. Finally, he nods. "Okay. What else?"

"The FBI had an entire task force assigned to Timmerman, all because of what he was working on. They said it was important to national security."

McCarty just nods, silently, so I go on. "And I believe that Timmerman was murdered because of that same work."

"Keep talking," he says.

"The same people that killed Timmerman are trying to kill his dog; somehow the dog represents a danger to them."

"What kind of dog?"

"Bernese mountain dog."

He nods. "I love those dogs; the markings are amazing. Can I see him?"

"He's not here," I lie. "At this point he's missing."

"That's the dog I saw on television this morning? The one who was kidnapped?"

"Yes. Is any of this making any sense? Maybe ringing a bell?"

He's still quiet for a few moments, hopefully thinking. "You know anything about DNA?"

"No."

"You got a pen and a piece of paper?"

"In my desk."

"I'll get it," says Sam, and he goes off to do that. He's back quickly and hands the pen and paper to McCarty, who sits down and starts writing on it. When he's finished, he shows me a drawing of what I take to be a strand of DNA.

"This is nature," he says. "Everything comes from this. You control this, you control the world."

"How can you control DNA?" I ask, not understanding this at all.

"By creating it. Timmerman was creating synthetic DNA. There were rumors that he was, and now I'd bet anything on it."

"Is that known to be possible?"

He nods. "Sure, everybody's trying it, and some think they're making good progress. But right now it's just a theory. A damn good one, but just a theory."

"What could you do with it?"

"Anything you want. See, if you can create DNA, then you program it however you want. Then you inject it into a cell, and once it gets inside, it's like it boots itself up. Like a computer program, you know? Then it gets the cell to do whatever it wants it to do. Whatever you want it to do."

"Give me an example," I say.

"You're not getting it," he says, and truer words were never spoken. "Everything is an example. You can duplicate life-forms, or you can create completely new ones."

"So it's cloning?"

He smiles. "Cloning is yesterday's news. If Timmerman pulled this off, it's no wonder somebody killed him for it. Shit, I'd kill him for it."

It's starting to dawn on me. "So Waggy . . . the Bernese . . ."

"Came from the lab" is how he finishes my sentence. "Did Timmerman own the dog's father or mother?"

I nod. "Father. He was a champion."

"So he took the father's DNA . . ."

I interrupt. "Isn't that cloning?"

He shakes his head. "No, because I'll bet Timmerman didn't use the father's DNA. He copied it; he created new, synthetic DNA just like it."

"Why?"

"Just to prove to himself that he could. Like a test."

"So why would someone then want to kill Waggy?"

"Maybe to keep anyone from knowing what Timmerman was doing," he says. "There must be something about the DNA that identifies it as synthetic."

I nod. "Which is why Timmerman sent his own DNA in to be tested. It must have been a copy as well, and he wanted to see if the lab would pick up on it."

"Now you're getting it," he says, as I feel myself beaming at the approval. "But the lab missed it, because they didn't know what they were looking for. It's completely understandable."

"But if he proved he could synthetically produce his own DNA, why did he have to use the process to create the dog?"

"Because copying DNA is one thing, but creating a living thing with it is far more complicated. And to exactly copy a champion show dog, that's about as good as it gets."

"So why would the FBI be watching Timmerman? What would they be afraid of?"

McCarty shakes his head as if disappointed. "Maybe you're not getting it after all. This is the ticket to creating anything . . . a new life-form, fuel, anything. For instance, you could create bacteria and viruses that we don't know how to deal with; you think the government might be interested in that?"

"Holy shit," Sam says, an appropriate comment considering the circumstances.

"Did you say fuel?" I ask. "This stuff can create fuel?"

He nods. "Sure, that's probably the main reason companies are pursuing it. You can tell cells to make biofuels. If Timmerman could figure out a way to do it cost-effectively, you know what that would be worth?"

"I can imagine," I say, though I'm not sure I can. "One thing I didn't mention. I think that there might have been a secondary explosion that took place in Timmerman's laboratory."

McCarty smiles and says, "Fuels have a tendency to do that."

• • • • •

I DON'T HAVE TIME TO CONSIDER the staggering implication of what McCarty had to say. I'm in danger of being late for court, and I'm aware that Hatchet would strangle me, DNA strand by DNA strand, for that offense. On the way in, I get a call from a local TV reporter asking me if I've heard that Waggy was stolen last night, and that Charles Robinson is out making statements accusing me of being behind the theft. He is threatening to go to the police and file charges, an empty threat since he has no evidence. At least I hope he has no evidence.

Since it's been all over the news this morning, I acknowledge that I've heard about it, and am outraged by Robinson's accusations. I deny any involvement; once I've committed a serious felony, lying to a reporter seems easy by comparison.

I tell the reporter that I will have more of a comment later, after court, but I manage to find the time to accuse Robinson of not adequately providing for Waggy's security, and I further threaten a lawsuit against Robinson on Steven's behalf if Waggy is not quickly found, safe and sound.

I make it to court with only ten minutes to spare, and I can see that Kevin was getting nervous that he might have to take over. We don't talk about the events of last night, but he obviously knows what happened.

I wish I didn't have to be here; it requires my total concentration, and I'd much rather be thinking about what I learned this morning. McCarty was credible. It may turn out to be a lunatic theory, but it had the ring of truth to it, and his confidence in what he was saying was contagious.

Hatchet makes no mention of the Waggy kidnapping; he probably doesn't care much either way, as long as it doesn't involve him.

Richard calls Philip Sandler, Walter Timmerman's attorney. He is there to testify about his preparation of Walter's will, and Steven's connection to that.

Sandler says that Timmerman called him three weeks before his death and mentioned that he was considering disinheriting Steven.

"Did he say why?" Richard asks.

"He had a contentious relationship with Steven, and he was particularly upset with him at that point."

"Did he share with you what he was upset about?"

"He felt that Steven was mistreating his stepmother, Diana. His view was that Steven never accepted her into the family."

"What happened after that phone call?" Richard asks.

"About a week later, he called and said that he and Steven had argued about it, and he definitely wanted to disinherit Steven."

"So he was taken out of the will entirely?" Richard asks.

"No, but he would only receive money if Diana were also not alive when the will was settled."

When Richard turns the witness over to me, my first question is, "Mr. Sandler, you said that Walter and Steven Timmerman had a contentious relationship. Would you say they never got along?"

"No, I wouldn't say that. It was up and down. Sometimes things were good, sometimes they weren't."

"And sometimes Steven was in the will, and sometimes he wasn't?"

He nods. "Yes."

"How many times did Walter Timmerman instruct you to take Steven out of the will?"

"Probably twenty times."

"And did you do so each time?" I ask.

"No, on a number of those occasions he called and told me he had changed his mind before I had a chance to do it."

"How many times did you actually do it?"

"Nine."

"And the first eight of those times, he subsequently instructed you to put his son back into the will?"

"Yes."

"Did he ever say that Steven had threatened him, or that he was afraid for his life if he kept Steven disinherited?"

"No."

"And as far as you know, Steven never physically assaulted his father?"

"I am not aware of any such thing."

I excuse the witness, and then catch a break when Hatchet announces that he has received a note that one of the jurors is feeling ill. That will give us some time without having to listen to, and try to deflect, the mounting evidence against Steven.

I go home and decide to take Tara for a long walk. I haven't done it for a while, because I didn't have the heart to leave Waggy at home alone. But now that Waggy is in the basement with Marcus, Tara and I arc free to be on our way. Walking Tara is the thing I do that for some reason most allows me to think clearly, and clear thinking is what is need right now.

Before I leave I go down to the basement to check on the unlikely duo. Marcus is throwing a tennis ball, and having Waggy chase it. What he does is run after the ball, often skidding to a hilarious stop on the slippery floor. Then he mouths it for a while, but neglects to bring it back to the person who threw it in the first place. Instead he looks up hopefully, as if wanting the person, in this case Marcus, to once again throw the ball that he does not have. It is up to Marcus to walk over and retrieve the ball before tossing it again.

Marcus is laughing at Waggy's antics, which brings to a total of one the number of times I've seen Marcus laugh. I ask him if everything is okay, and he nods and throws the ball again. This is working out better than I thought.

I realize that I haven't even mentioned to Waggy yet that he may be a creation of science rather than sex, but I think I should. I don't want him learning it from some stranger later in life.

I don't think I've ever seen a happier dog than Tara as we set out. I'm not sure if it's that we're going on the walk, or if it's that she finally will get some time away from her lunatic companion. But away we go, Tara's tail wagging and her nose sniffing, and me thinking.

There are two parallel tracks to this case. One is the trial itself, and the other is our investigation into whatever it was that Walter Timmerman was doing before he died. I am willing to believe that his work in some fashion caused the death of himself and his wife, mainly because it makes sense and it doesn't help me to believe otherwise.

If this becomes purely a matter of defending Steven, we are in deep trouble. Richard is presenting the jury with some very compelling evidence. Though I am poking some holes in that evidence and questioning its authenticity, it is basically me asking the jury whether they want to believe me or "their own lying eyes."

It still makes very little sense to me that Steven is in this position at all. If I believe that Walter was working on some powerful force that could have an international impact, and he was killed by some sinister entity intent on possessing or stifling that force, then where does Steven fit in? Why was it necessary to frame him? It was not an easy thing to do, and the process of doing it necessarily included the danger of detection.

I never thought I would say this after initially meeting Stanley McCarty, but I definitely believe he knew what he was talking about. His words were compelling, and he spoke them with an easy confidence. It also doesn't help me not to believe him; the area of investigation it opens is also the only one I have worth pursuing.

My instincts, which place Charles Robinson somewhere near the center of this, might well be confirmed by what McCarty had to say. As a trader of energy with international contacts, he would have been the logical person for his friend Walter Timmerman to turn to with his discovery.

But once Timmerman approached him, Robinson would have looked at him as a cash cow, the possible key to untold wealth and power. Why then, would he have killed him? Had they had a dispute over the direction they should take? Had Timmerman ultimately betrayed him and gone elsewhere?

As my father would say, "I'm not going to know until I know. And maybe not even then."

But one thing I do know: On the investigative track of this case, the time for playing defense is over. I cannot sit back and watch Steven go down the tube, or wait for someone to successfully kill Waggy. It's time to go on the offense, which means Charles Robinson's world is about to be shaken.

● ● ● ● ●

WHEN I GET BACK TO THE HOUSE, Pete

Stanton is waiting for me.

Robinson has demanded an investigation into the Waggy kidnapping, and Pete has internally maneuvered to be the one to conduct an interview with me. Laurie is with us when he questions me.

"Do you have a search warrant?" I ask.

He shakes his head. "No, not enough probable cause. I am here to interview you, which I know you'll consent to, because you are a citizen concerned with justice and the American way."

"That is beautiful. For the first time I feel understood."

"Did you steal the dog?" he asks.

"Is this off the record?" I ask.

"Off the record? Who do I look like, Bob Woodward? I'm a cop; nothing is ever off the record."

"I did not steal that poor animal, and I only hope you can find him and return him safely to Mr. Robinson. You and he are in my prayers."

"Where were you last night at around eleven o'clock?"

"Home and in bed with the police chief of Findlay, Wisconsin."

"We were snuggling," Laurie adds.

"Do you have any idea where the dog is?" he asks.

"No, but I'm considering hiring a team of investigators to help in the hunt. Any information we get will be turned over to you immediately. This heartless criminal must be brought to justice."

"You know what I think?" he asks. "I think you kidnapped the dog and he's down in the basement right now."

"But you didn't bring a search warrant?"

"No."

"And you aren't going to get one?"

"No."

"You policemen are relentless, you know that?"

Pete leaves, knowing full well what the truth is, and having no intention of attempting to expose it. I deeply appreciate that, and someday will tell him so.

Once he's gone, I call Cindy Spodek. I call her rather than Agent Corvallis mainly because on Friday evening if would be difficult to reach him, and I have Cindy's cell and home phone numbers. I also think it's probably best that she approach him on my behalf, because she'll lie and say that I'm credible and reliable.

Obviously she has caller ID, because she answers the phone with, "So, did you kidnap the dog?"

"That's how you answer your phone? By accusing your old friend of committing a felony?"

"Knowing you and what a dog lunatic you are, I would say there's a ninety-five percent chance you did it."

"I just want you to know that I'm deeply hurt, but for the purposes of this conversation, I'm going to move past that."

"My cup runneth over," she says. "What can I do for you, old friend?"

"I want you to set up a meeting with Corvallis about the Timmerman case."

"Aren't we into a 'been there, done that' situation?"

"I believe we are."

"It was a fascinating meeting, Andy, really it was. But I think I'm going to need a little more to get Corvallis in a room with you again."

"I'm going to give you Charles Robinson."

"The guy you stole the dog from? Why would I want him?" she asks.

"You wouldn't, but Corvallis would," I say, and then it dawns on me that she may not know anything about all this. She is not a member of the task force assigned to Timmerman, and may be on the outside of a need-to-know situation.

I ask her straight-out if she knows what is going on, and she admits that while she has some suspicions, she is basically in the dark.

"Would you like to be brought into the light?" I ask.

"I would."

"And can I count on you to keep everything I tell you in confidence, except the parts you don't have to keep in confidence?"

"Not knowing what the hell you are talking about, I'll say yes."

I proceed to tell her everything I know, and everything I suspect, about the Timmerman case. I'm glad to do so, because I'm pretty far out on a limb here, and Cindy is really smart. If she thinks I'm way off base, she'll tell me so and show me how.

She doesn't. Instead she just says, "You could be right about this, Andy. I'll call Corvallis; when do you want to meet?"

"Tomorrow."

"Tomorrow is Saturday," she says.

"Boy, you FBI people are really sharp. Cindy, I would like to get moving on this before the jury delivers a verdict."

"Okay, I'll call you back."

When I get off the phone, I update Laurie on what she said, and my request for a meeting tomorrow.

"If you get the meeting, I want to go with you," she says.

"Why?"

"You're starting to get into potentially dangerous territory, and dealing with danger is not exactly your forte."

"Danger is my middle name," I say.

"Robert is your middle name."

"No, I changed it while you were in Wisconsin. I thought Danger would be more appealing to chicks."

"I knew there was something exciting about you, I just couldn't place it."

I finally agree to let Laurie come with me to the meeting, because she's smart and I value her opinion. Also, because I really hate saying no to Laurie. At least I think I would; I've never actually tried it.

Laurie tells me that she taught Waggy a trick, which she wants to show me. We go down to the basement, and she tells me to get him excited, which I do by throwing a tennis ball. He is firmly into his nut-job routine when she demonstrates the trick.

She puts her hand toward the floor, palm-down, and says, "Quiet time, Waggy. Quiet time."

He doesn't even bother to look up, just continues to roll around with the ball, in wild excitement.

Laurie makes her voice even sterner. "Quiet time, Waggy. Quiet time."

Waggy yelps a few times as the ball rolls away from him, and then leaps on it, grabbing it in his mouth and violently shaking it and his head from side to side.

"It's a great trick," I say. "But you might want to perfect it before you do it on stage."

"Do you want to watch a movie?" she asks, ignoring the dig.

"Did you teach Waggy to load a DVD also?"

"That's for tomorrow," she says.

We go back upstairs and watch *The Natural,* one of Laurie's favorite movies. She's not a big sports fan, but for some reason she loves sports movies. We watch the flick, and drink some wine, and pet Tara. It is perhaps my favorite way to spend time, not counting the NFL.

When we're finished we go upstairs and make love, which on second thought is my favorite way to spend time, including the NFL.

Afterward Laurie looks at me, probably surprised that I haven't fallen asleep within eight seconds. "What are you thinking?" she asks.

"That I want you to move back here and marry me." These are words that I've said a thousand times, but they're usually in my head, and never actually come out through my mouth. This time I involuntarily speak them, loud and clear, and even Tara looks over in surprise.

"Excuse me?" Laurie asks, meaning she didn't hear me the first time or she wants to give me an easy out to pretend I never said it.

Since I have no way of retreating, I push ahead, rephrasing it as a question. "Will you move back here and marry me?"

Ten seconds that feel like ten years go by before she answers. "Is it all or nothing?"

"What do you mean?"

"I mean if I wanted to, could I choose one without the other?"

Is it possible she's considering this? Or even taking it seriously? "I don't know; I didn't think it through. But let's see . . . you can choose one, but only if it's the moving-back-here one."

"Can I think about this?"

"Sure. I'll go downstairs and have a sandwich."

"I don't mean think for a few minutes, Andy. I mean think it through."

"Sure. No problem," I say. "How long do you think it will take? Are we talking hours, or months?"

"Andy . . . ," she admonishes.

"Okay, sorry. I don't want to blow this. But if we meet with the FBI agent, can I introduce you as my fiancée?"

"No."

"Laurie, he's an FBI agent. We can't just tell him that we're sleeping together."

"Then we'll stop sleeping together," she says.

"On the other hand, what business is it of his? What is he, the sex police? I'm sick of government intruding in the bedrooms of private citizens like us."

"Andy . . ."

"What?"

"I love you. And thank you for asking me to marry you. Nobody's ever asked me that before."

"I've tried to a bunch of times, but I could never quite get up the nerve. I always assumed you'd say no."

"Maybe I will," she says, softly.

"And maybe you won't."

· · · · ·

CINDY CALLS ME at eight AM to tell me that Corvallis will see me this afternoon.

She will not be joining us, possibly because Corvallis knows we'll be talking specifics, and she isn't on the case. If she is upset or offended about it, she hides it well. It is simply how the bureau functions. I promise her that I'll tell her everything that goes on.

Laurie still wants to go with me, and we agree that I will introduce her as my investigator, without mentioning that she is a law enforcement officer in Wisconsin. That might complicate matters for Corvallis, so there's no point even going there.

This time Corvallis is all business. He seems to understand from last time that he can't push me around or intimidate me, and he makes no effort to do so. He seems fine with Laurie being there, but he does not have any of his staff sit in with us.

"You've got the floor," he says.

"Okay. Part of what I'm going to say I know for a fact, and part is what I believe. Just so you'll know, regardless of what you do, I'm going to act as if what I believe is absolutely true. It's the only way I can defend my client."

I continue, "Walter Timmerman was working to develop syn-

222

thetic DNA, which is why you were watching him so carefully. The implications of what he was doing were enormous, for reasons I don't have to tell you."

Corvallis doesn't react at all to what I am saying; he just stares impassively and listens.

"He went to Charles Robinson, a friend of his, to help him benefit from his discovery. My assumption is that Robinson was going to use his connections in the energy industry to capitalize on what could be an incredible new source of energy, one that could have a real impact on the geopolitical balance in the world.

"I don't know if Charles Robinson had Walter Timmerman killed. I doubt that he did, though it's possible they had a falling-out; perhaps one of them felt that he was being betrayed by the other. It's also possible that another party, perhaps one with an interest in maintaining the energy status quo, decided to remove Timmerman from the picture before he could complete his work.

"Once Timmerman was dead, the killers for some reason wanted all evidence of his work destroyed, so no one else could get it. That is why they blew up the house, and that is why they tried to kill the dog. Because the dog is a product of this invention"—I can't help but smile—"and has a high energy level of his own.

"So I'm not sure of Robinson's role in the murders, though the fact that he wanted possession of the dog is incriminating. He could well have planned to kill the dog, or at the very least see to it that his DNA was never tested. But the dog was taken from him, and at this point his whereabouts are unknown."

Corvallis speaks for the first time. "So what are you proposing?" he asks.

"I believe that whether or not Robinson is a murderer, he is at the center of this. I believe I can scare him with what I've learned, and maybe shake him into admitting something that both of us can use."

"How?"

"By meeting with him and confronting him. You can fit me with a wire, and you can be near the scene if things go bad."

He turns to Laurie, who to this point has not said a word. "And you'd be there as well?"

She shakes her head. "No, Robinson would be more likely to deal if it's just Andy. But I'll be with you, nearby, just in case."

He shakes his head. "We work alone."

"Not this time you don't," I say. "Ms. Collins has my full confidence, which at this point I can't quite say for you."

He thinks for a few moments. "Okay . . . I'll be in touch."

"When?" I ask.

"I have people I need to clear this with."

I nod. "And I have a client I need to defend, so put a rush on it."

Laurie and I leave, and once we get in the car she says, "He'll go for it."

I nod. "I think so, too. And if I was wrong about my theory, he'd have thrown us out of the office."

She nods her agreement.

"You were quiet in there," I say. "What were you doing . . . thinking about what we talked about last night?"

"Andy . . ."

"Because there's a lot to think about," I say. "Flower girls, bridesmaids, showers, shit like that. I think I'm going to have Tara give me away."

"No one has to give the man away."

"Oh."

"Andy, are you going to keep bringing this up?"

"Probably."

"Then I'm going to check into a hotel."

"Bring what up?"

• • • • •

RICHARD CALLS A STRING OF WITNESSES
who are so boring, the jury has trouble staying awake.

First up is Patrolman Marty Harris, who gave Steven's car a parking ticket on the street outside Mario's restaurant in Paterson on the night of the murder. The restaurant is located just two blocks from the exact spot where the murder took place, a fact that Richard uses twenty minutes and two maps to demonstrate.

The ticket was written at nine thirty-seven, as noted by Patrolman Harris on his ticket. This fits in quite well with the estimated time of death, which was around ten o'clock, a connection that Richard makes sure the jury understands.

When he turns him over to me after about an hour of tedium, there's really nothing about what he said for me to question. So I decide to question him about what he didn't say.

"Patrolman Harris, where was Steven Timmerman while you were writing the ticket?"

"I don't know."

"Are most people who park in that space usually in the restaurant, since that's the only place open on that street at night?" I ask.

"I would assume so."

"So you didn't see Steven Timmerman, before or after writing the ticket?"

"No."

"Did you see his father, Walter Timmerman?"

"No."

"Mr. Wallace showed a map, pointing out where the car was parked and where the body was found. Are you familiar with that area? Have you ever driven or walked by there?"

"Yes. Many times."

"The body was found behind a convenience store. If I asked you to drive to that store tonight, could you find it?"

"Of course," he says.

"Where would you park?"

I can see his mind racing as he contemplates the mistake that many witnesses make. He has said nothing wrong, but he believes that his next truthful answer will hurt the prosecution's side, so he tries to think of a way out. Of course, he should not be trying to manipulate matters, he should just tell the truth.

Which ultimately he does. "I would park in front of the convenience store."

"Not at Mario's restaurant, two blocks away?" I ask.

"No."

"Let me present you with a hypothetical. Suppose you were going to murder someone who was in your car, and you were planning to commit the murder behind the convenience store. Obviously you wouldn't want to be seen with that person, since that would make you a likely suspect after the body was found. Would that make you more or less likely to part two blocks away and walk with him?"

"I would park near the convenience store," he says.

"Thank you. Me too."

Next up is a clerk from the phone company named Nina Alvarez, who testifies about the phone call from Walter Timmerman to

Steven on the night of the murder. Steven had also told me about the call, but we could not find it in Walter's records. The explanation for that, as Ms. Alvarez quickly points out, is that it was not made from Timmerman's private cell phone, but rather from his business cell phone, listed under the account of Timco.

Through Richard's lens, Alvarez's testimony comes off as damning. The implication is that whatever was said between the two men, it resulted in a confrontation and murder two hours later. Richard's contention is that it was the trigger that ultimately resulted in Walter Timmerman's death.

In my cross-examination I ask Alvarez, "Do you know what Walter and Steven Timmerman talked about that night?"

"No, sir," she says.

"Could it have been about the Mets game the night before?"

"I can't say."

"Do you know that they talked at all?"

"I know that the call was answered and lasted twenty-four seconds."

"Could a friend of Steven's, or maybe a housekeeper, have answered the phone and taken a message?"

She nods. "It's possible, sir."

"Could the answering machine have answered, and Walter left a message?"

"It's possible, sir."

I hate to end the cross-examination, because I like being called "sir." It doesn't happen that often. But other than asking Ms. Alvarez her favorite color, there's nothing more for me to get from her, so I let her off the stand.

When court finally adjourns, I check my cell phone and listen to a message from Agent Corvallis agreeing to participate in my plan as it relates to Charles Robinson, and telling me that I should call him.

I call him immediately, and he says that I need to give them twenty-four hours' notice before any meeting, so as to give them time to set things up. We also talk about possible locations for the meeting, and how I should position things with Robinson.

Corvallis, now that he is on board, comes off as helpful and smart, qualities I am going to need to call on before this is over.

• • • • •

CHARLES ROBINSON TAKES MY CALL,

but he doesn't seem his old jovial self. "You decide to give up the dog? Because otherwise you're going to jail," is the first thing out of his mouth.

"The dog is what I wanted to talk to you about," I say.

"So talk."

"I think we should meet in person."

"Why? You can say what you've got to say now."

"What I've got to say concerns not only the dog, but also Walter Timmerman, and synthetic DNA."

There is silence for a few moments from Robinson. If the first words out of his mouth aren't *What the hell are you talking about?* then I'll have final confirmation that I'm right.

Those are not his first words. His actual first words are, "You think you can keep screwing around with me?" I can see him snarling through the phone.

"I think we can help each other," I say. "I think we can help each other a lot."

"You don't know what you're messing with," he says.

"If you don't meet with me, I'll be messing with the FBI by this time tomorrow."

He tells me to come over to his house in Closter, a town about half an hour from me, tonight. Corvallis had anticipated that, and told me it was fine, that the FBI could comfortably set up there. My guess is that means they've had previous surveillance on Robinson's house, but it's only a guess.

However, there is no way I'm going there tonight. I tell him I'll meet him at eight tomorrow night, and he reluctantly agrees. He has gone from surly and confrontational to nervous and anxious to meet me. It's a transformation that certainly works in my favor.

Once I'm off the phone, I call Corvallis and tell him what transpired. He's fine with it, and we pick a place to meet two hours before I'm to be at Robinson's. At that point I'll be fitted with the wire, and we'll go over final arrangements.

It is terrific for me to have Laurie here to discuss these things with, and she and I spend a few hours kicking around exactly what I should say to Robinson. I'm nervous about it, though of course I would never admit it to her.

"Andy," she says, "I know you realize this could be dangerous. Robinson could have been the one to hire Jimmy Childs, and he could see you as a danger to be eliminated."

"You just trying to cheer me up?"

"No, I'm trying to make you aware. Your safety is far and away the most important thing. If at any point your instincts tell you that you are in the slightest jeopardy, you get out of there immediately. Okay?"

I agree, though I neglect to mention that I have absolutely no faith in my instincts, at least not in this situation. In a courtroom, yes. When it comes to physical danger, no. If I bailed out of every situation in which I was physically fearful, I'd never leave the house.

Laurie points out another negative when she says, "I'm afraid there's no place for Marcus in this."

I nod. "I know. The FBI wouldn't let him within half a mile of the place. It's their show; I hope they know what they're doing."

"I'll be there with them," she says.

"Then I hope you know what you're doing," I say with a nervous smile. "You know, we could go down to city hall tomorrow at lunchtime, and if anything goes wrong tomorrow night, you could be the rich Widow Carpenter."

"You're an incorrigible idiot," she says.

"I'm aware of that," I say, and then turn serious for what I hope will be a brief moment. I tell her that she needs to know that she is the beneficiary of my will, and that Kevin drew it up and has the document itself. "You get everything, including and especially Tara."

"Andy, nothing is going to happen. I only brought it up because I want you to be careful."

"I know. I've been meaning to tell you about the will since I did it."

"When did you do it?"

"About three years ago," I say.

"Before I went to Wisconsin?"

I nod. "Yup."

"Did you take me out of the will when we were apart and not seeing each other?"

"Nope."

"We weren't even talking, and I was the beneficiary of your will?"

"Yup."

"You're a lunatic, you know that?"

"Yup."

• • • • •

TODAY IS CHARACTER DAY AT THE TRIAL.
It is standard procedure; the prosecutor calls a series of witnesses for
basically no other reason than to testify as to what a terrific person
the victim was. In this case it will take twice as long, because there
are two victims.

I barely cross-examine most of these witnesses, for two reasons.
First of all, I have basically nothing to get from them, and by not
questioning them I hope to decrease their importance. Second, I
don't want to look as if I'm attacking the victims and their memory;
juries don't look very fondly on that.

The only witness I spend any time at all with is Robert Jacoby,
the head of the DNA lab. Richard has called him as a friend of
Walter's, and he mouths every platitude there is on behalf of his dear
friend's memory.

When I get to examine him, I ask, "Mr. Jacoby, did you receive
an unusual request from Walter Timmerman a couple of months
ago?"

"Yes. He sent me a DNA sample to test, and it turned out to be
his own DNA."

"Did you ask him why he did that?"

"Yes, but he never responded."

I then get Jacoby to admit that Walter had been secretive about his research in recent months, and I let him off the stand. Maybe his answers will come in handy later, or maybe not.

I'm glad that today is such an insignificant court day, because my mind is very much focused on my meeting with Robinson tonight. It sure as hell is much more important than any of these witnesses.

All of this takes the entire morning, and after lunch Richard embarks on phase two, which involves calling witnesses to testify that Steven and the victims did not get along. The first witness he calls is an uncomfortable-looking Martha Wyndham.

"Ms. Wyndham, you worked for the Timmermans, did you not?" Richard asks.

"I did."

"In what capacity?"

"I was Walter Timmerman's executive assistant for six months until he died, at which point I began working for Diana Timmerman."

Since two bosses died on her within six months, Martha Timmerman is not exactly a good-luck charm, but Richard neglects to point that out. Instead he asks, "You worked out of their home?"

She nods. "I did."

"Do you know the defendant, Steven Timmerman?"

Martha looks over at Steven and says, "I do."

"Did you have occasion to see Steven when he was in the company of Walter Timmerman, or Diana Timmerman, or both?"

"Many times."

His questions force her to focus on those times when Steven argued with Walter, and she concedes that it happened fairly frequently. She glances occasionally at Steven, as if distressed that she has to be doing this to him.

She tries to repair the damage by saying, "Sometimes they got along very well. Walter could be difficult, especially with Steven. He had very specific expectations for him."

"And if they were not met?" Richard asks.

"He expressed his displeasure in very strong terms."

"And how did Steven respond?"

"He would get angry."

"Would he ever storm out?"

"Yes."

"Did you ever see him throw things in anger?"

She glances at Steven again. "Yes, he broke a lamp against a wall once."

Richard now gets Martha to turn to Steven's relationship with Diana, and even though she tries to couch it, it is obvious their interactions were a disaster.

"Did Steven ever tell you that he hated his stepmother?"

"Yes."

"What did he say about her effect on his father?"

"That she was destroying him, and that as smart as he was, he still couldn't see through it."

When it's my turn, I ask Martha, "Do you have any knowledge as to whether these problems between Steven and his father, as well as his stepmother, started before your arrival?"

"Oh, yes, they all said that. It had been going on much longer than that."

"Did Steven ever attack his father?"

She shakes her head. "I don't believe so."

"Did he ever attack his stepmother?"

"No, I don't believe so."

"Have you ever seen him commit or attempt to commit a violent act?"

"No."

"Thank you, no further questions."

The last witness for the day is Thomas Sykes, Timco's CEO by day, and Diana Timmerman's Hamilton Hotel lover by night. He doesn't have much to say, simply confirming the stormy relationships that Steven had with his father and mother.

I could question Sykes about his affair with Diana Timmerman, but I'm not sure what it gets me at this point. Instead, I basically ask Sykes the same questions I asked Martha Wyndham, and get the same responses, most notably the one about never having seen Steven commit a violent act.

"I have no further questions for this witness, Your Honor, but I do reserve the right to call him back to the stand as part of the defense case."

Hatchet is fine with that, and I let Sykes off the stand. I haven't embarrassed him with a revelation of the affair, but I'm not above doing so later.

In court, there's actually very little that I'm above.

• • • • •

W<small>HY DO</small> I <small>GET</small> <small>MYSELF</small> into these situations? I'm about to go into a meeting alone with a man whom the FBI and Laurie both think might try to kill me.

There's something wrong with this picture. I'm a lawyer, the person who is supposed to get involved after the violence, not during. There were no self-defense classes in law school, and we were never taught how to deal with a dangerous criminal while wearing a wire. The only time the word "wire" came up was when we were told that international corporate clients might pay our fees by "wire" transfer.

But here I am, in an FBI van at a rest stop off the Palisades Interstate Parkway, having a wire taped to my chest. I'm sweating so much that I'm afraid it will electrocute me. Laurie is watching all of this with an impassive stare, which I am sure masks very significant worry, if not outright dread. The only confrontations I can handle are verbal. If you wanted to buy a foxhole, I could handle the closing for you, but you wouldn't want me in there with you if things got dangerous.

My plan is not exactly well thought out. I want to get Robinson on record admitting that my theory about the synthetic DNA is correct. I don't expect him to admit to any murders; I still don't know if he committed or planned any. But I, and certainly Corvallis, would like to get him to implicate others.

Whether I accomplish this by threats or an inference that Robinson and I can turn this into a mutually profitable situation, I can't yet say. I'm going to play it by ear and take the conversation in the direction I deem most fertile in the moment. That is an area in which I feel comfortable.

Corvallis will be in the van with four other agents, two of whom work the technical equipment, and Laurie. Other agents will be spread out on the grounds near the house, ready to move in if I am in danger. I also will have a small panic button attached to my belt, a signal for them to storm the house and save the lawyer.

Once we are all set, and the various electronics are attached to me, I exit the van and get into my car. I wait ten minutes for the FBI people to go ahead and get in position, and then I drive to the house myself.

As I pull up to a house and property just a notch below that of Walter Timmerman's, I don't see the van or any agents. I hope that they are just good at concealment, because if they're not there I could be in major trouble. I feel like Michael Corleone before his meeting in the restaurant with Solozzo, depending on the gun to have been planted in the bathroom.

I park, take a deep breath, and go to the front door, which is wide open. This doesn't feel like a good sign, and it's not the only one. Coming through the open door is a stench that is unlike anything I have ever experienced.

In every movie I have ever seen where this situation occurs, there is a dead body waiting to be discovered by the hero. The only thing missing here is the hero, because if it's me then I'm miscast.

I turn and look around, hoping to see Corvallis or someone who will provide guidance. Seeing no one, I softly say, "The door is open and it smells awful." I'm sure they can hear me in the van, but the communication is only one way, so they can't answer me, and it does me no good.

I decide to go in, because not to do so is to leave and therefore make no progress. Besides, while the stench may mean a dead body, it also would mean the body has been dead for a while. Therefore, if someone murdered that body, he has had plenty of chance to leave already.

I walk through the foyer and living room, covering my nose with my sleeve and ridiculously calling out "hello!"—as if Robinson were going to come walking out saying, *Andy, welcome. I was cooking us fried horse manure for dinner. Smells delicious, doesn't it?*

When I get to the kitchen, I come upon what is easily the most disgusting sight I have ever seen . . . the most disgusting sight anyone has ever seen. What used to be Charles Robinson sits at the kitchen table, but he is no longer human. It is as if his enormous body has melted from the inside out, and he is covered with disgusting blotches of ooze and blood. Much of it has dripped to the floor.

I once saw the decapitated, burned body of a corrupt cop, and I later saw his head wrapped in plastic. Those were disgusting sights, but compared with this they were like a field of daffodils.

I start to run from the kitchen, simultaneously pressing the panic button and screaming, "Get in here! Get in here!" The words don't come out quite as clearly as I would like, because my vomit gets in the way.

When I reach the outside, I literally fall to the ground and gasp for air. Agents rush to me, no doubt thinking that I'm hurt, but I motion for them to go in. Corvallis then comes running to me with two agents and Laurie, and I gasp what has happened.

Laurie stays with me as everyone else goes inside. I'm still on the ground, gasping, trying to keep the remainder of my last twelve meals down. It is not my finest moment, but right now I can't worry about that. I just have to get control and figure out how not to be haunted the rest of my life by what I've just seen.

Within fifteen minutes, there are so many vehicles at the Robinson house you'd think the Yankees were playing the Red Sox in the backyard. I'm sure every FBI agent in the tristate area has been summoned, and I can see a bunch of people with forensics equipment.

Corvallis comes out and greets one of the arriving men as "Doctor," and he brings him into the house. If this guy can do anything for Robinson, I am going to make him my personal physician for life.

Crime scenes take forever, and as the closest thing to a witness, I know that I am going to have to wait around to be questioned. Two hours go by, during which Laurie and I stroll around the grounds. I tell her in detail what I saw, and the act of walking in the fresh air and being with her makes me feel considerably better.

Finally, Corvallis comes over to talk to me. "We need a statement," he says.

I just nod my understanding.

"You okay?" he asks, showing more concern than I expected. "It is pretty rough in there."

"What happened to him?" I ask.

"Let's do the statement first, okay?"

"Okay." This is the correct procedure; if he were to tell me anything that they learned, it could be viewed as prejudicing my statement.

I basically have little to say about the actual scene; all I did was walk in and discover the body. Everyone who followed saw exactly the same thing as I did, and I'm sure by now it has been memorialized by hundreds of pictures. But I do insist on including in the statement the reason that I was there in the first place; it will serve me well if I can ever get evidence of all this into the trial.

The statement is verbal and taped, and I promise to sign a transcript of it when they have it ready. I request that I see it before court tomorrow, and Corvallis says that will not be a problem. Then I renew my question to Corvallis. "What happened to Robinson?"

"It looks like iridium."

That's a little cryptic for me, so I ask him to elaborate.

"It's a poison, a favorite in international circles. The KGB had a particular preference for it, but others have used it as well. You don't want to know the details of what it does; you've gotten a firsthand look."

"How long was he dead?"

"We don't have a firm time on that yet. He was eating a meal, I assume the poison was in the food. The amount that would fit on the head of a pin would kill someone in forty-five seconds."

"Not a pleasant forty-five seconds," I say.

"Yeah. You guys okay getting home?" he says.

"Yes. You know I'm going to try to use all this at trial."

He smiles. "And the relevance?" He is pointing out that I'm going to have a tough time connecting Robinson's death to Steven's trial in a way to get Hatchet to admit it.

"I'm working on it, but it'll come in."

"We may be on different pages on that," he says, and then walks off.

He's probably right, but I'd know better if I knew what the hell page I was on.

• • • • •

ON THE WAY HOME I call Kevin and ask him to come over. That way, he, Laurie, and I can discuss at length the impact of tonight's events on our case, and the strategy we should employ to make the most of it.

The potential benefits are obvious. Walter Timmerman's work involved him with very rough people, so rough that the person he was in a form of partnership with was poisoned to death. This couldn't help but create the credible thought in a jury's mind that the perpetrator might have killed Walter as well.

Diana's death is more problematic, in that we have no evidence she was involved with Walter's work. However, the manner in which she died helps us. It also blew up Walter's lab, and could easily have killed Waggy, both of which fit into our theory.

Unfortunately, while this all makes sense to us, it is unlikely to impress the jury, because the jury is very unlikely to ever hear about it. We have no real way to connect Robinson to Walter's DNA work except our theory. We can't even factually prove that Walter was working in the weeks before his death, no less on something momentous.

We are going to have to try to get Corvallis to testify. He'll refuse; he already as much as said so tonight. But Hatchet can compel his testimony, albeit with assurances that he does not have to reveal classified, national security information. It's by no means definite that we can get Hatchet to go along, since we have little to advance as an offer of proof.

But we'll certainly try, and Kevin goes off to prepare a legal brief to present. Kevin is far better at this aspect of the law than I am, which is damning him with faint praise. The truth is, he's pretty much the best at it of anyone I've ever been around.

Among the things about this that bother me, and one that has bothered me from the beginning, is why such a great effort was made to frame Steven. These were murders that seem to have been committed from a distance by powerful entities, and it's hard to picture them as having been solved. For example, I would strongly doubt that an arrest will be made in the Robinson murder; nor do I believe that anyone will be framed for it. Why pick on Steven?

I also can't quite pin down Robinson's role in all this. It seems logical that he was Timmerman's way to connect to the type of people who would pay huge dollars for the right to use the synthetic DNA, probably to make biofuels. But Robinson would have made a fortune as well, so it seems unlikely he would have killed Walter.

More to the point, why would anybody have murdered Walter? If his work was the golden goose, why kill it? The only thing that comes to mind is an entity that was threatened by that work, perhaps someone who did not want the energy status quo threatened. But we are light-years away from making that connection in the real world, and the trial is winding down.

I call Richard and inform him of what happened at Robinson's house, and of my intention to try to get Corvallis to testify. The call is a courtesy similar to those he's extended to me in the past, but it in no way has a negative impact on our position. If I sprang the issue on him in court, he would just ask for a delay to prepare a response, and Hatchet would undoubtedly give it to him.

"Have you decided what to do about Waggy?" Kevin asks.

"Nothing for the time being," I say. "With Robinson gone the pressure is off, but if Waggy 'shows up' again, Hatchet could get on my back."

Once Kevin leaves I sit down in the den and do what I frequently do during a trial. I take the discovery documents and reread them. There are often things that I find that I've missed in previous readings, but that's not the main reason I do it. It keeps my mind alert to the details, so that if something comes up during court, I can remember it instantly and react.

I usually do it in segments; each night I'll read everything related to one particular area of evidence. Tonight I pore through everything about the night of Walter Timmerman's murder, including the forensics on the scene, the phone call Walter made to Steven, the location of Steven's car, et cetera.

Almost every time I do this I am bothered by the sensation that I am missing something, but in fact I rarely am. Tonight I have the same feeling, though the information is fairly dry and straightforward.

The Mets are playing the Dodgers on the West Coast tonight, and I turn on the game while I continue to read. The next thing I know Laurie is waking me, and a glance at the TV shows it to be the eighth inning. I slept through the first seven, and since fourteen runs have been scored, those seven innings couldn't have been very quickly played. Unfortunately, the Dodgers scored eleven of the runs.

Laurie leads me into the bedroom, and within five minutes we're both back asleep. She hasn't even decided what to do, and already we're an old married couple.

I get to court early and bring Steven up to date on everything that has transpired. Since he doesn't have access to the media in his cell, he has not heard about Robinson's death, and he is stunned.

When my meeting with Steven is over, an FBI agent, as promised, is waiting for me with a typed copy of my statement from last night for me to sign. I do so, and then make him wait while I have the court clerk make a Xerox of it for me.

Before the morning session begins, Richard informs me that he will be finishing his case today. That case is basically done, and the witnesses he calls will simply dot his I's and cross his T's.

His first witness is a prime example. A representative of the Metropolitan Transportation Authority named Helene Markowitz, she is merely there to testify that Steven's car went through the Lincoln Tunnel at seven forty-five that evening, thirty minutes after he received the phone call from his father.

"How can you be so precise about the time?" Richard asks.

"He has an E-ZPass chip on his car, so that tolls are automatically paid by his credit card without his having to stop. It records the time he goes through the tollbooth."

For some reason, her answer causes me to think of something I hadn't registered before. I quickly write a note and slide the paper over to Kevin. It says, "How did Walter Timmerman get to the murder scene?"

Kevin looks confused by the question and writes back, "The killer drove him there."

That is most likely true, especially since Walter Timmerman's Lexus was destroyed at the house. But something bothers me about Kevin's answer, something I can't quite place and don't have time to wonder about now.

Richard calls two more uneventful witnesses and then announces that the prosecution rests. I immediately request a meeting in chambers with Hatchet and Richard, so that I can present our request to have Corvallis come in and testify.

I lay out the entire situation for Hatchet, making my point that I need to be able to do the same for the jury. If I can demonstrate that Walter Timmerman was involved with very dangerous people, and in fact those people killed his friend and partner, Robinson, the jury would very likely find reasonable doubt as to Steven's guilt.

"Mr. Wallace," Hatchet says, "I assume you don't agree?"

"We certainly do not, Your Honor. It is a classic fishing expedition." Richard then goes on to give a response that is predictable and mostly correct. He points out that I have made no tangible offer of proof; instead I have presented a series of suppositions and theories. Even the one fact I can cite, Robinson's murder and my tangential role in it, is not relevant to this case, since I can make no real connection between that murder and Timmerman's.

"Your Honor," I say, "Mr. Wallace would be correct if I were arguing to take the information I currently have before the jury. I agree that I am not ready to do that, and I am not asking you to allow it. What I am simply asking is that you direct the FBI to testify to these facts, and to detail how their own, separate investigation relates to this trial. Then, if the relevance is proven, I would call him before the jury."

I take out the copy of my signed statement. "Here is a statement I gave to the FBI about last night's events. I signed it, and as you certainly know, if I was untruthful in this statement then I have committed a felony. It includes the negotiations I had with the FBI leading up to my visit to the Robinson house last night. The operation was conducted under their supervision, and certainly should be enough to compel their testimony."

Hatchet and Richard read the statement, which in typewritten form is six pages. When they are finished, Hatchet says, "Mr. Wallace?"

"Your Honor, this is an interesting story that changes nothing."

"With respect," I say, "it changes everything. And I would

submit that your calling Agent Corvallis to court for a closed hearing presents absolutely no risk. If he testifies under oath that I'm delusional, then all you've done is waste a few minutes of the court's time. But if I'm correct, then my client has a right for the jury to hear what he has to say."

I expect Hatchet to take the matter under advisement, but instead he says, "I will order that Agent Corvallis appear before this court at the earliest possible time, hopefully tomorrow morning. At that point I will decide whether or not to compel his testimony."

• • • • •

THE MOST IMPORTANT DECISION of any trial is getting close. That, of course, is whether to have the defendant testify on his own behalf. While it is a crucial decision, it is usually an easy one for a lawyer to make. I can't remember the last time I wanted a client to testify in his own defense. Too many things can go wrong, even when the defendant is innocent.

But it is also the one decision that the client must absolutely make on his own, albeit with advice from his attorney. If he decides not to testify, the judge will go so far as to question him in open court as to whether he was presented with the option, and declined voluntarily.

Kevin and I arrange to meet with Steven in an anteroom. Before we can even talk about his possible testimony, I tell him of our success in getting Corvallis into court.

"Will he tell the truth?" Steven asks.

"He won't lie. Whether we can get him to tell the truth is another matter. He will try not to say anything at all."

I bring up the matter of Steven testifying, and like most clients, he wants to do so. This is that rare time that I am leaning in the same direction. He is really the only person who can testify about his actions the night of his father's death. He can also talk about their relationship, and he comes off as likable and credible.

The other reason I am inclined to support his decision to testify is that the way this trial has gone, we need a Hail Mary pass. We have to do something to shake things up, or we are going to lose. Juries generally want to hear a defendant testify, and this might be the time to give them what they want.

Kevin tells Steven that he agrees as well, which is a surprise to me, since we haven't talked about it. I can't ever remember Kevin being in favor of a client testifying in his own behalf, and it's a sign that he thinks the situation is as dire as I do.

"But we don't have to decide this now," I say. "If you take the stand, you'll be the last one to do so, and a lot is going to happen before then."

"Are we losing?" Steven asks.

"We haven't had our turn at bat yet."

"I had this fantasy that the prosecution was going to present their case, and it would be so weak the judge would just end the trial right there."

"It's called a motion to dismiss," I say. "I'm going to make one tomorrow morning, but the judge will turn us down. We need to make our case."

"And can we effectively do that?"

"I don't know."

He smiles, but it's not exactly a happy smile. "I was hoping you'd tell me what I wanted to hear. You should learn to bullshit more, you know?"

"I know," I say, "it's one of my weaknesses."

Kevin and I head home to finish preparations for our defense case. We need to go over every detail, even though we've been over the same ground many times before, so that we are completely prepared for any eventuality.

It's basically an issue of confidence for me. If I feel completely sure of the subject, then I can more comfortably freewheel, and thus be more effective. If I am in any way unsure of the details, I have a tendency to get more conservative.

Conservative is not what we need now.

The focus of the evening is altered when the court clerk calls to say that Agent Corvallis will be in court tomorrow morning at nine. We now have to turn our full attention to that argument, since if we fail we have no real hope of getting anything about Walter's work or Robinson's murder before the jury. And without that, we are in deep trouble.

So we work until midnight, pausing only to have dinner with Laurie. She's made my favorite, pasta amatriciana, and in the face of that, preparation will have to wait. I have my priorities.

I arrive at court at eight thirty in the morning, and I learn that Hatchet has summoned Richard and me into his chambers for a pre-hearing chat.

"I have been told by FBI attorneys that there are serious national security implications involved in what Agent Corvallis is doing. I have turned down their request to withdraw my order for him to appear, but I have agreed that the hearing this morning will be closed, and the transcript will be held under seal," he says.

"That's fine with me, Your Honor." I say.

"I'm so relieved," Hatchet says. "You know how I covet your approval. Mr. Wallace?"

"Obviously we believe that Agent Corvallis should not be compelled to testify at all, but since we have for the moment lost that argument, we have no problem with it being closed and the transcript kept under seal."

When we get back into the courtroom, Agent Corvallis has already arrived with four FBI attorneys. He gives me a big smile and handshake when he sees me, then introduces me to the smiling attorneys. Everybody's so happy; you'd never know they were there to try to bury Steven Timmerman.

Steven is brought in, since defendants have the right to be present for every aspect of their trial. Hatchet then enters and convenes the hearing, spending a few minutes setting the ground rules. I will question Agent Corvallis first, and Richard will follow.

I am in an unusual situation here: The truth is I know very little about the FBI's investigation of Walter Timmerman. I have theories, many of which have been mostly confirmed, but I don't know the meat and potatoes of it. Thus, I can wind up doing that which lawyers religiously try to avoid, asking questions I don't know the answer to.

"Agent Corvallis, have you been leading an FBI investigation focused on Walter Timmerman?"

"Yes."

"When did that investigation begin?"

"About six months ago," he says.

"What motivated it?"

"Walter Timmerman was doing some work that was potentially significant to the national security of the United States."

"What was the nature of that work?" I ask.

"I'm not at liberty to say."

"Are you aware if he enlisted the help of his friend Charles Robinson in connection with that work?"

"Yes. He did."

I ask Corvallis to confirm that I approached him with my suspicions about Timmerman and Robinson, and he acknowledges that I did.

"Did I tell you the kind of work I thought Walter Timmerman was doing?"

The FBI lawyer objects, in an effort to preempt me from mentioning what the actual work was. Hatchet sustains and instructs me not to do so, then lets Corvallis answer the question.

"Yes, you did. I did not indicate whether your theory was accurate or not."

"But you know what he was doing in the last months of his life?" I ask.

"I do."

I then take him through the events of the other night, starting with my being fitted for a wire, our planning of the confrontation, and then finding Robinson dead in his house. He completely confirms the truth of my narration.

"Do you believe that Charles Robinson's death was related to my upcoming meeting with him?"

"I do."

"And he was aware that my meeting related in some way to Walter Timmerman's work?" I ask.

"Yes."

"And Charles Robinson was killed by dangerous people?"

Corvallis smiles. "Most certainly."

"And Walter Timmerman was involved with the same people?"

"Perhaps indirectly, but yes."

It's time to ask the key question. "Is it conceivable that those same people played a role in Walter Timmerman's death?"

"No."

Of all his possible answers, no is my least favorite. I sense a disaster looming, but I press on, mainly because I have no choice.

"It's not conceivable?"

"That is correct, to the best of my knowledge."

"Is it conceivable that different people murdered Walter Timmerman than murdered Charles Robinson, but that Timmerman was killed because of his work?"

"No, it is not conceivable," he says.

I'm getting frustrated; I sincerely doubt that Corvallis would lie under oath, but his answers are hard to believe.

"Do you know who murdered Walter Timmerman?" It's a dangerous question, but with the jury not present, I feel I can take the chance, especially since I know that Jimmy Childs committed the murder.

"I have no personal knowledge of it, though you have presented me with your account of it."

"Then how can you be so sure it was not work-related?"

Corvallis looks over at his attorneys, and then speaks to Hatchet. "I would like to alert my attorneys to intervene if I start to say too much."

"That's fine, but not necessary. Attorneys are born with that instinct," Hatchet says.

Corvallis nods and turns back to me. I can feel the bomb about to go off. "The bureau has devoted substantial resources to this investigation, in concert with other agencies," he says. "We have people in place who have therefore accumulated significant information, though I can't say how, or what much of that information is."

He pauses, probably for effect. "But I can tell you with certainty that the people whom Walter Timmerman was dealing with, who murdered Charles Robinson, were not involved in Timmerman's death. I can further say that it would have been totally counterproductive for them to have killed him; they were in fact extraordinarily upset when he died. I am close to certain that Walter Timmerman did not die as a result of his work."

I'm finished; there is nothing left for me to ask, no other avenues to probe. Hatchet turns Corvallis over to Richard, who mercifully has no questions for him.

Hatchet also seems to understand that the only kind thing to do is to quickly put us out of our misery. After a brief preamble, he says, "The defense had requested Agent Corvallis's testimony in the stated belief that it would implicate one or more other possible perpetrators, and would therefore be crucial testimony to present to the jury.

"Agent Corvallis has testified, under oath in these proceedings, that he is aware of no other possible perpetrators, and that the theory of the defense, to the best of his knowledge, is incorrect.

"It is therefore the ruling of this court that the testimony of Agent Corvallis will not be required nor permitted. Agent Corvallis, thank you for appearing here today.

"The defense will begin presenting its case tomorrow morning."

• • • • •

KEVIN, LAURIE, AND I are all realists. It is one of the key reasons we work so well together. When things are going bad, we recognize it and confront it if we have to. And right now this case has gone world-class bad.

We were counting on Corvallis testifying; it was essentially our only way of getting our theory of the case before the jury. Now we know that we won't have him, and we have to change our plan of attack. Unfortunately, we have nothing decent to change it to.

The only approach left to us is to attack the details of the prosecution's case at the edges, to find minor inconsistencies and make them seem like major flaws. Jurors will want to look at the big picture, and we will be giving them nitpicks, because we have no other bullets in our gun.

Our case will open on the night of Walter Timmerman's murder, and our plan tonight is to dissect it, moment by moment, and show holes in the prosecution's case. We take out every document and piece of information that we have and spread it out on the dining room table, in case we need to refer to any of it.

"Okay, so let's start at the beginning," I say.

Kevin nods. "Good. Steven is at home in New York, and his father calls him and asks him to meet him in Paterson."

Laurie, who has been reading the transcripts on a daily basis, nods and says, "And there's testimony that he went through the toll-booth about half an hour later. He went to Mario's, waiting to meet his father."

"Wait a minute. Kevin, remember that note I passed you the other day? I asked how Walter got to the murder scene."

Kevin nods. "And I told you the killer brought him there."

"Then where did he meet the killer?"

"What do you mean?" he asks.

"Well, he didn't drive to where the killer was; the documents show his car was in the garage when the house was destroyed. He sure as hell didn't take a bus to downtown Paterson. So how did the killer get to him? When and where did they meet that night?"

"Maybe he took a cab."

"Why would he?" Laurie says. "He had a car. And if a cab picked him up a couple of hours before he was murdered, it likely would have come out already. The media coverage the day after the murder was substantial, I assume?"

"Very substantial," I say.

"I admit it's an interesting question," Kevin says. "But what does it ultimately mean? We know that Jimmy Childs killed him, so what's the difference how he got to him?"

"Because maybe he had help," I say. "Maybe it's a way to get Robinson back into the case. Let's get the security guard logs at the house gate from that night. Maybe Robinson came there at the time in question and drove off with him."

"We should be so lucky," Kevin says, but promises to subpoena the records first thing in the morning.

Unfortunately, the morning comes way too quickly. I was hoping we could skip it entirely, along with the next few months. But that's not how it works out, and before I know it Hatchet is taking his seat on the bench.

I make the obligatory yet pathetic motion to dismiss, and Hatchet immediately denies it. He tells me to call our first witness, and I call Jessica Santorini, a bartender at Mario's.

After establishing that she was at the restaurant that night, I ask her if she remembers seeing Steven there.

She nods. "I do. He was sitting at the bar."

"About how long was he sitting there?"

"I'm not sure of the exact time, but it was quite awhile. I remember because all he had was one or maybe two drinks, and I kept asking him if he wanted something else. He said no, and I think he said he was waiting for somebody."

"Did you talk about anything else?"

"I'm not sure; it was pretty busy that night."

On cross-examination, Richard asks her, "Did the defendant pay by credit card or cash?"

"Gee, I wouldn't know," she says.

Richard introduces the restaurant's record that night, which show no credit card payment by Steven. "If he didn't pay by credit card, then it must have been cash, correct? There's no other choice, is there?"

"No, that's it."

"So there's no way to identify his check?" he asks.

She shakes her head. "Not really."

"And no way to know what time he left?"

"No."

"Thank you."

I bring in a waitress and a patron at the restaurant that night, both of whom basically say the same thing: They're pretty sure they remember Steven, but they can't say for sure when he left.

We're not exactly generating headlines here.

At lunch, a court messenger brings Kevin an envelope, and he opens it and takes out some papers. "The security gate logs from that week," he announces, as he tries to locate the night in question.

"Robinson? Tell me he was at the house that night," I say, hoping it will show Robinson can be shown to have arrived at the house and left with Walter Timmerman."

"No," Kevin says, looking up at me. "But Thomas Sykes was. He arrived at a quarter to seven."

The name surprises me. "Could he have been shacking up with Diana at that house?"

"Either that or he came to see Walter," he says. "There's no way to tell from this whether Walter was home."

"Does it say if Sykes left alone?"

Kevin shakes his head. "No." Then, "So what have we learned?"

"We've learned something; we just don't know what it means, or if it has any value. We'll figure it out tonight."

I go outside and use my cell phone to call Laurie. "How are you feeling?" I ask.

"I feel fine," she says.

"Ready to go to work?"

I can see her smile through the phone. "You'd better believe it," she says.

• • • • •

"LET'S MAKE SOME ASSUMPTIONS about Thomas Sykes," I say. "Let's assume that he was not at the house that night for a quickie with Diana Timmerman. And let's further assume that he was involved in the murder of her husband."

"We have nothing to base that on," says Kevin.

"I would say almost nothing. We do at least know he was at the house that night, and we know he was having an affair with Timmerman's wife. But I'll concede the point; we aren't close to implicating him. I'm just suggesting we assume the worst, and try to figure out the pieces. If it doesn't fit, then we'll move on."

"Okay," Kevin says. "Sykes went to the house, grabbed Walter Timmerman, and drove him to Paterson, where Jimmy Childs was waiting to shoot him."

Laurie says, "The head of security, Durant, says that if Walter Timmerman had been in Sykes's car when he left there should be a notation to that effect." I had asked Laurie to interview Durant while we were in court today, and she did so.

"He was in the trunk, or tied up in the back if Sykes had an SUV." They both stare at me as if I'm an idiot, so I say, "Assumptions. Assumptions."

258

"Fine," Laurie says, going along. "He tied him up, and then when they got away from the house, he forced Walter to call Steven."

Another piece, something I had completely missed until now, clicks into place, and I can feel my excitement starting to grow. "What happened to his phone?" I ask.

I pick up my own phone without waiting for an answer to my question, but before I dial I ask Kevin to dig out all the cell phone records. "The ones in discovery and Sam's as well."

I dial Billy Cameron, the public defender who was representing the young man originally accused of the Timmerman murder. He's not home, but when I tell his wife who I am and that I am calling on an urgent matter, she gives me his cell number.

"Billy? Andy Carpenter."

"Let me guess: They nailed you on the dognapping and you need me to arrange bail."

"No, if that happened I would call someone competent. But I do have a question I need you to answer."

"Shoot," he says.

"Your client was picked up with Timmerman's wallet. Did he have anything else of Timmerman's on him?"

"I don't think so. Like what?"

"Like his cell phone."

Billy thinks for a moment. "No. I would remember that. I can check the files when I'm in the office, but I'm pretty sure he didn't have it."

"Thanks, Billy. That's what I needed."

"I just got back to town yesterday. How's the case going?"

"Getting better all the time."

When I get off the call, Kevin is ready with the cell phone information. "Sam's documents never showed the call on Timmerman's cell phone, but that was explained in court. The phone company rep said that the call was made from Timmerman's business phone,

259

under the Timco account. I was never much interested in checking on whether the call took place, because Steven had confirmed to us that he received it."

"What if it was Sykes's phone?" I ask, and by now I'm almost yelling. "Everybody assumed it was Timmerman's phone because it came up as Timco, but Sykes's phone would show the same thing. He's the goddamn CEO. We need to call Sam and get records from that cell phone. And I need Steven's home phone records for the last year."

"Okay, let's take a step back and look at the big picture," Laurie says. "Why would Sykes want Walter Timmerman dead?"

"To take over the business entirely?" Kevin asks. "Or maybe so that Diana Timmerman could inherit her husband's money, and then Sykes could marry her?"

"That didn't work out too well," I say.

Kevin is getting into this. "It could also have to do with Timmerman's work. Sykes is a scientist; maybe he found out about it and wanted to take it over for himself. For all he knew, Timmerman was working alone and in secret. If Timmerman were to die, Sykes might be able to walk in and take over without anyone knowing. Especially because Timmerman's lab was in his house, and Sykes would have access through Diana."

"So why blow up the house?" Laurie asks.

That's a tough one, but I take a shot at it. "Maybe Sykes had already gotten what he needed, and he didn't want anyone else to get it as well. And maybe this way he was able to get rid of Diana, who was the only witness to what he was doing."

"Holy shit," Laurie says, thereby exposing her delicate side. "I just had a thought; try this out. Maybe Sykes killed Timmerman for personal reasons, and then someone else blew up the house. Maybe with Timmerman dead, someone wanted to make sure no one had access to his work."

"What are you basing that on?" I ask.

"Childs never told Marcus he killed Walter Timmerman, remember? All he told him was that he blew up the house and tried to kill Waggy. We just assumed he didn't admit to killing Walter because Marcus didn't ask the question, but maybe it was because it never happened."

The three of us just look at one another for at least sixty seconds, as we all come to grips with the fact that, at the very least, we've come up with a very viable theory.

"Now, how are you possibly going to prove all this?" Laurie asks.

"We don't have to prove it," I say. "We all think this is possible, right? We just have to get the jury to think like us."

We talk for another hour, and then Kevin heads for home. As Laurie and I are about to get into bed, I say, "You ready for a stake-out, and maybe a phone call?"

"Sure," she says.

"Good. Go to Sykes's office, and when he leaves, give him a call on the cell phone number we got from Sam's records."

"What do you want me to say?"

"Sorry, wrong number. I just need to make sure it's his cell phone, and that he carries it with him."

I explain what I'm talking about without taking too long, since it's delaying my getting into bed with Laurie. But I do make the mistake of putting forth one more conversational gambit. "I know I'm not supposed to talk about this, but it's great having you here and involved. It felt like old times tonight."

She smiles. "I'm enjoying it. I feel like I'm back in the action."

"You know, if multiple murder and depravity is your thing, there's really nothing like New Jersey."

• • • • •

I DON'T HAVE TO adjust our witness list to include Thomas Sykes. That's important, and far more than a convenience. This way Sykes already understands the possibility that he will be called, and will not be surprised when he is. He will also not be un-duly alerted, and will not feel he is a target. For us to have a chance, I'm going to have to take Sykes apart on the stand, and I want him unprepared for the onslaught.

I'm not a big fan of fair fights.

I call Sykes in his office before the start of court in the morning, and I am surprised and pleased that he is already there. "Mr. Sykes, I just want to alert you that you will be handed a subpoena today requiring your appearance in court tomorrow."

"For what purpose?" he asks.

"You'll be a witness for the defense. I had hoped to avoid calling you, but it doesn't seem like I have a choice."

"What do you hope to get from me?" he asks.

"I'm going to talk to you about the lifestyles of both victims, unfortunately including your relationship with Mrs. Timmerman."

"You're going to slime the victims?" he asks. "Is that your style? I had been told you were better than that."

262

"I choose to call it defending my client," I say. "See you tomorrow."

I think the call went pretty well, and that Sykes will have no reason to think I have any agenda other than the one I just mentioned.

When Steven is brought into court, I consider whether to alert him to what is going on. I decide against it; it might raise false hopes, and we're dealing with a very long shot. Besides, there are only a few minutes before Hatchet comes in, and Steven would have an hour's worth of questions.

Kevin is not in court this morning; he is making sure that the subpoena is served, and getting some other information that we need. It's nice for him; this way he doesn't have to be embarrassed by the pathetic string of witnesses we have planned for today.

The first of those witnesses is Dr. John Holland, a professor of criminology at the John Jay College of Criminal Justice in Manhattan. Holland is a leading expert in blood spatter, and his work as an expert witness probably allows him to quadruple his annual salary as a college professor.

My goal with Holland is to affirmatively establish the points I made when I cross-examined the prosecution's forensic witness. "How likely is it that the person who shot Walter Timmerman from point-blank range was splattered with blood, brain matter, and skull fragments?" I ask.

"At that range it is a certainty," he says.

"And if he then got into his car, and transferred trace amounts of the splatter to the interior of the car, how likely is it that the transferred material would be only blood?"

"Virtually no chance," he says, and I let him go on to explain. He likens it to making a pasta sauce, starting with marinara and adding ground meat, olive oil, Worcestershire sauce, cream, and assorted other ingredients. If you eat some, there's no way you're going to have only pure marinara running down your chin. With this explanation, he manages to effectively make his point while equally effectively making the jury nauseous.

Richard's cross-examination is short, as if he doesn't think the witness is worth spending a lot of time with. He talks about the bleeding that would take place after the initial splatter, and how blood that was virtually pure could have pooled on the ground.

On balance, the witness certainly favors us, but I'm sure that Richard has experts in reserve whom he can call in rebuttal. I'm also sure he doesn't think he will need to, and at this point he's right.

Just before lunch Laurie comes in and passes me a note telling me that the phone call went perfectly, and a few minutes later Kevin arrives as well, with the documents we need. The stage is basically set for tomorrow, except for preparation tonight.

I just wish it were tomorrow already.

My afternoon witnesses are perfunctory at best. I call two associates of Walter Timmerman, who testify as to how secretive about his work he was in the months before he died. They describe the behavior as uncharacteristic, and both refer to Timmerman as a normally collaborative man when it came to his science.

Finally, I bring in an officer at Timmerman's bank, who testifies to the twenty-million-dollar wire transfer he received weeks before his death. The money came from a numbered Swiss account, and therefore the source is impossible to trace. He admits that it was the first time Timmerman had ever received a transfer of this type. While he is too circumspect to admit that it is suspicious, I believe that the jury will find it so. Of course, it's a bit of a stretch for them to believe that someone would send him twenty million dollars and then kill him.

Like he does every night, Kevin comes by for dinner and so that we can prepare together. Usually, we are on the same page when it comes to getting ready for a trial day, but when we are facing a crucial witness we are complete opposites.

Kevin thinks we should have a mock session, where he plays the witness role, in this case Sykes, and I fire questions at him. That way he believes I can hone my approach and only follow the lines of questioning that have been proven to work in this fashion. He wants us to analyze what Sykes might say from every angle, and prepare questions designed to overcome his defenses.

While I see the logical merit of Kevin's argument, it just isn't my style. I need it to be free-flowing; I can't be restricted by meticulously pre-planned tactics.

The only thing bothering me right now is my inability to see how I can get the murder of Charles Robinson connected to Sykes and therefore before this jury. My theories aren't well developed enough to have included a motive for Sykes to have killed Robinson. Perhaps it was a fight over the fruits of Walter Timmerman's labor, but it feels like I'm stretching.

After Kevin leaves, Laurie and I talk some more about the case, until I've reached my saturation point. When we're ready to go to bed, Laurie says to me, "Big day tomorrow."

I nod. "Yeah. Especially for Steven."

"Do lawyers have to abstain from sex the night before a big game, like athletes?" she asks.

"On the contrary, it's encouraged. It clears the mind and makes questions crisper and clearer."

"Is that right?"

"Absolutely. The more sex, the better the lawyer. That's why so many hookers have become Supreme Court justices."

"Then by tomorrow morning they'll be calling you Chief Justice Carpenter."

We need a Perry Mason moment.

Actually, what we really need is Perry Mason, but since he must be pushing 130 years old, we probably have a better chance at getting one of his moments.

A Perry Mason moment is when the witness cracks under the relentless pressure of a brilliant defense attorney and confesses to the crime right on the stand. A perfect example of it was when Tom Cruise asked, "Did you order the code red?" and Jack Nicholson screamed back at him, "You're goddamn right I did!"

The first thing I do when the court session is convened is ask for a meeting with Hatchet and Richard in chambers. I tell them, "My first witness is going to be Thomas Sykes, and I would like him designated as a hostile witness."

Hatchet seems surprised. "He is hostile to the defense?"

"He's going to be," I say. "We believe that Thomas Sykes murdered Walter Timmerman, and we are going to use his testimony to show the credibility of that theory."

"Whoa," Richard says. "I thought you were blaming some international bad guys after Timmerman's work. Where is this coming from?"

I smile. "I'm afraid you're going to have to wait for the show to open. But it's legit, Richard."

"Does the prosecution wish to lodge an objection to my declaring this witness hostile?" Hatchet asks.

"No objection. But I would remind Your Honor that defense counsel cannot make reckless charges without foundation."

"It's lucky you're here to remind me of things like that," Hatchet says, drily. "If I didn't have you, I'd have to invent you."

We get back to court, and when Steven is brought in I greet him in what I think is the same way I do everyday. But no sooner have I said hello than he asks, "What's going on?"

"What do you mean?"

"Something's up," he says. "There's something about you that's different today."

"Just keep your fingers crossed," I say, before Hatchet comes in and we're all rising to our feet.

Sykes takes the stand, and Hatchet reminds him that he is still under oath from his last trip there.

"Mr. Sykes, Walter Timmerman was the founder of Timco, the company you currently preside over as CEO. Is that correct?"

"It is."

"And how many years did you know Mr. Timmerman?" I ask.

He thinks for a moment before answering. "Twenty-two."

"He was instrumental in your career advancement?"

"Yes. Very."

"Mr. Sykes," I say, "do you remember when I came to visit you in your office?"

"I do."

"And do you recall that I told you I had evidence that you had been having an affair with Walter Timmerman's wife, Diana?"

"Yes. I recall that."

Sykes seems pretty much at ease. This is what he expected was coming, and he is prepared for it.

"And did you admit that you were having an affair with Diana Timmerman?"

"I said that we were in love," he says, lying through his teeth. "I told you that it wasn't anything we had planned; it just happened."

"So you admit to the relationship here, under oath, as well?"

"Yes."

"Did you also tell me that it was your belief that Walter Timmerman was also unfaithful to his wife?" I may be stretching this too far, but I want Sykes to be totally confident of where I'm going, so when I strike it will be a shock to him.

"Yes, I told you that, but I also said I only suspected it, and had no firm information about it."

"Mr. Sykes, did you kill Walter Timmerman?"

He snaps back in the chair as if I had punched him in the chest. "What? No. Of course not. How could you ask me something like that?"

"Mr. Sykes, the way it works here is that I ask the questions and you answer them. Until now, I thought you had that down pat."

Richard objects to my mistreating the witness, and Hatchet sustains. Business as usual.

"Where were you the night of the murder?" I ask.

"I was at home," he says.

I introduce the Timmerman house security log from that night as a defense exhibit, and then show it to Sykes. I get him to read that it shows him arriving at the house at six forty-five in the evening.

"Is that accurate? Did you arrive there at that time?"

He seems to be trying to figure out the best answer, and finally nods. "Yes, apparently so. It was months ago, and I had forgotten. I was only there a short time, and I think I went straight home from there. Though I may have run a couple of errands."

"Why did you go there that night?"

"To see Mrs. Timmerman," he says.

"Was Walter Timmerman at home?"

"He was not."

"Did you know where he was?" I ask.

"No."

"Did his wife know where he was?"

"I don't know." His answers are getting shorter as his worry increases. Some people do the opposite; they feel if they talk enough, they can make the problem disappear in a sea of words. Sykes's reaction is the opposite; I'm going to have to pry the words out of his mouth with a crowbar.

"But she wasn't worried about his returning and walking in on you?"

"She did not seem worried. No. And we were not doing anything we needed to worry about."

"Is it possible that Walter Timmerman was at home, and that you forced him into the trunk of your car and drove him to Paterson?"

Richard objects before Sykes can answer, and Hatchet admonishes me. I didn't expect to get an answer, which would have been an outraged *no* anyway. What I wanted was to get my theory in front of the jury, so they'd have a road map to follow.

"Mr. Sykes, may I see your cell phone, please?"

I see a flash of real worry, if not panic, in his eyes. "It's turned off."

"That would be a good answer if the question had been, *Mr. Sykes, what is the current status of your cell phone?* But what I asked was if I could see it."

He takes it out of his pocket, and I get permission from Hatchet to have him turn it on. I then get Hatchet's approval to have the court clerk dial a number, which I have her read off one of the discovery documents. As soon as she does, Sykes's cell phone starts to ring.

"Please answer it," I say.

He does so, but doesn't look happy about it. "Yes," he says, and the court clerk confirms that she hears Sykes's voice through the phone.

"Mr. Sykes, based on the documents that were provided by the prosecution and submitted to the court, your phone is the one that called Steven Timmerman at seven twenty on the night of the murder. It was registered to Timco, so the prosecution assumed, I believe incorrectly, that Walter Timmerman made the call. Did you call him?"

If he says no he will clearly be lying, so he tries "yes."

"What was the purpose of that call?"

"Mrs. Timmerman had told me she was concerned about Walter; she didn't know where he was, and that was unlike him."

"But she wasn't concerned thirty minutes before, when you were there?" I ask.

"That's correct. Maybe something happened; maybe she learned something. I didn't ask. I called Steven to see if he knew where his father was."

"You were out at the time? Is that why you used your cell phone?" I ask.

"Yes. I was in the car, as I said, I was probably running some errands."

"But you knew his number?"

"Yes."

"Because you had called him before?" I ask.

"Yes."

I introduce more documents into evidence, and then hand them to Sykes. "These are Steven Timmerman's phone records from that number for the last year. Please look at them and tell the jury which calls that you made to him. Take your time."

He looks through the papers for about three minutes and then hands them back to me. "I don't see any. But I know I called him a number of times. Maybe it was more than a year ago."

"But you called him often enough that you remember the number?"

"Yes."

"Maybe you can help me. I haven't called Steven at home because he has been in a jail cell since he was wrongly accused. When he's released I'll need to call him to discuss my fee, so what is his number? Just so I'll have it."

He hesitates, and then says, "I can't remember now. It's hard to think clearly when I'm being attacked like this."

"When you called Steven, what did he say?"

"That he had no idea where his father was; that they hadn't been in much contact lately."

"So when he was no help, who did you call next?"

"I don't remember."

"Your phone records show no other calls that night."

"Then I didn't make any."

"So you were worried about Mr. Timmerman, you got no information from Steven, and that eased your mind enough not to call anyone else?"

"I said that Diana was worried about him. She probably made the other calls. These were not very significant events at the time, Mr. Carpenter. My recollection is not clear."

"Okay. I'll change the subject to something hopefully clearer. Let's talk about money. I was reading the terms of Walter Timmerman's will, and basically he left his estate and share of the company to his wife, Diana. Are you aware of that?"

"I've read it in the newspapers."

"If she were not alive when the estate was settled, the money would then go to Steven. Are you aware of that?"

"Vaguely."

271

"But if Steven were not in a position by law to receive the money, say if he were in jail for killing his father, Walter Timmerman's stock goes back into the company. Did you know that?"

"I did not."

"Therefore, all the other shareholders would then automatically have a bigger piece of the company. By my figuring, and correct me if I'm wrong, your personal stake in the company would increase by over eighty million dollars."

"I have not given it a moment's thought," he says.

"Wow. You must be really rich," I say, and am pleased when a few jury members laugh at the absurdity of it. "Most people would give at least half an hour's thought to getting eighty million dollars."

"I am fortunate enough to be well off financially. No amount of money would make me harm my partner and friend."

"You don't consider sleeping with his wife harmful to him?"

"That is something I deeply regret."

I consider whether to delve into the likelihood that Sykes knew about Walter's DNA work, and that taking it over was a motivation for murder. I decide against it, because it would just be me accusing and him denying, and I have nothing factual to catch him on.

I let Sykes off the stand, and Richard attempts to rehabilitate him. It gives him a chance to once again vehemently deny any wrongdoing, and to rail against the injustice of being asked about minor incidents that happened a long time ago, and then having the inference drawn that his inability to answer accurately should be incriminating.

We definitely won this round, but I just don't know if we won it by a big enough margin.

• • • • •

PERRY MASON HAS LEFT THE BUILDING.

Actually, I'm not sure he was ever here. Sykes did not break down and admit his guilt, nor did I get enough out of him that his guilt was obvious.

But I made a lot of progress, and no fair-minded observer could have come away with anything near certainty that Sykes was not involved in the murder. Sykes had few good answers, only denials and evasions, and in my mind he should now be universally viewed with suspicion.

The real question is whether that suspicion of Sykes will result in reasonable doubt about Steven's guilt. I believe that it should; if a person thinks there's a chance that Sykes did it, then that same person by definition has to have a reasonable doubt as to whether or not Steven did.

This is the crucial question we must answer, because the time has come to decide whether or not Steven will testify. Kevin and I meet with him, and it's the first time I can ever recall starting such a meeting without having a clear point of view of my own.

"I think we made substantial progress with Sykes," I say, "and

I can augment that in my closing argument. But there's no way to know for sure."

Kevin was more impressed than I was by the progress I made, and he says so. He is therefore now taking the position that Steven should not testify.

"Tell me the positives and negatives," Steven says.

I nod. "Okay, let's start with the positives. You can testify that you spoke to your father that night on Sykes's phone, and you can say why you went to Mario's. I can't say those things in closing arguments; I can only talk about evidence already introduced. You can also tell the jury directly and in your own words that you did not commit these crimes."

"And the negatives?"

"You will be asked about the evidence against you, like the blood and the gun, and you'll have no answers to give, since you don't really know how that evidence came into existence. You'll also be asked about problems you've had with your father and stepmother, and in the hands of a good prosecutor like Richard, you'll look bad in the process. On cross-examination, Mother Teresa could be made to look like Tony Soprano."

"Anything else?" he asks.

"Yes, it would be nice to end this on Sykes, so that he is fresh in the minds of the jury. If you testify, he'll fade somewhat into the background. When a defendant testifies, it alters the entire trial in one direction or the other."

"So what's your recommendation?" Steven asks

As I've been talking, I've been developing a point of view. "On balance, I would recommend that you not take the stand."

"Okay . . . you're calling the shot."

I shake my head. "No, you're calling it. This has to be your decision and only your decision."

He nods. "I understand that. And my decision is to trust your judgment."

All there is for me to do now is prepare my closing argument, and that is what I have on tap for tonight. It's another area in which I like to be freewheeling and spontaneous, but I also have to make sure I don't miss anything, because I'll have only one bite at the apple.

What I do is write the general subjects I want to cover on a piece of paper, and then I think about them one at a time. If there are any details I'm unsure of, I refer to what is now the mountain of notes and documents that make up the case file. But basically I know what there is to know, and what it is I want to say.

Laurie knows enough to leave me by myself during this prep time. I'm on my own at this point, and no one can really help.

I'm not thrilled with how things are going with Laurie. She hasn't come to a decision, which I pessimistically view as a negative sign. I know she has always liked to think things all the way through until she is comfortable, and I'm much more spontaneous. But it still doesn't feel right.

Also, I'm feeling like I did when waiting for Laurie to decide whether or not to go to Wisconsin two years ago. If she leaves, it will feel somewhat like she is walking out on me again. We might have difficulty surviving that.

I am starting to believe that I brought it up too soon, yet for some reason I'm not sorry I did. But at this moment I can't let myself worry about it either way.

Whether Laurie lives in Wisconsin or New Jersey is fairly insignificant compared with whether Steven lives at home or in state prison.

Even to me.

• • • • •

"WHEN WE FIRST CONVENED HERE,
I told you this was a simple case," is how Richard begins his closing statement. "And nothing has been said since to change my mind. Steven Timmerman was quarreling bitterly with his father, and he resented him terribly for marrying a woman that Steven hated.

"The defense has pointed out that those arguments happened frequently over time, and this was also not the first time Walter had threatened to disinherit his son. And all of that is true.

"But resentments have a way of building over time. They simmer in some people, getting more and more powerful, more and more dangerous. And then one day, sometimes even after a perceived slight that is far less than previous ones, a person can snap, can decide that they can take no more.

"That is what happened here. In addition to the anger, you have clearly seen that Steven Timmerman had motive, almost half a billion dollars' worth of motive. You have learned that he was seen two blocks from where the brutal murder happened, in a place where he had never been seen before.

"Scientific evidence has demonstrated beyond doubt that

Walter's blood was in Steven Timmerman's car, and you have been told that the murder weapon was found in his loft.

"As if all of that were not enough, you have learned that Steven Timmerman was an expert in the kind of explosives that blew up his parents' house and killed his stepmother. The stepmother whom witness after witness has said that he hated.

"I have unfortunately been involved in a great many murder cases, and let me tell you, ladies and gentlemen, they rarely are as uncomplicated as this.

"Now, at the last minute, the defense pointed their fingers at Thomas Sykes and said, 'He did it.' And when, in the face of an unexpected barrage of accusations, Mr. Sykes displayed nervousness and faulty memory, they said, 'Aha! There's proof of his guilt.'

"Let's be clear on something, ladies and gentlemen. There is no physical evidence against Mr. Sykes, not a shred. No blood, no murder weapon, no parking ticket showing him in downtown Paterson. He is not an explosives expert, nor has the defense even attempted to give a motive for why he would kill the woman that he loved.

"Mr. Carpenter told you at the opening of the trial that Steven Timmerman's record was clean, that there was no hint of violence in his past. Well, believe me, the same thing is true in spades for Thomas Sykes.

"So I ask just one thing of you. Please stick to the facts, and make your decision according to what makes sense. That's all. Thank you."

Obviously it's important to hear the prosecution's closing arguments, because I can then adjust my remarks to counter it, but I often wish I didn't have to hear them at all. Richard has done a terrific job, and if I were a member of the jury I would probably be thinking, *Hang the bastard*. But I have to put that out of my mind, or I'll be too defensive and therefore too cautious.

"Ladies and gentlemen, Richard Wallace is a fine attorney, and he's done a fine job presenting his case, but he simply could not be more wrong. There is nothing simple about this case. Nothing at all.

"The perpetrator of these murders wanted it to appear simple. He planted such obvious clues that a person in his first year at the police academy could have followed them. All signs pointed to Steven Timmerman, so let's go get him, full speed ahead.

"Of course, for it all to be true and real, Steven Timmerman would have to be not just a murderer, but also a moron. He would have had to leave his victim's blood in his car and never bothered to wash it out.

"He would have had to make the decision to kill his stepmother by blowing up her house with an explosive when everyone knew of his expertise using that explosive. Why do that? Why not shoot her, or poison her, or stab her? Why do it the one way that would point clearly to him?

"Then, to cap off this run of stupidity, he would have had to hide the gun in the one place it could be traced to him. After wiping off the fingerprints, no less.

"But that last one didn't work out so well, because the police couldn't find it. So someone had to call anonymously and tell them to go back and look in the table. Who was that person? Someone Steven told? Otherwise, how could they have known? Could Steven be that dumb? Could anyone be that dumb?

"Steven Timmerman is not dumb, and he is not resentful, and he is not violent. He took very little from his father, choosing instead to work his trade. It is ludicrous to think that he murdered so as to gain what he had spent so long turning down.

"Now I want to talk to you about Thomas Sykes. Thomas Sykes admits to an affair with Diana Timmerman. He was at Walter Timmerman's house two hours before he was murdered, and his phone was used to place what can only be described as a suspicious call to Steven Timmerman, the first time he had ever called him.

"And Thomas Sykes stood to make eighty million dollars if Walter and Diana Timmerman died. But he would make that only if Steven Timmerman were not in a position to claim his rightful inheritance. What a coincidence.

"And, ladies and gentlemen, sometimes all the facts are not readily available, and the ones that are can only take you so far. So you have to go with your gut feelings about people and the way they act.

"Thomas Sykes looked like a deer caught in the headlights on the witness stand. He was trapped, and he sounded like it, and he looked like it.

"Now, you may not know with certainty that Thomas Sykes murdered Walter Timmerman. I'm not saying you should; he has not been investigated by the authorities, and there is much more for all of us to learn.

"But consider this: Judge ~~Henderson~~ HATCHET will explain to you that to find Steven Timmerman guilty, you must do so beyond a reasonable doubt. If you think that there is a chance, even a relatively small one, that Thomas Sykes is guilty, then you must have a reasonable doubt as to Steven's guilt.

"It's as simple as that.

"Steven Timmerman is a victim. He's lost his father, and he's lost his freedom. His father is gone forever, but you have the power to give him his freedom back. Thank you."

When I take my seat, Steven puts his hand on my shoulder and softly says, "Thank you; I think you were fantastic."

"I wish you were on the jury," I say.

He smiles. "So do I."

• • • • •

I'LL NEVER AGAIN describe waiting for a verdict as the most stressful thing I have ever faced. Not after sitting in that hospital room while Laurie was in a coma, fighting for her life. Nothing compares to that, but waiting for the jury to rule is no day at the beach.

I'm naturally pessimistic when it comes to this point in the trial, and Kevin is naturally optimistic. The truth is that neither of us knows what the hell he is talking about. Jury verdicts are impossible to predict.

It's an accepted maxim that the longer the jury is out, the better for the defense. That is because defense teams usually consider a hung jury to be a victory, and the longer a verdict watch goes, the more likely that somebody on one side or the other is holding out.

Of course, like everything else, this accepted maxim is by no means always accurate. I have seen juries vote to acquit in an hour, and vote to convict after two weeks.

So the way I deal with my stress is to hang out and try not to think about the verdict. The longest I have successfully avoided those thoughts is about twenty minutes, but as I recall they were a very peaceful twenty minutes.

I make it a point to visit Steven once a day, though it's unlikely I make him feel any better. I scrupulously don't give him my opinion as to the outcome; instead I mouth meaningless phrases like "I'm cautiously hopeful" and "We're not going to know until we know." Real profound stuff.

We're in the third day of waiting when Laurie comes into the den. It's in the morning, and she knows I like to obsess and agonize in the den in the morning. After lunch I prefer obsessing and agonizing in the living room, and after dinner my choice is to obsess and agonize while pacing around the house. The variety appeals to me.

Laurie generally knows enough to leave me alone at these times, so her entry is a small surprise. I worry for a moment that she is going to tell me that the jury has reached a verdict, but I haven't heard the phone ring. I'm not sure why I hate being told that a decision has been reached, but it might be that it's because at that moment it feels officially out of my control.

"Hi," she says. It's not a particularly interesting way to open a conversation, but the tone in her voice indicates that she has something on her mind.

"Uh-oh," I say as I stand up and gird for the worst. For some reason I gird better standing.

"I know you don't like to talk when you're waiting for the jury, but I've figured things out as well as I'm going to, and I know you were anxious to have this conversation, so . . ."

So intense was my focus on the jury that the situation with Laurie had almost been totally out of my mind, but now it is staring me in the face. I don't want to hear bad news now, but if I don't hear what she has to say, I'll agonize and obsess about it as well. That won't be good; when it comes to obsessing and agonizing, I'm basically monogamous. One thing at a time.

"Say it really fast," I tell her. "Whatever it is, say it really fast."

She laughs. "You're impossible, you know that?"

"You're not going fast enough."

"I want to live here, with you."

Did she say what I think she said? "Did you say what I think you said?"

"If you think I said I want to live here with you, then yes."

I go over and kiss her, mainly because that way she won't be able to talk and tell me she changed her mind. Then I ask, "What about getting married?"

"That's up to you," she says. "I'm fine with it, but I don't need it. We love each other, and I want to spend the rest of my life with you, and that's enough for me." She smiles. "Besides, I'm already in the will."

I kiss her again. "What made you decide to live here?"

"Probably what I went through. Life is too precious, and it's too damn short. I hope we each have a hundred years left, but if we don't, or even if we do, I want to spend it with the person I love."

"And will you be my investigator again? Coincidentally, a position just opened up."

She smiles. "Maybe. I haven't thought that through. And I'm going to have to spend some time in Findlay, transitioning to my replacement. And I'll want to visit a lot; I have so many great friends there."

"I understand; that's perfect."

"I feel good about this, Andy. I'm very happy with what I decided."

"You're the second happiest person in the room," I say.

We kiss again, and the phone rings. I answer it, and Rita Gordon, the court clerk, says, "Andy, they've reached a verdict."

I hang up and turn to Laurie. "You're now the happiest person in the room."

• • • • •

"I'VE NEVER EXPERIENCED anything like this," Steven says when I see him before court. "I never really realized it was possible to be this scared."

I'm not about to tell him that his fear is unwarranted, because it isn't, and because he wouldn't believe me anyway. There is nothing like this in any other area of our society. In a few minutes, twelve strangers are going to tell Steven that they've decided he can live in freedom, or in misery. And then they'll go home, and that will be that.

Richard and his team arrive a few minutes after we do, and as he walks in, we make eye contact. I get up and meet him off to the side of the room, and we shake hands.

"Good luck," he says.

I nod. "The same to me."

He smiles. "There's always more at stake on your side of the table, Andy. I know that. I want to win, but I'm sure not anxious for you to lose."

I ask him something that I never, ever ask anyone, especially a prosecutor. "Do you think he did it?"

"Probably," Richard says. "Am I certain beyond a reasonable

283

doubt? I don't think so. But I'm comfortable whichever way it goes."

"Will you do me a favor?" I ask.

"If I can."

"When this is over, no matter how it goes, will you try to get a judge to issue a search warrant on Thomas Sykes?"

"For what?" he asks.

"Trace evidence in his car, and his computer."

"Why his computer?"

"There's an e-mail that was sent to Walter Timmerman by the head of a DNA lab. It would be important to know if Sykes ever saw it. I'll tell you all about it when we have more time."

The bailiff signals to us that Hatchet is about to come in. "Right now we have no time," Richard says.

"Will you do it?"

"I'll certainly give you a chance to talk me into it."

That'll have to be good enough for now. I go back to the defense table, my heart beginning its pre-verdict pounding. Hatchet comes in and announces that the jury has, in fact, reached a verdict.

He calls them in, and they file in slowly, not looking at us. That's usually either bad news, or good news. Jury-predicting doesn't become any easier as you get closer to hearing their verdict.

Hatchet goes through some court business, which I can barely focus on. He then gives the obligatory warning that he will not tolerate any disorderliness in the courtroom once the verdict is read.

He asks the jury foreman if they have reached a verdict, and the woman confirms that they have. She hands the verdict form to the bailiff, who brings it to Hatchet. Hatchet looks at it for a few moments, probably delighting in the fact that he is now the only person other than the jury to know what it says.

Finally, he hands it back to the bailiff, and asks Steven to stand. Steven, Kevin, and I rise as one, and we each have a hand on one of

Steven's shoulders. In my case it's more to hold myself upright than to make him feel better.

The bailiff starts to read, at a pace of what seems like one word every twenty minutes. "In the matter of the State of New Jersey versus Steven Timmerman, count one, the first-degree murder of Walter Timmerman, the jury hereby finds the defendant, Steven Timmerman, not guilty."

Steven's head goes down and he grips both of our arms, in a gesture I would more expect if he had lost. But I can see that he is smiling and crying at the same time, and I could easily do the same. Because I am all man, though, I just stick to smiling.

I listen carefully as the other counts are read, and they are all "not guilty." Steven turns and hugs me and then Kevin. This is one time I think the good guys came out on top.

It had been out of my mind, but at this very moment it hits me that Laurie is going to live with me. Steven goes free and Laurie comes back.

I've had worse days.

IT'S A SACRED TRADITION that we celebrate winning verdicts at Charlie's. It's my favorite place in the world to be, so I pick the place as a victory present to myself. It's always just the client, the defense team, and people who helped in the defense. So in this case it's Laurie, Kevin, Edna, Steven, Martha Wyndham, and myself.

Marcus is not here because he's at the house, still guarding Waggy. We have no proof that Waggy is no longer a target, so we can't take a chance on leaving him unprotected. Marcus didn't seem to mind; I ordered in four pizzas to make it more palatable to him.

Tomorrow I am going to have Waggy miraculously turn up at the Passaic County Animal Shelter, where Willie is going to discover him and then take him out. By tomorrow night he'll be going crazy everywhere in my house, and not just the basement.

Tonight Vince and Pete are here as well, less for the sacred-tradition aspect than for the free-beer-and-food aspect. Their attendance is also less significant because they happen to be here every night.

I can't even imagine the joy and relief that Steven must be feeling. My guess is that it would be like jumping out of an airplane after being told there was a decent chance your parachute wasn't going to open. The chute would decide whether you would live or die, and all you could do is wait for the decision.

Steven raises a glass of champagne and says, "To Andy and Kevin, fantastic lawyers and even better people."

Other people make toasts as well, and the more we drink the less eloquent they get. I finally stand with my beer bottle raised and say, "I have an announcement to make. Laurie Collins and I may or may not be getting married." A cheer goes up, but the state of inebriation in the room is such that they would cheer if I announced it was going to be cloudy tomorrow.

Steven comes over to me later in the festivities and says, "You haven't sent me a bill yet."

"I will," I say.

"Do you have a recommendation for a lawyer I should use to deal with my father's will?"

I know someone who is very good at probate, and I give Steven his name.

"So you thinks Sykes is guilty?" he asks.

"I think he killed your father," I say.

"But not Diana?"

That something that's still bothering me. The only reasons I can think of for Sykes blowing up the house would be to kill Diana and destroy Walter's laboratory, so that no one could get access to his work.

Neither rationale completely holds up to close scrutiny. If he married Diana, they would have walked away with over four hundred million, compared with the eighty million Sykes would get as part of the company. On the other hand, Diana could have been in the process of dumping him, and he might therefore have faced the prospect of getting nothing.

As far as the laboratory goes, Sykes had full access to the house through Diana. He could easily have destroyed the lab without taking the house down with it. Of course, this theory also has an *on the other hand* attached to it. Sykes could have had Childs use the overkill of a bomb purely as a further way to frame the explosives expert, Steven.

"I'm not sure if he killed Diana," is how I answer Steven. "But maybe we'll learn more about that."

"How?"

I mention that I've asked Richard to seek search warrants against Sykes, and how I will be pushing that when I meet with him tomorrow. Steven seems happy to hear it; he naturally wants his father's killer caught.

Martha Wyndham, Laurie, and Kevin come over and join the conversation. "Why do you guys look so serious?" Laurie asks. "The trial is over. You won."

"Winning isn't enough for us," I say. "We want to dominate."

"I wish Waggy were here," Martha says. "He certainly played a key role."

"I agree completely," says Steven. "And is it proper for me to ask what you've decided about him?"

"If he ever turns up, and I'm very optimistic that he will, I'm going to file a motion with the court awarding him to you—"

Steven interrupts: "That would be great." He says it with real enthusiasm, which makes me feel like I made the right choice. Tara won't admit it, but she's going to miss Waggy as much as I will. Or maybe she won't.

"—though I would be reluctant to give him up until I felt certain he's no longer a target."

"Makes sense."

"But if you ever go on vacation, Waggy doesn't get boarded; he comes to stay at our house," Laurie says. I have to admit, I love the way she says "our house."

Steven smiles. "You got a deal."

"And I get visitation rights," Martha says.

Steven nods. "Whenever you want."

I can tell the evening is coming to an end, because Vince signals for the waiter to bring me the check. Steven grabs it and pays it, bringing the grand total of times I haven't gotten stuck with the check at Charlie's to one.

When we get home, Marcus has brought Waggy up to the living room, and he is playing with him and Tara. I think he's going to miss the Wagster as much as the rest of us.

"You really think he's still in danger?" Laurie asks.

"To tell you the truth, I have no idea. There's just too much I don't know about this whole case. But for now I don't want to take a chance with him."

"When he goes to live with Steven, are you going to get Tara another friend? I think she likes the company."

I shrug. "Maybe; I've been thinking about it. But it would be a dog closer to Tara's age."

She nods. "Good idea."

I'm pretty much ready to go upstairs with Laurie, but Marcus doesn't seem to be planning to leave. "Marcus, can I get you anything?" I ask.

"Nunh."

"We're going to go to sleep, okay?"

"Yuh."

Laurie whispers to me. "Andy, do you think we should? Is it right to just leave him here?"

I nod. "Yuh and yuh."

• • • • •

My meeting with Richard Wallace

isn't even necessary. By the time I get there, he already has gotten the police department to prepare the search warrants on Thomas Sykes, which will be presented to a judge and then hopefully executed. They're for his home, his car, and his office, and basically they're hunting for trace evidence and incriminating documents and computer records.

It's an entirely different situation than would have occurred if Steven had been found guilty. Then there would have been almost no way Richard could have convinced his boss to try to pin the crime on Sykes. Once Steven had been convicted, they would not have had the stomach to do something that might have overturned that conviction.

"I buy that he killed Walter Timmerman," Richard says, "but not the house. It doesn't feel right. If he was going to do that, why not do it when both of them were home? He could have killed them both with one bomb, and it would have been even easier to place it on Steven."

"Because I think Sykes wanted a chance to get a look at that lab, without Walter around."

"How could he have been sure that Diana would be home when he set the bomb off? She could have been at the goddamn beauty parlor."

It's a good point, and one I hadn't thought of. "That'll have to go to the bottom of a long list of things I don't know," I say.

"Unless he called and she answered the phone; that would have been the key to detonate the bomb."

I think back to that day. "No, she was having Martha tell people she wasn't available. And she gardened a lot; even if she was home, she could have left the house at any time."

"Maybe we'll learn something with the warrants," Richard says.

"Or maybe it'll raise more questions."

He looks at me strangely. "You seem awfully downbeat for a winner."

I smile. "I know; I hate unresolved cases, especially when the fact that they're unresolved means a murderer may walk."

Richard promises to keep me informed as best he can about the results of the search warrant, but I'm aware that it will be in the hands of the police, and it will only be brought to him if charges seem justified.

On the home front, Laurie and I are making plans for a trip to Findlay. The doctor isn't quite ready for her to travel yet, but he said he'll likely retract that restriction in a couple of weeks.

Laurie figures it will take about three weeks to help in the job transition; she has already notified the city manager of her decision to leave, and fortunately her second in command is a likely successor. She also has to make arrangements to sell her house and transport her things.

Laurie has a million friends there, and because the chief of police is widely known and admired, I'll likely be viewed as the villain who's taking her away. It's a small price for me to pay.

We're going to drive there so that we can take Tara with us

without having to put her in a crate under the plane. I'm hoping to have Waggy with Steven by then; the idea of spending a long road trip with Waggy cooped up in the car is chilling.

For a long time I have been spending most of my waking hours pathetically trying to figure out a devious way to get Laurie to move back here. Now that it's happening, I'm going to have a lot of free thinking time on my hands.

The media reported on the search warrant being executed on Thomas Sykes, and Sykes's lawyer issued a statement saying that his client was being unduly persecuted and harassed. He said that now that the authorities were too inept to convict Steven, they were looking for a scapegoat, and poor Sykes was the guy they chose.

Steven has come over twice in the last three days to visit with Waggy and hang out. I'm just waiting for the Sykes matter to resolve itself one way or the other, and then I'll send Waggy off to Manhattan and his new life.

If New Yorkers think they're in the city that never sleeps now, wait till they have to live with Waggy.

Steven is over when Richard Wallace calls me. "Trace evidence from Sykes's car shows Walter Timmerman's blood and brain matter."

I am about to say, *Maybe Walter Timmerman accidentally cut open his brain once when he was in that car,* but I think better of it, because Steven is standing there, and after all, it was his father. I'm sensitive that way.

"Glad to hear that," I say. "Are you going to arrest him?"

"His lawyer has been notified and is going to bring him in tomorrow morning so that he can surrender himself and avoid the perp walk," Richard says. "Money has its privileges."

I can tell Richard is unhappy with this arrangement; he thinks Sykes should be publicly arrested just like Steven was. But obviously word came down for it to be handled that way, so there's nothing he can do. For that reason I don't voice my own complaint.

Steven's heard enough of the call that I can't keep it from him. "They got him?" he asks.

I nod. "Looks like it. He's turning himself in tomorrow morning."

Steven makes a fist in satisfaction. "Boy, I was hoping for that. I was afraid it wouldn't happen, but I was really hoping."

"This is not something you should talk about until it actually happens. It might get out to the media, but it shouldn't come from you."

Steven nods. "No problem."

When Steven leaves, I tell Laurie the news about Sykes, and my hope that he will confess and fill in the blanks in my knowledge about all that has happened.

"What do you think the chances are of that?" Laurie asks.

"Zero."

● ● ● ● ●

I WAKE UP IN THE MORNING and turn on the news. Thomas Sykes's picture is on the screen, next to a talking anchorman who actually looks a little like him. I'm not surprised to see the photograph, until I realize that it is only seven AM, much earlier than I would have thought Sykes would turn himself in. Maybe he wanted to do it with as little fanfare as possible.

"Sykes's body was found by his attorney, Lawrence Wilborn," the anchorman says. "Our information is that Wilborn called nine-one-one immediately, but that Sykes was pronounced dead at the scene. The police are not commenting, but it is believed that the cause of death was a self-inflicted bullet to the head."

I immediately call Richard, who does not answer either his office or cell phone. I don't know his home number, but I'm sure he's not at home anyway. Richard and everybody he works with is going to have a tough week coming up, as everybody points the finger at everyone else for letting Thomas Sykes sit at home and blow his brains out. Richard was opposed to the move, but I'm sure he'll still be in the line of fire.

My next call is to Pete Stanton. Sykes's house is not in his jurisdiction, so he is not directly involved, but he promises to call around and see what he can find out.

He calls back in fifteen minutes. "Sykes called his lawyer at four AM and told him that he'd better get over there right away. The lawyer lives only ten minutes away, but Sykes was already dead. One bullet, gun pressed to the temple. Definitely appears to be a suicide."

I thank Pete and hang up. Sykes's taking his own life is not particularly hard to believe. He had to know he was facing virtually certain life in prison, so this would have represented the easy way out to him.

Sykes's death doesn't exactly leave me bemoaning the injustice of it all. I have no doubt that he was a murderer, and his departure will not leave a void that society must fill.

But I can't say I'm happy about it. I wanted answers. If Walter Timmerman's blood and brains splattered over Sykes, then he must have pulled the trigger. Why not Childs? Why hire Childs to blow up the house and kill Waggy, but not shoot Timmerman?

I also want to know what role Charles Robinson played in all this, and who killed him. If Sykes shot Walter, blew up Diana, and poisoned Robinson, he's an unusually versatile murderer.

And did Sykes know about Walter's work and kill for it, or was this all about his money? It seems like an unusual coincidence for Sykes to have gone on this murder spree just at the time that Walter was working secretly with synthetic DNA. Walter's had all that money a long time; why kill him now?

I verbalize all of this to Laurie, who has been watching the coverage on television. She has no answers to my questions, but adds another little twist. "I don't think Sykes killed himself," she says.

"Why not?"

"Mostly it's my instinct," she says. "But I can try to explain it. If Sykes was thinking logically, he would have thought there was a decent chance to beat the charge. Steven beat the same charge, with much more evidence against him. Sykes had a lot of money and good lawyers. And he was a person of privilege, used to getting what he wanted. I don't think he would have given up this fast."

"Maybe he wasn't thinking logically," I say.

"Then he wouldn't have called his lawyer. What did it gain him? He wasn't hoping the lawyer would stop him, because it sounds like he died within minutes of making the call. But calling the lawyer made it look more like a suicide. If I'm right, that's what the real killer wanted."

"This is fascinating," I say. "I hope you're getting to the part where you tell me who the real killer is."

She smiles. "I'm afraid you'll have to tune in next week for that. But I will give you a clue."

"Please do."

"Look for someone who has a connection to all the main players involved . . . Timmerman, Sykes, and Robinson."

It's amazing how I can focus on a problem forever without getting anywhere, and then somebody says something that completely clears away the fog. Laurie's right, I need to be looking for someone with a connection to the big three. And I just may know who that is.

"Robert Jacoby," I say.

"The guy who runs the DNA lab?"

"Yes. He knew Walter and Sykes very well, they were his country-club buddies. What if he realized what Walter was doing when he sent in his own DNA? Our expert said he could have realized it was synthetic if he knew what he was looking for. Well, maybe he did."

"And went after it for himself," she says.

"Right. He would know exactly what to do with it, and how to profit from it. And he could have used Robinson in the same fashion Timmerman did, to connect with the people who would pay for it."

"So why kill Robinson?"

"Maybe he went off the reservation and tried to screw his partner. I can't answer that yet. But what if Sykes, Robinson, and Jacoby were in it together? When Sykes was going to go down for the murders, Jacoby thought Sykes would rat him out, so he killed him as well."

"It's all possible, Andy. But it's also completely made up; we just created an entire conspiracy out of our own heads."

I smile. "But we've got two pretty good heads."

"Sykes could have killed himself."

"I have to assume he didn't. Otherwise I have nowhere to take this."

"You don't really have to take it anywhere, you know. You won the case."

I think about that for a moment. The way I do my job, the way I've always done my job, is to think of it as a competition, a game. I won't feel like I've won the game unless I've figured it out. Laurie already knows this about me, so I smile and say, "The game isn't over yet."

"And if you win the game it means a murderer gets caught," she says.

"That's what makes it a really great game."

• • • • •

I CALL AGENT CORVALLIS and request a meeting. He doesn't seem particularly enamored of the idea, and it takes a veiled threat that I will publicly discuss everything I know about Walter Timmerman's work, and the FBI's involvement in it, before he agrees. He says that he'll be out of town tomorrow, but he'll give me fifteen minutes the day after.

I file papers with the probate court with my decision to award Waggy to Steven. The court accepts it within forty-eight hours, and of course there is no reason not to. Diana Timmerman and Charles Robinson are no longer around to contest it, and Steven is the heir to the rest of his father's fortune.

A delighted Steven picks Waggy up, and I see he's already stopped at a pet store to get dog food, dishes, beds, and toys. I should mention that he'll also need about a ton of doggy Ritalin, but I'll let him find that out for himself.

As Steven and his new best friend prepare to leave, Tara looks on fairly impassively. Life for her is going to get more peaceful, but also more boring. I'm not sure how she feels about that, and it's hard to tell based on her interaction with Waggy. They just sniff each other a little bit, and then Tara decides to lie down.

"Wags," I say, "it's been great having you. Feel free to visit anytime. My home is your home."

I go to give him a hug, but he will have none of it, wriggling free and jumping into the backseat of the car. Waggy has never been much of a sentimentalist.

Steven has thanked me about four hundred times since the trial, but feels compelled to do so even more effusively this time. He adds a hug, not knowing I'm not a fan of guy hugs. Waggy and I have that in common.

"What are your plans for him?" I ask. "Are you going to show him?"

"No. Waggy and I talked about it," he says. "We've decided he's not going to be a champion. He's just going to have fun and be a dog."

I'm glad to hear that, although I'm pretty sure Waggy would find a way to have fun no matter what he did.

I remind Steven to be careful with Waggy, since we can't be one hundred percent positive that whoever went after him won't try it again. Hopefully it was Sykes. He promises to be alert, and they're off to New York. Within a couple of weeks, Waggy will be making disparaging New Jersey jokes like all other New Yorkers.

Once Steven leaves, I head for the city myself, where I'm meeting with Corvallis at the FBI's Midtown office. I park the car on West 49th Street in one of the ubiquitous rip-off parking lots. If Corvallis really gives me just fifteen minutes, then I'll be paying about four bucks a minute.

Corvallis starts off the meeting by telling me why he shouldn't be meeting with me. "You've made my life more difficult," he says. "If not for you, Robinson might still be alive, and we could still be watching him. But hell, you're just doing your job, and you're not a bad guy, so . . ."

I put my hands to my eyes. "Stop it," I say, "I promised I wouldn't get emotional."

He laughs. "All right, what the hell do you want?"

"I've got a theory I wanted to run by you. I don't think Thomas Sykes killed himself."

"Based on what?" he asks.

I tell him my reasons, or at least Laurie's reasons, and then add, "And I think Robert Jacoby has been behind this from the beginning."

"Who the hell is Robert Jacoby?" he asks.

I'm not thrilled with the question. Corvallis really does seem puzzled as to Jacoby's identity, and given how close he has been to this case, that doesn't bode well for the accuracy of my theory. "He's the head of a DNA lab."

Corvallis nods as if he now remembers where he heard the name, and I continue. "He knew Timmerman, Robinson, and Sykes, and Timmerman sent him his own DNA to see if Jacoby would pick up on the fact that it was synthetic. I think he did pick up on it and saw an opportunity."

"I can't help you with that," he says. "I know very little about the guy. But I can help you with something else."

"What's that?" I ask.

"Sykes definitely committed suicide. No question about it."

"How do you know that?"

He frowns. "You may not realize this, but we do have an idea what we're doing. And we even have forensics experts. The gunpowder residue on Sykes's hands shows he pulled the trigger. If somebody else was holding his hand while he did, it would have distorted the pattern. So unless he complied when someone simply instructed him to shoot himself in the head, then it's a suicide."

It certainly wouldn't stun me if Corvallis were lying about this, but I don't know why he would. "So it's the considered opinion of the FBI that Sykes blew up the house and killed Diana Timmerman?"

"Could be," he says.

"Are you actively trying to find out who did it if he didn't? Or is murder not a significant enough crime for you guys to deal with?"

"In this case it is a local crime unless we get information to the contrary. So it's up to the local authorities. Our involvement in this matter is over."

"So you're not worried that someone might have gotten their hands on Walter Timmerman's work?"

He smiles. "I think it's fair to say that we've prepared for that."

I nod my understanding. "You got to Timmerman's lab in the house first, didn't you? After he was murdered?"

Corvallis doesn't respond, so I continue. "When I met Diana Timmerman at the house that day, she complained that the police had already searched the house three times. Yet the discovery reports show only one search. That's because your people were in there the other two times, without telling the locals about it."

"You're quite a fascinating storyteller," he says. "I'm just sorry the fifteen minutes are up."

"I'm taking a ten-minute extension. I'd bet that not only did your scientists get up to speed on Timmerman's work, but once you did you changed it to throw off anybody who got into that lab after you."

"You're on a roll," he says.

"You were sorry when the house blew up," I say. "Not because Diana Timmerman died, but because you were watching it to see who went in there. And you weren't worried, because you had gotten to the lab first.

"And because you were all over that house, that's how you know it isn't Jacoby. If it was you would have picked him up already. You know who was there every minute, which is why it could have been Sykes. But I don't buy it. Sykes lost the inside track at four hundred million when Diana Timmerman died. Just because he had access and could have planted the bomb doesn't mean . . ."

"Is the story finally over?" he asks.

"Holy shit . . . ," I say. "I need to use your phone."

He doesn't give me permission and I don't wait for it. I grab the phone and dial Steven Timmerman's number. It rings five times before the machine picks up. I can't take the chance to leave a message.

I hang up and grab a notepad and paper from Corvallis's desk. I talk as I write down Steven's address. "I believe Martha Wyndham is behind this; she has been from the beginning. Please get some agents to this address; it's Steven Timmerman's apartment. If I'm right, she's going to try to kill Steven and his dog. Please."

I start to move toward the door as he stands up. "What about you?" he says.

"I'll meet you there."

• • • • •

I TELL THE CABDRIVER that I'll give him a hundred dollars if he can get me to Steven's apartment in less than ten minutes. Based on his driving after that, my promise is a highly motivating one.

I didn't wait to go with Corvallis, because by the time he got downstairs and had a car brought around, it would have taken much too long. Certainly there is no way he is going to beat this cab.

I could be wrong again, but I should have known it was Martha Wyndham all along. She may well be working for someone else, but she's been in the middle of everything from the beginning. And if I'm right, she won't wait long to go after Steven.

It certainly answers the question of how the person who detonated the bomb knew that Diana Timmerman would be in the house. Martha was there, just starting to drive away, and she could have dialed the number from her car. And Martha had suggested I let Waggy live in that house while I decided who to award him to. It would have saved Jimmy Childs the trouble of trying to kill Waggy.

She was also there the day before the poison was thrown in our yard. We hadn't been walking Waggy, in an effort to hide his

303

location. But Martha saw him, and I believe that set the attempted poisoning in motion.

And Martha was one of very few people with access to Walter's lab, and the knowledge of what he was doing. When she blew up the lab she must have felt she and her people had learned all there was to learn, of course having no idea that the FBI had been there first.

As often happens when I get myself in these situations, I don't have a concrete plan for what I'll do when I get to Steven's house.

I call his number on my cell phone, and I'm surprised when he answers. "Hello," he says. He doesn't sound tense or upset, which is a relief.

"Steven, it's me, Andy."

"Andy, how are you? Checking up on Waggy?"

"Steven, have you heard from Martha Wyndham?"

"She's right here. She came to visit and take Waggy for a walk."

If there was a worse thing I could have heard him say, I'm hard-pressed to think of it now. I never should have made this call. "Steven, listen to me very carefully, and don't say anything. Martha has been behind this all along, and you are in danger. Now pretend that I asked you over for dinner this weekend, and you'd like to come."

He hesitates a moment and then says, "Dinner Saturday? Sure, I'd like that."

"I'm going to be there with the police in just a couple of minutes. When we get off the phone, I want you to very casually go into the bathroom, and then lock yourself in. Do not come out no matter what."

My hope is that Martha, realizing the police are on their way, will take Waggy and leave, and not worry about dealing with Steven. Even if she has a gun, she would be unlikely to use it to shoot open the bathroom door. It would attract too much attention. I hope.

"Don't worry about Waggy, just go into the bathroom. Now say something friendly about dinner."

"Sounds great," he says. "What time should I be there?"

"I'm going to hang up now. Pretend to wrap up the call and then say good-bye. And Steven, you need to act as if nothing is wrong."

I hang up and try to figure out my next step. There is certainly no way for me to storm the apartment, even if I were so inclined. It's on the fourth floor, and there's only a single staircase leading up to it. I would think somebody up there could hold off a SWAT team, so it's unlikely that an unarmed, chickenshit lawyer is going to fight his way in. Besides, once Steven is barricaded in the bathroom, Martha is likely to be making a hasty exit.

I reach the apartment in what must be record time, and I jump out and drop the fistful of money through the window in the driver's lap. I go up the five steps to the door, and am confronted with the realization that I have no idea what to do now.

I look around and cannot see any arriving federal agents; for the moment it's only me. I also have no key to get into the building, so I decide to buzz every other apartment, and hope somebody lets me in. There are twelve total apartments in the building, including Steven's, so I buzz the other eleven. Through the intercom, four people ask who it is, and in each case I say "UPS." At least one of them presses their buzzer, and the door opens.

I'm inside, and still without the slightest idea what to do. I leave the door ajar behind me, to make it easy for Corvallis and his agents to get in should they ever show up. I decide to walk up the stairs and hopefully listen through the door into Steven's apartment; at least that way maybe I can find out if Martha's still there.

I'm on the second-floor landing when a door opens on one of the floors above, and I hear the telltale sound of Waggy's feet scratching and trying to get traction on the slippery floor.

I hear Martha say, "Take it easy. Calm down." She's got more chance of her command being obeyed if she tells him to fly, or sing the national anthem.

They reach the stairs and are heading my way. It's pretty dark in here, which is the only thing working to my advantage. I back up against the wall, so she won't see me until they almost reach me. Unfortunately, as I do I hit my head against a fire extinguisher hanging on the wall. It makes a noise that I'm afraid she has heard.

"Is anybody down there?" Martha calls out, and when there is no answer, I hear them coming down the steps again.

My heart is pounding as they approach, so loud that it seems like it is echoing in the stairwell. Martha has a gun in her hand as she passes the point at which she should have seen me. But she does not see me, because she is intent on Waggy as she strains to keep him in check on the leash. He is dragging her forward so fast that she seems in danger of falling down the steps.

"Waggy! Stop it!" she screams as I jump out from behind her. I hit her from behind, and that, coupled with the forward motion that crazy Waggy is already generating, sends all three of us tumbling down the steps.

We land in a heap at the bottom, and I am conscious of Waggy yelping in pain. I feel a searing pain in my shoulder, but I don't know what has happened to Martha.

"Glad you could join us." It's Corvallis's voice, and when I look up he is holding his gun on Martha. Surrounding him are three other agents, also with their guns at the ready. It might be slight overkill, because Martha appears to be unconscious.

"Steven," I say. "Four B."

Corvallis makes a motion, and two of the agents run up to the fourth floor. I get to my feet and follow them, my shoulder hurting as badly as anything has ever hurt me.

Steven's door is open when I get there, and I'm cringing at what I'm going to find. Cringing hurts my shoulder, as does talking, climbing stairs, and breathing. Thankfully, the cringing proves to be unnecessary, as the agents have gotten Steven to open the bathroom door and have brought him into the living room.

"Is Waggy okay?" is the first thing Steven asks when he sees me.

That's my kind of guy.

• • • • •

THE DRIVE TO WISCONSIN is as comfortable as it gets. It feels like Laurie, Tara, and I are a family, and we're going on a family vacation. It makes me think that we should get an RV, leave everything behind, and just travel the country, and I mention that to Laurie.

"I don't think you get good television reception on those things," Laurie says. "And you've got the football season and the World Series coming up."

So much for the RV idea.

I separated my shoulder in the fall down the steps, and the doctor said it would take about eight weeks to heal. Fortunately, it was my left shoulder, because I work the remote control with my right hand.

Waggy walked with a limp for a couple of days after the fall, or more accurately he ran with a limp. He's fine now, and driving Steven crazy.

Before we left I shared with Steven what I know about the murders. Once Martha was taken into custody, Corvallis was more willing to fill in some of my blanks. He hadn't been aware of her involvement, and even seemed somewhat grateful to me for exposing her.

308

I was right that Walter and Robinson were going to sell his discovery to energy interests for a fortune, though I was wrong that Jacoby had any involvement in the scheme. Corvallis wouldn't tell me who was going to be the purchaser, but it may well have been a foreign government. Whoever it was placed a highly skilled agent, who turned out to be Martha, on the inside of Timmerman's world so that they could monitor things to their satisfaction. Whether or not Timmerman was aware of who she was, I don't know.

Their plan was jolted when Sykes and Diana killed Walter for his money, as they planned to marry after he was dead. Faced with this situation, Martha copied all of Walter's work in the lab, and used Jimmy Childs to plant the explosives in the house. She blew it up, unaware that the FBI had gotten to that lab first and left her with incorrect, worthless information.

She poisoned Robinson so that he could not reveal anything to the FBI, and after that all that was left to erase any trace of Walter's work was to have Childs kill Waggy, which of course almost resulted in Laurie's death.

But that is now behind us, as are New Jersey, Pennsylvania, and Ohio. We'll be in Wisconsin soon, and Laurie will do what she needs to do, and then we'll all go home together.

We're leaning toward getting Tara a friend.

A calm, normal friend.

Just for a change of pace.